PUFFIN IN BLOOM is a charming assortment of classic novels with coming-of-age themes. Cover artist Anna Bond of Rifle Paper Co. is best known for her signature floral patterns; and just as a flower blossoms, a child comes into her own. This selection of literature will help inspire and engage during the later years of childhood, and is a collection both young and old will cherish forever.

ANNA BOND of Rifle Paper Co., a worldwide stationery and gift brand, is an artist known for her whimsical designs, which often include hand-painted illustrations and lettering. She works with her husband in Winter Park, Florida.

THE PUFFIN IN BLOOM COLLECTION
with cover illustrations by Anna Bond

Anne of Green Gables
L. M. Montgomery

Heidi
Johanna Spyri

A Little Princess
Frances Hodgson Burnett

Little Women
Louisa May Alcott

HEIDI

'*Can you remember whether* you'd had a dream? One perhaps that seemed very real?'

'Oh yes.' Heidi's eyes met his. 'I dream every night that I'm back with Grandfather and can hear the wind whistling through the fir trees. I know in my dream the stars must be shining brightly outside, and I get up quickly and open the door of the hut—and it's so beautiful. But when I wake up I'm always still here in Frankfurt.'

HEIDI

BY
JOHANNA SPYRI

Cover illustration by Anna Bond
Translated by Eileen Hall
Interior illustrations by Cecil Leslie

PUFFIN BOOKS
An Imprint of Penguin Group (USA)

PUFFIN BOOKS
Published by the Penguin Group
Penguin Group (USA) LLC
375 Hudson Street
New York, New York 10014

USA * Canada * UK * Ireland * Australia
New Zealand * India * South Africa * China

penguin.com
A Penguin Random House Company

First published in 1880
This translation first published 1956
Copyright © 1956 by Puffin Books
Reissued in this edition by Puffin Books, an imprint of Penguin Young Readers Group, 2014

Endnotes copyright © 2009 by Penguin Books
Cover illustration © 2014 by Anna Bond of Rifle Paper Co.

Set in Minion by Palimpsest Book Production Limited, Falkirk, Stirlingshire

British Library Cataloguing in Publication data
A CIP catalogue record for this book is available from the British Library.

Puffin Books ISBN 978-0-14-751402-8

Printed in the United States of America

20 19 18 17 16

Contents

1

Up the Mountain

The pretty little Swiss town of Mayenfeld lies at the foot of a mountain range, whose grim rugged peaks tower high above the valley below. Behind the town a footpath winds gently up to the heights. The grass on the lower slopes is poor, but the air is fragrant with the scent of mountain flowers from the rich pasture land higher up.

One sunny June morning, a tall sturdy young woman was climbing up the path. She had a bundle in one hand and held a little girl about five years old by the other. The child's sunburnt cheeks were flushed, which was not surprising, for though the sun was hot she was wrapped up as though it was mid-winter. It was difficult to see what she was like for she was wearing two frocks, one on top of the other, and had a large red scarf wound round and round her as well. She looked like some shapeless bundle of clothing trudging uphill on a pair of hobnailed boots.

After climbing for about an hour, they came to the little

village of Dörfli, half way up the mountain. This was the woman's old home, and people called to her from their houses all the way up the street. She did not say much in reply but went on her way without stopping until she reached the last house. There a voice from within hailed her. 'Half a minute, Detie,' it said, 'I'll come with you, if you're going any farther.'

Detie stood still, but the little girl slipped her hand free and sat down on the ground.

'Tired, Heidi?' Detie asked her.

'No, but I'm very hot,' the child replied.

'We'll soon be there. Just keep going, and see what long strides you can take, and we'll arrive in another hour.'

At that moment a plump, pleasant-faced woman came out of the house and joined them. The little girl got up and followed as the two grown-ups went ahead, gossiping hard about people who lived in Dörfli or round about.

'Where are you going with the child, Detie?' the village woman asked after a while. 'I suppose she's the orphan your sister left?'

'That's right,' Detie replied. 'I'm taking her up to Uncle. She'll have to stay with him now.'

'What, stay with Uncle Alp on the mountain? You must be crazy! How can you think of such a thing? But of course he'll soon send you about your business if you suggest that to him.'

'Why should he? He's her grandfather and it's high time

he did something for her. I've looked after her up to now, but I don't mind telling you, I'm not going to turn down a good job like the one I've just been offered, because of her. Her grandfather must do his duty.'

'If he were like other people that might be all right,' retorted Barbie, 'but you know what he is. What does he know about looking after a child, and such a young one too? She'll never stand the life up there. Where's this job you're after?'

'In Germany,' said Detie. 'A wonderful job with a good family in Frankfurt. Last summer they stayed in the hotel at Ragaz where I've been working as chambermaid. They had rooms on the floor I look after. They wanted to take me back with them then, but I couldn't get away. Now they've come back and have asked me again. This time I'm certainly going.'

'Well, I'm glad I'm not that poor child,' said Barbie, throwing up her hands in dismay. 'Nobody really knows what's the matter with that old man, but he won't have anything to do with anybody, and he hasn't set foot in a church for years. When he does come down from the mountain, with his big stick in his hand – and that doesn't happen often – everybody scuttles out of his way. They're all scared stiff of him. He looks so wild with those bristling grey eyebrows and that dreadful beard. He's not the sort of person one would want to meet alone on the mountain.'

'That's as may be, but he's got to look after his grandchild now, and if she comes to any harm that'll be his fault, not mine.'

'I wonder what he's got on his conscience to make him live all alone up there, and hardly ever show his face,' Barbie wondered. 'There are all sorts of rumours, but I expect you know the whole story. Your sister must have told you plenty about him, didn't she?'

'Yes, she did, but I'm not telling. If he heard I'd been talking about him, I should catch it all right.'

But Barbie did not mean to lose this excellent opportunity of getting to know more about the old man. She came from Prättigau, farther down the valley, and had only lived in Dörfli a short while, just since her marriage, so she still had much to learn about her neighbours. She was very anxious to know why the old man lived up on the mountain like a hermit, and why people were reluctant to talk about him as they did, freely enough, about everyone else. They didn't approve of him, that much was certain, but they seemed afraid to say anything against him. And then, why was he always called 'Uncle Alp'? He couldn't be uncle to everyone in the village, but no one ever called him anything else, even Barbie used that name too. And here was her friend Detie, who was related to him and had lived all her life in Dörfli, until a year ago. Then her mother had died, and she had found a good job in a big hotel at Ragaz. She had come from there that morning with Heidi, with the help of a lift on a hay cart as far as Mayenfeld.

Now Barbie took her arm, and said coaxingly, 'You could at least tell me how much of what they say is true, and how much only gossip. Come on now, do explain why he's so against everyone, and why everyone is afraid of him. Has he always been like that?'

'That I can't say for certain. I'm only twenty-six and he must be seventy or more, so I never knew him in his young days. All the same, if I could be sure that you wouldn't pass it on to everyone in Prättigau, I could tell you plenty about him. He and my mother both came from Domleschg.'

'Go on, Detie, what do you take me for?' protested Barbie, half offended. 'We aren't such gossips as all that in Prättigau, and anyway I'm quite capable of holding my tongue when I want to. Do tell me. I promise not to pass it on.'

'All right then – but mind you keep your word!'

Detie glanced round to make sure that Heidi was not within earshot, but she was nowhere to be seen. She must have stopped following them some way back, and they had been too busy talking to notice. Detie stood still and looked in all directions. The path twisted and zigzagged down the mountainside, but she could see down it almost as far as Dörfli and there was nobody in sight anywhere along it.

'Ah, there she is,' cried Barbie suddenly, 'can't you see her?' She pointed to a little figure far below. 'Look, she's climbing up the slopes with Peter and his goats. I wonder why he's taking them up so late today. Well, he'll keep an eye on her all right and you can get on with your story.'

'Peter needn't bother himself,' said Detie. 'She can look after herself, though she's only five. She's got all her wits about her. She knows how to make the best of things too, which is just as well, seeing that the old man's got nothing now but his hut and two goats.'

'I suppose he was better off once?' asked Barbie.

'I should just think he was. Why, he had one of the best farms in Domleschg. He was the elder son, with one brother, a quiet respectable fellow. But old Uncle wanted nothing but to ape the gentry and travel about all over the

place. He got into bad company, and drank and gambled away the whole property. His poor parents died, literally died, of shame and grief when they heard of it. His brother was ruined too, of course. He took himself off, dear knows where, and nobody ever heard of him again. Uncle disappeared too. He had nothing left but a bad name. No one knew where he'd gone to, but after a while it came out that he had joined the army and was in Naples. Then no more was heard of him for twelve or fifteen years.' Detie was enjoying herself. 'Go on,' Barbie cried breathlessly.

'Well, one day he suddenly reappeared in Domleschg with a young son, and wanted some of his relations to look after the boy. But he found all doors closed against him. Nobody wanted to have anything to do with him.'

'Whew!' came in a whistle from Barbie.

'He was so angry he vowed he would never set foot in the place again. So he came to Dörfli and settled down there with the boy, who was called Tobias. People thought he must have met and married his wife down in the south. Apparently she died soon afterwards, though nothing is known for certain. He had saved a little money, enough to apprentice his boy to a carpenter. Tobias was a good sort and everyone in the village liked him – but no one trusted the old man! It was said that he had deserted from the army at Naples, so as to avoid some trouble about killing a man – not in battle, you understand, but in a brawl. All the same we accepted him as a member of the family. His grandmother and my mother's grandmother were sisters, so we called him Uncle, and as we're related to almost everyone in Dörfli, one way or another, the whole village soon called him Uncle too. Then, when he went to live right up there on the mountain, it became Uncle Alp.'

'And what happened to Tobias?' Barbie asked eagerly.

'Give me a chance! I was just coming to that,' Detie snapped at her. 'Tobias was apprenticed to a carpenter in Mels, but as soon as he had learnt his trade, he came home to Dörfli and married my sister Adelheid. They had always been fond of each other. They settled down very happily together as man and wife, but that didn't last long. Only two years later he was killed by a falling beam while he was helping to build a house. Poor Adelheid got such a shock when she saw him carried home like that, that she fell ill with a fever, and never walked again. She had not been very strong before and used to have queer turns when it was hard to tell whether she was asleep or awake. She only survived him by a few weeks. That set tongues wagging of course. People said it was Uncle's punishment for his mis-spent life. They told him so to his face, and the pastor told him he ought to do penance to clear his conscience. That made him more angry than ever, and morose too. He wouldn't speak to anyone after the pastor's visit, and his neighbours began to keep out of his way. Then one day we heard that he'd gone to live up on the mountain and wasn't coming down any more. He's actually stayed up there from that day to this, at odds with God and man, as they say. My mother and I took Adelheid's baby girl to live with us. She was only about a year old when she was left an orphan. Then, when mother died last summer I wanted to get a job in the town, so I took Heidi up to Pfäffersdorf and asked old Ursula to look after her. I managed to get work in the town right through the winter, as I'm handy with my needle and there was always someone who wanted sewing or mending done. Then early this year that family from Frankfurt came again, the people I waited on last year, and now, as I told you, they want me to go back with them, and they're leaving the day after tomorrow. It's a first-rate job, I can tell you.'

'And you're going to hand that child over to the old man, just like that? I'm surprised that you can even think of such a thing, Detie,' Barbie told her reproachfully.

'Well, what else can I do?' demanded Detie angrily. 'I've done my best for her all these years, but obviously I can't saddle myself with a five-year-old child on this job. Look, we're half way up to Uncle's now,' she went on. 'Where are you going, Barbie?'

'I want to see Peter's mother. She does spinning for me in the winter. So this is where I leave you. Goodbye, Detie, and good luck.'

Detie stood watching as Barbie went towards a little brown wooden hut sheltering in a small hollow a few yards from the path. It was so dilapidated that it was a good thing that it got some protection from the full force of the mountain gales. Even so, it must have been wretched to live in, as all the doors and windows rattled every time the wind blew and its rotten old beams creaked and shook. If it had been built in a more exposed position, it would certainly have been blown down into the valley long ago.

This was Peter the goatherd's home. He was eleven, and every morning he went down to Dörfli to fetch the goats and drive them up to graze all day in the fragrant mountain meadows above. Then, in the evening, he brought them down again, leaping with them over the hillside almost as nimbly as they did. He always gave a shrill whistle through his fingers when he reached the village so that the owners could come and collect their animals. It was usually children who answered the call – not even the youngest was afraid of these gentle goats.

During the summer months this was the only chance Peter had of seeing other boys and girls. For the rest of the time, goats were his only companions. He spent very little time at home with his mother and his old blind grandmother who lived with them. He used to leave the hut very early, after bolting his breakfast of a piece of bread and a mug of milk, and he always stayed as long as possible with the children in Dörfli, so he only got back in time to gobble his supper and tumble straight into bed. His father had been the goatherd before him, but he had

been killed several years ago, when felling a tree. His mother's name was Bridget, but she was seldom called anything but 'the goatherd's mother', and his grandmother was just Grannie to everyone, old and young alike.

For several minutes after Barbie had left her, Detie looked anxiously about for the two children with the goats, but there was no sign of them. She climbed a little farther up the path to get a better view and then stopped to look again. She was getting very impatient.

The children had strayed far away from the path, for Peter always went his own way up the mountain. What mattered was where his goats would find the best bushes and shrubs to nibble. At first Heidi had scrambled up after him, puffing and panting, for her load of clothes made climbing hard, hot work. She did not complain, but she looked enviously at Peter, running about so freely on bare feet, in comfortable trousers; and at the goats whose nimble little legs carried them so lightly up the steep slopes and over bushes and stones. Then suddenly she sat down and pulled off her boots and stockings. She unwound the thick red scarf and quickly unbuttoned her best dress, which Detie had made her wear on top of her everyday one, to save carrying it. She took off both dresses and stood there in nothing but a little petticoat, waving her bare arms in the air with delight. Then she laid all the clothes together in a neat pile and danced off to catch up with Peter and the goats. He had not noticed what she was doing, and when he caught sight of her running towards him like that, he smiled broadly. He looked back and saw the pile of clothing she had left on the grass, and grinned from ear to ear, but he said nothing. Heidi felt much happier, and free as air, and began to chatter away, asking him a string of questions. He had to tell her how many goats he had, where he was taking them, and what he was going to do when he got there. Presently they reached the hut and came within Detie's view. As soon as she spotted them she called out shrilly:

'What on earth have you been doing, Heidi? What a sight you look! What have you done with your frocks? And the scarf? And those good new boots I bought you to come up here in, and the stockings I knitted for you? Wherever have you left them all?'

Heidi calmly pointed to the place where she had undressed. 'There they are,' she said. Her aunt could see something lying there, with a red spot on top, which was the scarf.

'Oh, you naughty little thing!' she cried crossly. 'What on earth made you take your clothes off like that? What's the meaning of it?'

'I didn't need them,' replied Heidi, as if that were quite sufficient explanation.

'You stupid child, haven't you any sense at all?' scolded Detie. 'And who do you think is going down to fetch them for you now? It would take me a good half hour. Peter, you run back and get them for me, and be quick about it. Don't stand there gaping, as if you were rooted to the ground.'

'I'm late as it is,' said Peter. He made no attempt to move but stood with his hands in his pockets as he had done all the time Detie had been shouting at Heidi.

'Well, you won't get very far, if you just stand there, staring,' said Detie. 'Look here's something for you.' She made her tone more persuasive, and held out a bright new coin. The sight of this stirred him to action, and he dashed off with giant strides down the steep slope. He snatched up the pile of clothes and was back with them in no time. Detie had to admit that he had earned his reward. He tucked the coin away, deep down in his pocket, with a very broad grin, for such riches did not often come his way.

'Now you carry the things up to Uncle's for me. You're going that way I know.' And Detie began to climb the steep path behind the goatherd's hut.

Peter was quite willing and followed on her heels,

holding the bundle under his left arm and swinging the stick he used for the goats in his right hand. It took nearly an hour to reach the high pasture where Uncle Alp's hut stood on a little plateau. The little house was exposed to every wind that blew, but it also caught all the sunlight and commanded a glorious view right down the valley. Three old fir trees with huge branches stood behind it. Beyond them the ground rose steeply to the top of the mountain. There was rich grazing land immediately above the hut, but then came a mass of tangled undergrowth, leading to bare and rugged peaks.

Uncle Alp had made a wooden seat and fixed it to the side of the hut looking over the valley. Here he was sitting peacefully, with his pipe in his mouth and his hands on his knees as the little party approached. Peter and Heidi ran ahead of Detie for the last part of the way, and Heidi was actually the first to reach the old man. She went straight up to him and held out her hand. 'Hallo, Grandfather,' she said.

'Hey, what's that?' he exclaimed gruffly, staring searchingly at her as he took her hand. She stared back, fascinated by the strange-looking old man, with his long beard and bushy grey eyebrows. Meanwhile Detie came towards them, while Peter stood watching to see what would happen.

'Good morning, Uncle,' said Detie. 'I've brought you Tobias's daughter. I don't suppose you recognize her as you haven't seen her since she was a year old.'

'Why have you brought her here?' he demanded roughly. 'And you be off with your goats,' he added to Peter. 'You're late, and don't forget mine.' The old man gave him such a look that Peter disappeared at once.

'She's come to stay with you, Uncle,' Detie told him, coming straight to the point. 'I've done all I can for her these four years. Now it's your turn.'

'My turn, is it?' snapped the old man, glaring at her. 'And when she starts to cry and fret for you, as she's sure to do, what am I supposed to do then?'

'That's your affair,' retorted Detie. 'Nobody told me how to set about it when she was left on my hands, a baby barely a year old. Goodness knows I had enough to do already, looking after Mother and myself. But now I've got to go away to a job. You're the child's nearest relative. If you can't have her here, do what you like with her. But you'll have to answer for it if she comes to any harm, and I shouldn't think you'd want anything more on your conscience.'

Detie was really far from easy in her mind about what she was doing, which was why she spoke so disagreeably, and she had already said more than she meant to.

The old man got up at her last words. She was quite frightened by the way he looked at her, and took a few steps backward.

'Go back where you came from and don't come here again in a hurry,' he said angrily, raising his arm.

Detie didn't wait to be told twice. 'Goodbye, then,' she said quickly. 'Goodbye, Heidi,' and she ran off down the mountain, not stopping till she came to Dörfli. Here even more people called out to her than before, wanting to know what she had done with the child, whom they all knew.

'Where's Heidi? What have you done with Heidi?' they cried from their doorways and windows.

Detie replied, more reluctantly each time, 'She's up at Uncle Alp's. Yes, that's what I said. She's with Uncle Alp.' It made her uneasy to hear the women call back to her, from all sides, 'How could you do it, Detie!' 'Poor little mite!' 'Fancy leaving that helpless little creature up there with that man!' Detie was thankful when she was out of earshot. She did not want to think about what she had done, for when her mother was dying, she had made Detie promise to look after the child. She comforted herself with the thought that she would be better able to do so if she took this job where she could earn good money, and hurried away as fast as she could from all those people who would try to make her change her mind.

2

At Grandfather's

As soon as Detie had disappeared, the old man sat down again on the bench. He stared at the ground in silence, blowing great clouds of smoke from his pipe, while Heidi explored her new surroundings with delight. She went up to the goat-stall which was built on to the side of the hut, but found it empty. Then she went round to the back and stood for a while listening to the noise the wind made whistling through the branches of the old fir trees. Presently it died down, and she came back to the front of the hut, where she found her grandfather still sitting in the same position. As she stood watching him, hands behind her back, he looked up and said, 'What do you want to do now?'

'I want to see what is inside the hut,' she answered.

'Come on, then,' he said, and he got up and led the way indoors. 'Bring the bundle of clothes in with you,' he added.

'I shan't want them any more,' she declared.

The old man turned and looked sharply at her, and saw her black eyes shining with anticipation.

'She's no fool,' he muttered to himself, and added aloud, 'Why's that?'

'I want to be able to run about like the goats do.'

'Well, so you can,' said her grandfather, 'but bring the things inside all the same. They can go in the cupboard.'

Heidi picked up the bundle and followed the old man into a biggish room which was the whole extent of his living quarters. She saw a table and a chair, and his bed over in one corner. Opposite that was a stove, over which a big pot was hanging. There was a door in one wall which the old man opened, and she saw it was a large cupboard with his clothes hanging in it. There were shelves in it too. One held his shirts, socks, and handkerchiefs, another plates, cups, and glasses, while on the top one were a round loaf, some smoked meat, and some cheese. Here, in fact, were all the old man's possessions. Heidi went inside the open cupboard and pushed her bundle right away to the back so that it would not easily be seen again.

'Where shall I sleep, Grandfather?' she asked next.

'Where you like,' he replied.

This answer pleased Heidi, and as she was looking round the room for a good place she noticed a ladder propped against the wall near her grandfather's bed. She climbed up it at once and found herself in a hay loft. A pile of fresh, sweet-smelling hay lay there, and there was a round hole in the wall of the loft, through which she could see right down the valley.

'I shall sleep up here,' she called down. 'It's a splendid place. Just come and see, Grandfather.'

'I know it well,' he called back.

'I'm going to make my bed now,' she went on, 'but you'll have to come up and bring me a sheet to lie on.'

'All right,' said her grandfather, and he went to the cupboard and searched among his belongings until he found a piece of coarse cloth, which he carried up to her. He found she had already made herself a sort of mattress and pillow of the hay, and had placed them so that she

would be able to look through the hole in the wall when she was in bed.

'That's right,' said the old man, 'but it needs to be thicker than that,' and he spread a lot more hay over hers so that she would not feel the hard floor through it. The thick cloth which he had brought for a sheet was so heavy that she could hardly lift it by herself, but its thickness made it a good protection against the prickly hay stalks. Together they spread it out, and Heidi tucked the ends under her 'mattress' to make it all neat and comfortable. Then she looked at her bed thoughtfully for a moment, and said, 'We've forgotten something, Grandfather.'

'What's that?' he asked.

'A blanket to cover it, so that I can creep under it when I go to bed.'

'That's what you think, is it? Suppose I haven't got one?'

'Oh, well then, it doesn't matter,' said Heidi, 'I can easily cover myself with hay,' and she was just going to fetch some more when her grandfather stopped her. 'Wait a bit,' he said, and he went down the ladder, and took from his own bed a great sack made of heavy linen which he brought up to the loft.

'There, isn't that better than hay?' he asked, as they put it over the bed. Heidi was delighted with the result.

'That's a wonderful blanket, and my whole bed's lovely. I wish it was bedtime now so that I could get in it.'

'I think we might have something to eat first, don't you?' said her grandfather. Heidi had forgotten everything else in her excitement over the bed, but at the mention of food, she realized how hungry she was, as she had eaten nothing all day except a piece of bread and a cup of weak coffee before setting out on her long journey. So she replied eagerly, 'Oh, yes.'

'Well then, if we are agreed, let us go and see about a meal,' and he followed Heidi down the ladder. He went to the stove, lifted the big pot off the chain and put a smaller one in its place, then sat himself down on a three-legged stool and blew up the fire with the bellows till it was red and glowing. As the pot began to sing, he put a large piece of cheese on a toasting fork and moved it to and fro in front of the fire until it became golden yellow all over. At first Heidi just stood and watched with great interest, then she thought of something else and ran to the cupboard. When her grandfather brought the steaming pot and the toasted cheese to the table, he found it was laid with two plates, two knives, and the round loaf. Heidi had noticed these things in the cupboard and knew they would be needed for the meal.

'I'm glad to see you can think things out for yourself,' he said, 'but there is something missing.'

Heidi looked at the steaming pot and went back to the cupboard. She could see one mug there and two glasses, so she took the mug and one of the glasses and put them on the table.

'That's right. You know how to be helpful,' said her grandfather. 'Now where are you going to sit?' He himself was in the only chair so Heidi fetched the three-legged stool and sat down on that.

'You've got a seat all right, but rather a low one, and even with my chair you would not be high enough to reach the table.' So saying, the old man got up and pushed his chair in front of Heidi's stool and put the mug filled with milk on it, and a plate on which was a slice of bread covered with the golden toasted cheese. 'Now you have a table to yourself and can start to eat,' he said. Then he perched himself on a corner of the big table and began his own meal.

Heidi took up the mug and drained it thirstly. After that she drew a deep breath – for she had been too busy drinking to breathe – and set the empty mug down.

'Is the milk good?' asked her grandfather.

'The best I've ever drunk,' replied Heidi.

'You must have some more then,' and he refilled her mug.

She ate her bread and cheese, which tasted delicious, and every now and then she took a drink. She looked as happy and contented as anyone could be.

After the meal her grandfather went to the goat-stall and Heidi watched him sweep the floor with a broom and then put down fresh straw for the animals to sleep on. When that job was done he went into the shed, which was built on to the side of the hut, and sawed off several round sticks of wood. Then he bored holes to fit them in a strong flat piece of board, and when he had fitted them all together, the result was a high chair. Heidi watched him, silent in her amazement.

'Do you know what this is?' he asked, when he had finished.

'It's a chair specially for me,' she said wonderingly. 'And how quickly you made it!'

'She's got eyes in her head and knows how to use them,' thought the old man. Next he busied himself with some small repairs in the hut, driving in a nail here and there, tightening a screw in the door and so on. Heidi followed at his heels, watching him with the closest attention, for everything was new and interesting to her.

Thus the afternoon passed. A strong wind sprang up again, whistling and rustling through the fir trees. The sound pleased Heidi so much that she began dancing and jumping about, and her grandfather stood watching her from the door of the shed. Suddenly there was a shrill whistle and Peter appeared in the midst of his herd of goats. Heidi gave a cry of delight and rushed to greet her friends of the morning. As the goats reached the hut they all stood still, except for two graceful animals, one brown and one white, which detached themselves from the others and went up to the old man. Then they began to lick his hands for he was holding a little salt in them, as he did every evening to welcome them home.

Peter went away with the rest of the herd, and Heidi ran to the two goats and began to pat them gently. 'Are these ours, Grandfather?' she asked. 'Both of them? Do they go into the stall? Will they always be here with us?' Her questions followed so closely on each other that her grandfather could hardly get an answer in edgeways. When the goats had finished the salt, the old man said, 'Now go and fetch your mug and the bread.' She obeyed and was back in a flash. Then he filled her mug with milk from the white goat and gave it to her with a slice of bread.

'Eat that and then go to bed,' he said. 'If you want a nightdress or anything like that, you'll find it in the bundle your aunt brought. Now I must see to the goats. Sleep well.'

'Good night, Grandfather,' she called, as he walked off with the animals. Then she ran after them to ask what the goats' names were.

'The white one is called Daisy and the brown Dusky,' replied her grandfather.

'Good night, Daisy, good night, Dusky,' called Heidi after the goats, who had disappeared into their stall. She ate her supper on the bench outside the hut. The wind was so strong, it almost blew her away, so she finished her bread and milk quickly and went indoors and up to bed. There she was soon sleeping as soundly as if she was tucked up in the finest bed in the world.

Her grandfather also went to bed before it was dark, for he always got up with the sun, and that came over the mountain tops very early in the summer. During the night the wind blew so hard that it shook the whole hut and made its beams creak. It shrieked down the chimney and brought one or two of the old fir trees' branches crashing down. So after a while the old man got up, thinking, 'The child may be frightened.'

He climbed up the ladder and went over to her bed. Just then the moon, which had been covered by scudding clouds, shone straight through the hole in the wall on to

Heidi's face. She was fast asleep under her heavy coverlet, one rosy cheek resting on her chubby little arm, and with such a happy expression on her face that she must surely have been dreaming of pleasant things. He stood looking down at her till clouds covered the moon again, darkening the room. Then he went back to bed.

3

A Day with the Goats

Heidi was awakened next morning by a shrill whistle and as she opened her eyes a beam of sunlight came through the hole in the wall, making the hay shine like gold. At first she could not think where she was, then she heard her grandfather's deep voice outside and remembered joyfully that she had come to live in the mountains. She had been glad to leave old Ursula, who was very deaf and felt the cold so much that she sat all day by the kitchen fire or the living-room stove. Heidi had had to stay indoors where the old woman could see her, though she often longed to run outside and play. Now she jumped out of bed, full of excitement at all the new experiences awaiting her. She dressed herself as quickly as possible, then climbed down the ladder and hurried outside. Peter was waiting there with his herd and her grandfather was just bringing Daisy and Dusky from their stall. She went to say good morning to them all.

'Do you want to go up to the pasture with Peter?' asked the old man. This idea clearly delighted her. 'You must have a wash first, or the sun will laugh to see you look so black.'

He pointed to a tub full of water, standing in the sun beside the door, and Heidi went over to it at once and began to splash about. Uncle Alp went indoors, calling to Peter, 'Come here, General of the goats, and bring your knapsack with you.' Peter held out the little bag which contained his meagre lunch, and watched with big eyes as the old man put in a piece of bread and a piece of cheese, both twice as big as his own.

'Take this mug too, and fill it for her twice at dinner time. She doesn't know how to drink straight from the goat as you do. She'll stay with you all day, and mind you look after her and see she doesn't fall down the ravine.'

Heidi came running in. 'The sun can't laugh at me now,' she said. Her grandfather smilingly agreed. In her desire to please the sun, she had rubbed her face with the hard towel until she looked like a boiled lobster.

'When you come home tonight, you'll have to go right inside the tub like a fish, for you'll get black feet running about with the goats. Now off you go.'

It was very beautiful on the mountain that morning. The night wind had blown all the clouds away and the sky was deep blue. The sun shone brilliantly on the green pasture land and on the flowers which were blooming everywhere. There were primroses, blue gentian, and dainty yellow rock-roses. Heidi rushed to and fro, wild with excitement at sight of them. She quite forgot Peter and the goats, and kept stopping to gather flowers and put them in her apron. She wanted to take them home to stick among the hay in her bedroom, to make it look like a meadow.

Peter needed eyes all round his head. It was more than one pair could do to keep watch on Heidi as well as the goats, for they too were running about in all directions. He had to whistle and shout and swing his stick in the air to bring the wandering animals together.

'Where have you got to now, Heidi?' he called once rather crossly.

'Here,' came her voice from behind a little hillock some distance back. It was covered with primulas which had a most delicious scent. Heidi had never smelt anything so lovely before and had sat down among them to enjoy it to the full.

'Come on,' called Peter. 'Uncle said I wasn't to let you fall over the ravine.'

'Where's that?' she called, without moving.

'Right up above. We've still a long way to go, so do come on. Hear the old hawk croaking away up there?'

Heidi jumped up at this last remark and ran to him with her apron full of flowers.

'You've got enough now,' he said, as they started to climb again. 'Don't pick any more, otherwise you'll always be lagging behind, and besides, if you keep on, there won't be any left for tomorrow.'

Heidi saw the sense of this, and anyway her apron was almost full. She kept close to Peter after that, and the goats went on in a more orderly fashion too, for now they could smell the fragrant herbs they loved which grew on their grazing ground, and were anxious to reach them.

Peter usually took up his quarters for the day at the very foot of a rocky mountain peak. On the steep slopes above, there were only a few bushes and stunted fir trees, and the summit itself was just bare rock. On one side was the sheer drop over the ravine which Uncle Alp had spoken of. When they reached this place Peter took off his knapsack and laid it, for safety, in a little hollow, for there were sometimes strong gusts of wind and he had no wish to see his precious food go bowling down the mountain. Then he lay down in the sun to rest after the strenuous climb. Heidi put her apronful of flowers in the same little hollow. Then she sat down beside Peter and looked around her. The valley below was bathed in sunlight. In front of them a snowclad mountain stood out against the blue sky and to the left of this was a huge mass of rock, with jagged twin peaks. Everything was very still. Only a gentle breeze set the blue and yellow flowers nodding on their slender stems.

Peter fell asleep and the goats climbed about among the bushes. Heidi sat quite still, enjoying it all. She gazed so intently at the mountain peaks that soon they seemed to her to have faces and to be looking at her like old friends. Suddenly she heard a loud noise. Looking up, she

saw an enormous bird, circling overhead with outstretched wings and croaking harshly as it flew. 'Peter, Peter, wake up!' she cried. 'Here's the hawk.' Peter sat up and together they watched as the great bird soared higher and higher into the sky and finally disappeared over the grey peaks.

'Where's it gone to?' asked Heidi, who had never seen a bird as big as that before and had watched its flight with great interest.

'Home to its nest,' replied Peter.

'Does it live right up there? How wonderful! Why does it make such a noise?'

'Because it has to,' explained Peter briefly.

'Let's climb up and see where it lives,' she proposed.

'Oh, no, we won't! Even the goats can't climb as high as that, and don't forget Uncle told me to look after you,' he said with marked disapproval. To Heidi's surprise he then began whistling and shouting, but the goats recognized the familiar sounds and came towards him from all directions, though some lingered to nibble a tasty blade of grass, while others butted one another playfully. Heidi jumped up and ran among them, delighted to see them so obviously enjoying themselves. She spoke to each one, and every one was different and easily distinguishable from the others.

Meanwhile Peter opened his bag and spread its contents out in a square on the ground, two large portions for Heidi and two smaller ones for himself. Then he filled the mug with milk from Daisy and placed it in the middle of the square. He called to Heidi, but she was slower to come than the goats had been. She was so busy with her new playmates that she had ears and eyes for nothing else. He went on calling till his voice re-echoed from the rocks and at last she appeared. When she saw the meal laid out so invitingly, she skipped up and down with pleasure.

'Stop jigging about,' said Peter, 'it's dinner time. Sit down and begin.'

'Is the milk for me?'

'Yes, and those huge pieces of bread and cheese. I'll get you another mugful from Daisy when you've drunk that one. Then I'll have a drink myself.'

'Where will you get yours from?' she inquired.

'From my own goat, Spot. Now start eating.'

She drank the milk, but ate only a small piece of bread and passed the rest over to Peter, with the cheese. 'You can have that,' she said. 'I've had enough.' He looked at her with amazement for he had never in his life had any food to give away. At first he hesitated, thinking she must be joking, but she went on holding it out to him and finally put it on his knee. This convinced him that she really meant what she said, so he took it, nodded his thanks and settled down to enjoy the feast. Heidi meanwhile sat watching the goats.

'What are they all called, Peter?' she asked presently.

Peter did not know a great deal, but this was a question he could answer without difficulty. He told her all the names, pointing to each animal in turn. She listened attentively and soon knew one from the other. Each had little tricks by which it could easily be recognized by anyone looking at them closely, as she was doing. Big Turk had strong horns, and was always trying to butt the others, so they kept out of his way as much as possible. The only one to answer him back was a frisky little kid called Finch, with sharp little horns, and Turk was generally too astonished at such impudence to make a fight of it. Heidi was particularly attracted to a little white goat called Snowflake, which was bleating most pitifully. She had tried earlier to comfort it. Now she ran up to it again, put her arm round its neck, and asked fondly, 'What's the matter, Snowflake? What are you crying for?' At that, the goat nestled against her and stopped bleating.

Peter had not yet finished his meal, but he called out between mouthfuls, 'She's crying because her mother doesn't come up here any more. She's been sold to someone in Mayenfeld.'

'Where's her grandmother then?'

'Hasn't got one.'

'Or her grandfather?'

'Hasn't one.'

'Poor Snowflake,' said Heidi, hugging the little animal again. 'Don't cry any more. I shall be up here every day now, and you can always come to me if you feel lonely.' Snowflake rubbed her head on the little girl's shoulder, and seemed to be comforted.

Peter had now finished eating, and came up to Heidi who was making fresh discoveries all the time. She noticed that Daisy and Dusky seemed more independent than the other goats and carried themselves with a sort of dignity. They led the way as the herd went up to the bushes again. Some of them stopped here and there to sample a tasty herb, others went straight up, leaping over any small obstacles in their path. Turk was up to his tricks as usual, but Daisy and Dusky ignored him completely and were soon nibbling daintily at the leaves of the two thickest bushes. Heidi watched them for some time. Then she turned to Peter, who was lying full length on the grass.

'Daisy and Dusky are the prettiest of all the goats,' she said.

'I know. That's Uncle – he keeps them very clean and gives them salt and he has a fine stall for them,' he replied. Then he suddenly jumped up and ran after his herd, with Heidi close behind, anxious not to miss anything. He had noticed that inquisitive little Finch was right at the edge of the ravine, where the ground fell away so steeply that if it went any farther, it might go over and would certainly break its legs. Peter stretched out his hands to catch hold of the little kid, but he slipped and fell, though he managed to grasp one of its legs and Finch, highly indignant at such treatment, struggled wildly to get away. 'Heidi, come here,' called Peter, 'come and help.'

He couldn't get up unless he let go of Finch's leg which he was nearly pulling out of its socket already. Heidi saw at once what to do, and pulled up a handful of grass which she held under Finch's nose.

'Come on, don't be silly,' she said. 'You don't want to fall down there and hurt yourself.'

At that the little goat turned round and ate the grass from her hand, and Peter was able to get up. He took hold of the cord, on which a little bell was hung round Finch's neck. Heidi took hold of it too, on the other side, and together they brought the runaway safely back to the herd. Then Peter took up his stick to give it a good beating, and seeing what was coming, Finch tried to get out of the way.

'Don't beat him,' pleaded Heidi. 'See how frightened he is.'

'He deserves it,' Peter replied, raising his arm, but she caught hold of him and exclaimed, 'No, you're not to! It will hurt him. Leave him alone!' She looked at him so fiercely that he was astonished and dropped the stick.

'I won't beat him if you'll give me some of your cheese again tomorrow,' he said, feeling he ought to have some compensation after the fright the little goat had given him.

'You can have it all, tomorrow and every day,' promised Heidi, 'I shan't want it. And I'll give you some of my bread as well, but then you must never beat Finch or Snowflake or any of them.'

'It's all the same to me,' said Peter, which was his way of saying that he promised. He let Finch go and it bounded back to the herd.

It was getting late and the setting sun spread a wonderful golden glow over the grass and the flowers, and the high peaks shone and sparkled. Heidi sat for a while, quietly enjoying the beautiful scene, then all at once she jumped up, crying, 'Peter, Peter! A fire, a fire! The mountains are on fire, and the snow and the sky too. Look, the trees and the rocks are all burning, even up there by the hawk's nest. Everything's on fire!'

'It's always like this in the evening,' Peter said calmly, whittling away at his stick. 'It's not a fire.'

'What is it then?' she cried, rushing about to look at the wonderful sight from all sides. 'What is it, Peter?'

'It just happens,' he said.

'Oh, just see, the mountains have got all rosy red! Look at the one with the snow on it, and that one with the big rocks at the top. What are their names, Peter?'

'Mountains don't have names,' he answered.

'How pretty the rosy snow looks, and the red rocks. Oh dear,' she added, after a pause, 'now the colour's going and everything's turning grey. Oh, it's all over.' She sat down, looking as upset as if it was indeed the end of everything.

'It'll be the same again tomorrow,' explained Peter. 'Now

it's time to go home.' He whistled and called the goats together and they started the downward journey.

'Is it always like this up here?' asked Heidi hopefully.

'Usually.'

'Will it really be the same tomorrow?'

'Yes, it will,' he assured her.

With this she was content and as she had so much to think about, she didn't say another word till they reached the hut and saw her grandfather sitting under the fir trees, on the seat he had fixed there so that he could watch for the return of his animals. The little girl ran towards him, followed by Daisy and Dusky, and Peter called 'Good night, Heidi. Come again tomorrow.' She ran back to say goodbye and promised to go with him next day. Then she put her arms around Snowflake's neck and said, 'Sleep well, Snowflake. Remember I'll be coming with you again tomorrow and you're not to cry any more.' Snowflake gave her a trusting look and scampered off after the other goats.

'Oh, Grandfather,' Heidi cried, as she ran back to him, 'it was lovely up there, with all the flowers and then the fire and the rosy rocks. And see what I've brought you.' She shook out the contents of her little apron in front of him, but the poor flowers had all faded and looked like so much hay. She was terribly upset.

'What's happened to them? They weren't like that when I picked them.'

'They wanted to stay in the sun and didn't like being shut up in your apron,' he explained.

'Then I'll never pick any more. Grandfather, why does the hawk croak so loudly?'

'You go and jump in the washtub, while I milk the goats,' he replied. 'Then we'll have supper together indoors and I'll tell you about the hawk.'

As soon as Heidi was settled on her new high chair with her grandfather beside her and a mug of milk in front of her, she repeated her question.

'He's jeering at all the people who live in the villages down below and make trouble for one another. You can imagine he's saying, "If only you would all mind your own business and climb up to the mountain tops as I do, you'd be a lot better off."' The old man spoke these words so fiercely that it really reminded Heidi of the croaking of the great bird.

'Why haven't mountains got names?' she asked next.

'But they have,' he told her, 'and if you can describe one to me so that I can recognize it, I'll tell you its name.'

So she told him about the mountain with the twin peaks and described it very well. Her grandfather looked pleased. 'That's called Falkniss,' he said. Then she described the one covered with snow and he told her its name was Scesaplana.

'You enjoyed yourself, then?' he asked.

'Oh yes,' she cried, and told him all the wonderful things that had happened during the day. 'The fire in the evening was the best of all. Peter said it wasn't a fire, but he couldn't tell me what it really was. You can though, Grandfather, can't you?'

'It's the sun's way of saying goodnight to the mountains,' he explained. 'He spreads that beautiful light over them so that they won't forget him till he comes back in the morning.'

Heidi liked this explanation very much, and longed for another day to begin so that she could go up and watch the sun's goodnight again. But first she had to go to bed, and all night long she slept peacefully on her mattress of hay, dreaming of mountains and flowers and of Snowflake bounding happily about in the midst of it all.

4

A Visit to Grannie

All through that summer Heidi went up to the pasture every day with Peter and the goats, and grew brown as a berry in the mountain sunshine. She grew strong and healthy and was as happy and carefree as a bird in her new life. But when autumn came, strong winds began to blow, and her grandfather said to her, 'Today you must stay at home. A little thing like you might easily get blown over the side of the mountain by a gust of wind.'

Peter was always very disappointed when Heidi could not go with him. He had grown so used to her company that he found it terribly dull to be by himself again, and of course he missed the good bread and cheese she always shared with him. The goats were twice as troublesome, too, when she was not there. They seemed to miss her and scattered all over the place, as though they were looking for her.

But Heidi was happy wherever she was. Of course she loved going up the mountain where there was always so much to see, but she also enjoyed going round with her grandfather, watching him at his carpentry and all the other jobs. She specially liked to see him make the goat's milk cheese. He rolled up his sleeves and plunged his arms deep into a big pot of milk which he stirred thoroughly with his hands until in due course he produced the delicious round cheeses. But what she liked most of all was the noise the wind made in the old fir trees. She often left what she was doing to go and stand under them with her face turned up, listening and watching the swaying branches as the wind whistled and whirled through them. The wind blew right through her too, though now that the weather was cooler she wore socks and shoes and put on a dress once more. That strange music in the tree tops had a special fascination for her and she could not stay indoors when she heard it.

All at once it turned really cold and Peter arrived in the mornings blowing on his hands to warm them. Then one night it started to snow and in the morning everything was white. It snowed until there was not a single green leaf to be seen, and of course Peter didn't bring the goats up. From the window Heidi watched with delight as the snowflakes fell, faster and faster, and the snow drifted higher and higher till the hut was buried up to the window sills and it was impossible to go out. She hoped it would go on falling until the hut was completely covered, so that they would have to light the lamp during the day, but that did not happen. Next morning her grandfather was able to dig his way out, and shovelled the snow away from the walls, throwing up great piles of it from his spade as he worked. Then in the afternoon he and Heidi sat down by the fire, each on a three-legged stool, for of course he had long ago made one for her. They were interrupted by a great banging at the door, as though someone was kicking it. Then it was opened, and there stood Peter, knocking the snow off his boots before coming in. He had had to fight his way through high drifts and it was so cold that the snow had frozen on to him, and still clung to his clothes. But he had kept bravely on, determined to get to Heidi after not seeing her for a whole week.

'Hullo,' he said and went straight over to the stove. He didn't say anything more but stood beaming at them, well pleased to be there. Heidi watched in astonishment as the heat of the stove began to thaw the snow so that it trickled off him in a steady flow.

'Well, General,' said the old man, 'how are you getting on now that you've had to leave your army and start chewing a pencil?'

'Chewing a pencil?' exclaimed Heidi with interest.

'Yes, in the winter Peter has to go to school and learn to read and write. That's no easy matter you know, and it sometimes helps a bit to chew a pencil, doesn't it, General?'

'Yes it does,' agreed Peter.

Immediately Heidi wanted to know just what he did at school. Peter always found it difficult to put his thoughts into words and Heidi had so many questions to ask that no sooner had he managed to deal with one than she was ready with two or three more, most of them needing a whole sentence in reply. His clothes were quite dry again before she was satisfied. The old man listened quietly to their chatter, smiling from time to time. As they fell silent he got up and went over to the cupboard.

'Well, General, you've been under fire, now you'll need some refreshment,' he said.

He soon had supper ready and Heidi put chairs round

the table. The hut was less bare now than when she first arrived, for Grandfather had made one bench which was fixed to the wall and other seats big enough for two people, for Heidi always liked to be close beside him. Now they could all sit down in comfort, and as Peter did so, he opened his round eyes very wide at the huge piece of dried meat Uncle Alp put on a thick slice of bread for him. It was a long time since he had had such a good meal. As soon as they had finished eating Peter got ready to go, for it was growing dark.

'Goodbye,' he said, 'and thank you. I'll come again next Sunday, and Grannie says she would like you to come and see her.'

Heidi was delighted at the idea of going to visit someone, for that would be something quite new, so the first thing she said next morning was 'Grandfather, I must go and see Peter's Grannie today. She'll be expecting me.'

'The snow is too deep,' said Uncle Alp, trying to put her off.

But the idea was firmly in her head, and day after day she said at least half a dozen times that she really must go or Grannie would be tired of waiting for her. On the fourth day after Peter's visit the snow froze hard and crackled underfoot, and the sun was shining brightly, straight on to Heidi's face as she sat on her high chair eating her dinner. Again she said, 'I must go and see Grannie today, or she'll think I'm not coming.'

Her grandfather left the table and went up to the loft, from which he brought down the thick sack off her bed. 'Come on, then,' he said, and they went out together.

Heidi skipped delightedly into the shining white world. The branches of the fir trees were weighed down with snow which sparkled in the sunshine. Heidi had never seen anything like it.

'Just look at the trees,' she cried, 'they're all gold and silver.'

Meanwhile Grandfather had dragged a big sledge out of the shed. It had a bar along one side to hold on to, and it was steered by pressing the heels against the ground on one side or the other. To please Heidi he went round with her to look at the snow-clad trees. Then he sat down

on the sledge with her on his knees, well wrapped up in the sack to keep her warm. He held her tightly with his left arm and, taking hold of the bar with his right hand, pushed off with both feet. They went down the mountain so fast that Heidi felt as though she was flying, and screamed with delight. They stopped with a jerk just outside Peter's hut. Grandfather set her on her feet and took off the sack.

'Now go in,' he said, 'but start for home as soon as it begins to get dark.' Then he turned back up the mountain, pulling the sledge behind him.

The door Heidi opened led into a small kitchen, in which there was a stove and some pots on a shelf. A second door opened into another low little room. Compared with Grandfather's hut with its fine big room and the hay loft above, this place seemed wretchedly cramped. She went in and saw a woman sitting at a table mending a jacket which she recognized as Peter's. In one corner another woman, old and bent, was spinning. Heidi went straight to her and said, 'Hullo, Grannie, here I am at last. I expect you thought I was never coming.'

Grannie raised her head and felt for Heidi's hand. When she had found it, she held it in her own for a while and then said, 'Are you the child from Uncle Alp's? Are you Heidi?'

'Yes, and Grandfather has just brought me down on the sledge.'

'Fancy that. And yet your hand is so warm. Bridget, did Uncle Alp really bring her himself?'

Peter's mother left her mending to come and look at the child. 'I don't know, mother,' she said, 'it does not sound likely. She must be mistaken.'

Heidi looked her straight in the eye and said firmly, 'I'm not mistaken. It was Grandfather. He wrapped me up in my blanket and brought me down himself.'

'Well, well. Peter must have been right after all in what he told us about Uncle Alp,' said Grannie. 'We always thought he'd got it all wrong. Who would have believed it? To tell the truth, I didn't think the child would last three weeks up there. What does she look like, Bridget?'

'She's thin, like her mother was, but she's got black eyes and curly hair like Tobias and the old man. She's really more like them, I think.'

Heidi looked about the room while the women were talking, and her sharp eyes missed nothing.

'One of your shutters is hanging loose, Grannie,' she remarked. 'Grandfather would soon mend it, and it'll break the window if nothing's done about it. Look how it bangs to and fro.'

'I can't see it, my dear, but I can hear it very well, and everything else that creaks and clatters here when the wind blows through the cracks. The place is falling to pieces and at night, when the other two are asleep, I am often afraid that some time it may fall on us and kill us all. And there's no one to do anything about it. Peter doesn't know how.'

'Why can't you see the shutter?' asked Heidi, pointing. 'Look, there it goes again.'

'I can't see at all, child, it's not only the shutter,' said the old woman with a sigh.

'If I go out and pull the shutter right back so that it's really light in here, you'll be able to see, won't you?'

'No, not even then, light or dark makes no difference to me.'

'But if you come out in the shining white snow, I'm sure you'll see then. Come and see.' Heidi took the old woman's hand and tried to pull her up, for she was very upset at the thought of her never seeing anything.

'Let me be, child. I can't see any better even in the light of the snow. I'm always in the dark.'

'Even in summer, Grannie?' Heidi persisted anxiously. 'Surely you can see the sunshine and watch it say good-night to the mountains and make them all red like fire. Can't you?'

'No, child, nor that either. I shall never see them again.'

Heidi burst into tears. 'Can't anyone make you see?' she sobbed. 'Isn't there anyone who can?'

For some time Grannie tried in vain to comfort her. Heidi hardly ever cried, but when she did it was always difficult to make her stop. The old woman got quite worried and at last she said, 'Come here, my dear, and listen to me. I can't see, but I can hear, and when one is blind, it is so good to hear a friendly voice, and yours I love already. Come and sit beside me and tell me what you and Grandfather do up on the mountain. I used to know him well, but I haven't heard anything of him for years, except what Peter tells us – and that's not much.'

Heidi dried her tears. She saw a ray of hope. 'Just wait till I tell Grandfather about you. He'll be able to make you see, and he'll mend the hut too. He can do anything.'

Grannie did not contradict her, and Heidi began to chatter away telling everything she did up there, both in summer and in winter. She told how clever Grandfather was at making things, how he had made stools and chairs and new mangers for the goats, and even a bath tub, and a milk bowl, yes, and spoons – all out of wood. Grannie understood from her voice how eagerly she must have watched him at work.

'I'd like to be able to make things like that myself one day,' Heidi ended up.

'Did you hear that, Bridget?' Grannie asked her daughter. 'Fancy Uncle doing all that!'

Suddenly the outer door banged and Peter burst into the room. He pulled up short and stared when he saw Heidi, then gave a very friendly grin as she greeted him.

'What, back from school already?' asked Grannie. 'It's years since I've known an afternoon pass so quickly. Well Peterkin, how are you getting on with your reading?'

'Just the same,' he replied.

'Oh dear,' she sighed, 'I hoped you might have something different to tell me by now. You'll be twelve in February.'

'What to tell you? What do you mean?' asked Heidi, all interest.

'Only that perhaps he'd learned to read at last. There's an old prayer book up on the shelf, with some beautiful hymns in it. I haven't heard them for a very long time and can't repeat them any more to myself. I keep hoping Peterkin will be able to read them to me. But he doesn't seem able to learn. It's too difficult for him.'

'I think I must light the lamp,' said Bridget, who had been darning all this while. 'The afternoon has passed so quickly I hadn't noticed it was getting dark.'

Heidi jumped up at that. 'If it's getting dark I must go,' she cried. 'Goodbye, Grannie.' She said goodbye to the others and was just leaving when Grannie called anxiously, 'Wait a minute, Heidi, you can't go alone. Peter will come with you and see you don't fall. And don't stand about and let her get cold. Has she something warm to put on?'

'No, I haven't,' Heidi called back, 'but I shan't be cold,' and she ran off so fast that Peter could hardly keep pace with her.

'Bridget, take my shawl and run after her,' cried Grannie in distress, 'she'll freeze to death in this bitter cold,' and Bridget took it and went after them. But the children had only gone a very little way up the mountain when they saw Uncle Alp striding towards them, and almost at once they were together.

'Good girl, you did as you were told,' he said. Then he wrapped her in the sack again, picked her up in his arms, and turned for home. Bridget was just in time to see what happened, and she went back indoors with Peter to describe the surprising sight to her mother.

'Thank God the child is all right,' exclaimed the old woman. 'I hope Uncle Alp will let her come to see me again. Her visit has done me a deal of good. What a kind heart the little one has and how pleasantly she chatters.' Grannie was in very good spirits. 'I hope she comes again,' she said several times that evening, 'it would be something to look forward to.'

'Yes, indeed,' agreed Bridget each time, while Peter grinned broadly, and said, 'Told you so.'

And out on the mountain Heidi was chattering away inside the sack to her grandfather, though he couldn't hear a word through its eightfold thickness.

'Wait till we're home and then tell me,' he said.

As soon as they were indoors and Heidi had been unwrapped she began, 'Tomorrow we must take a hammer and some big nails down to Peter's house, so that you can mend Grannie's shutter and lots of other things too, because her whole house creaks and rattles.'

'Oh, we must, must we? Who told you to say that?'

'Nobody told me. I just know. The shutters and doors

and things are all loose and bang about, and then Grannie gets very frightened and can't sleep. She's afraid the house will fall down on top of them. And she can't see, and she says no one can make her better, but I'm sure you can, Grandfather. Fancy not being able to see, and being frightened too! We'll go and help her tomorrow, won't we?' She was clinging to the old man and looked up at him confidently. He gazed back for a moment and then said, 'Well, we can at least stop the banging and we'll do that tomorrow.'

Heidi was delighted and went skipping round the hut, chanting, 'We'll do it tomorrow! We'll do it tomorrow!'

Uncle Alp kept his promise. On the following afternoon they went down on the sledge again and Heidi was set down outside the cottage. 'Go in now,' he said, as before, 'but come away when it begins to get dark.' Then he laid Heidi's sack on the sledge and disappeared round the side of the building.

Heidi had hardly set foot inside the door before Grannie called out from her corner, 'Here she comes again!' She stopped spinning and held out both hands. Heidi ran to her and pulled up a little stool beside her, sat down and began to chatter away. Suddenly there came a series of loud bangs on the wall which so startled Grannie that she almost knocked her spinning-wheel over.

'This time the place is really falling down,' she cried tremulously. Heidi took hold of her arm and said, 'Don't be afraid, Grannie. That's only Grandfather with his hammer. He's mending everything so that you won't be frightened any more.'

'Is it true? God has not forgotten us after all. Can you hear it, Bridget? It really does sound like a hammer. Go out and see who it is, and if it's Uncle Alp ask him to come in so that I can thank him.'

It was Uncle Alp of course. Bridget found him nailing a wedge-shaped piece of wood on to the wall. 'Good day, Uncle,' she said. 'Mother and I are grateful to you for helping us like this, and Mother would like to thank you herself if you'll step inside. I'm sure no one else would have done as much for us and we won't forget it . . .'

But he interrupted her roughly. 'That's enough,' he said. 'I know quite well what you really think of me. Go indoors. I can see for myself what wants doing.' Bridget turned away, not liking to disobey him, and he went on hammering away all round the walls. Then he climbed up on to the roof and mended some holes there, till he had used up all the nails he had brought with him. By this time it was growing dark, and he took the sledge out of the goat-stall where he had left it, just as Heidi came to find him. He wrapped her up and carried her as he had done the evening before, though he had also to drag the sledge behind him. He knew it would not be safe for her to ride up on it without him beside her, for the wind would soon have blown the coverings away and she would have been frozen.

So he pulled it after him with one hand, holding Heidi safe and warm in the other arm.

So the winter went on. Poor, blind Grannie was happy again after many sad, dark years, for now she always had something pleasant to look forward to. Every day she listened for Heidi's light step and when the door opened and the little girl came in, she always said, 'Praise be, here she is again.' Then Heidi would sit down and chatter merrily away. These hours passed so quickly that Grannie never once had to ask Bridget, 'Isn't the day nearly over?' Instead, after Heidi had left, she often remarked, 'Wasn't that a short afternoon?' and Bridget would agree that it seemed no time since she had cleared away after dinner.

'God keep the child safe and Uncle Alp in a good humour,' was the old woman's constant prayer. She often asked Bridget if the child looked well. To that Bridget was always able to reply, 'She looks like a rosy apple.'

Heidi grew very fond of Peter's Grannie, and when she understood that no one could make her see again, she was very sad. But as Grannie told her over and over again that she didn't mind being blind nearly so much when Heidi was with her, she came down on the sledge with her grandfather every fine day. He always brought his hammer and nails and any other materials needed, and gradually he repaired the whole cottage, so that Grannie was no longer frightened by noises at night.

5

Two Unexpected Visitors

A winter passed and then another happy summer, and Heidi's second winter on the mountain was nearly over. She began to look forward eagerly to the spring, when warm winds would melt the snow and all the blue and yellow flowers would bloom again. Then she would go up to the pasture once more, and that she always enjoyed more than anything. She was now seven and had learnt a great many useful things from her grandfather. She knew how to handle the goats, and Daisy and Dusky ran after her like pet dogs, bleating with pleasure at the sound of her voice. Twice during the winter Peter had brought up messages from the schoolmaster in Dörfli, to say that Uncle Alp must send the child who was living with him to school. She was quite old enough, and ought in fact to have started the winter before. Both times Uncle Alp replied that if the schoolmaster had anything to say to him, he could always be found at home – but he did not mean to send the child to school. These messages Peter delivered faithfully.

When the March sun began to melt the snow on the slopes, the first snowdrops came out. The trees had shaken off their burden of snow and their branches were swaying freely in the wind. Heidi spent her time between the hut, the goat-stall, and the fir trees, and kept running to report to her grandfather how much bigger the patch of green grass had grown. One morning, just as she was dashing out of the hut for about the tenth time, she saw an old man standing on the threshold, dressed in black and looking very solemn. He saw she was startled and said in a friendly voice, 'You needn't be afraid of me. I'm fond of children. Come and shake hands. I'm sure you must be Heidi. Where's your grandfather?'

'He's indoors, making wooden spoons,' she told him, and showed him in.

He was the old pastor from Dörfli who had been a neighbour of Uncle Alp's when he lived there. 'Good morning, my friend,' he said, as he went up to him.

Uncle Alp looked up in surprise, and got to his feet. 'Good morning, pastor,' he replied. Then he pulled forward a chair, adding, 'If you don't mind a hard seat, take this one.'

'I haven't seen you for a long time,' said the pastor, when he had sat down.

'Nor I you,' was the reply.

'And now I've come to talk to you about something. I expect you can guess what.' He paused and glanced at

Heidi who was standing by the door, looking at him with interest.

'Run and take some salt to the goats, Heidi, and stay with them until I fetch you,' said her grandfather, and she did as she was told at once.

'That child should have gone to school this winter, if not last,' the pastor went on. 'The teacher sent you a warning, but you didn't take any notice. What do you intend to do with her, neighbour?'

'I don't intend to send her to school.'

The pastor stared at Uncle Alp, who was sitting with his arms folded and a very stubborn expression on his face.

'Then what will become of her?' he asked.

'She'll grow up with the goats and the birds. They won't teach her any bad ideas, and she'll be very happy.'

'She's not a goat, nor a bird, but a little girl. She may not learn anything bad from such companions, but they won't teach her to read or to write, and it's high time she began. I've come to tell you this in all friendliness, so that you can think it over during the summer and make your plans accordingly. This is the last winter when the child can stay up here without any education. Next winter she must come regularly to school.'

'She'll do no such thing,' said the old man obstinately.

'Do you really mean that nothing we can say will make you see reason about this? You've been about the world and must have seen and learnt a great deal. I should have credited you with more sense, neighbour.'

'Would you indeed,' said Uncle Alp drily, but his voice showed that he was not quite easy in his mind. 'Do you think I'm going to send a little girl like Heidi down the mountain every day next winter, no matter how cold or stormy it may be? And have her come back at night when it is often blowing and snowing so hard that it's difficult for a grown man to keep his feet? Perhaps you remember the queer spells her mother used to have. Such a strain might well make this child develop something of the same sort. If anyone tries to force me to send her, I'm quite prepared to go to law about it. Then we'll see what will happen.'

'You're right so far,' agreed the pastor amiably. 'It wouldn't be possible to send her to school from here. And you're fond of her, I can see. Won't you, for her sake, do what you should have done long ago – come back to Dörfli to live? What sort of a life do you lead up here, at odds with God and man? And there's not a soul to help you if you were in any trouble. I can't imagine how even you survive the cold in winter, and I'm amazed that the child can stand up to it at all.'

'The child has young blood and a warm bed, I'd have you know,' Uncle Alp replied. 'And I can always find plenty of wood. My shed is full of it and the fire never goes out the whole winter through. I've no intention of coming back to Dörfli to live. The people there despise me and I them, so it's better for us to keep apart.'

'It is not good for you,' said the pastor. 'I know what you are missing. Believe me, people don't feel so unkindly towards you as you think. Make your peace with God, neighbour, and ask His forgiveness, where you know you need it. Then come back to Dörfli, and see how differently people will receive you, and how happy you can become again.'

He stood up and held out his hand. 'I shall count on seeing you back among us next winter, old friend,' he said. 'I should be sorry if we had to put any pressure upon you. Give me your hand and promise you'll come down and live among us again and be reconciled to God and to your neighbours.'

Uncle Alp shook hands with him, but said slowly, 'I know you mean well, but I can't do what you ask. That's final. I shan't send the child to school, nor come back to the village to live.'

'May God help you, then,' said the pastor and he went sadly out of the hut and down the mountain.

He left Uncle Alp out of humour. After dinner when Heidi said as usual, 'Now it's time to go to Grannie's,' he only replied, 'Not today,' and didn't say another word that day. Next morning she asked again if they were going to Grannie's, and he only said gruffly, 'We'll see.' But before the dinner dishes had been cleared away they had another visitor. This time it was Detie. She was wearing a smart hat with a feather and a long dress which swept the ground as she walked – and the floor of the hut was not particularly good for it. Uncle Alp looked her up and down in silence. However Detie was all amiability, and started to talk at once.

'How well Heidi looks,' she exclaimed. 'I hardly recognize her! You've certainly looked after her all right. Of course I always intended to come back for her because I know she must be in your way, but two years ago I just didn't know what else to do with her. I've been on the lookout for a good home for her ever since, and that's why I'm here now. I've heard of a wonderful chance for her. I've been into it all thoroughly and everything's all right. It's a chance in a million! The family I work for have got some very rich relations who live in one of the best houses in Frankfurt. They've a little girl who's paralysed on one side and very delicate. She has to be in a wheel-chair all the time and has lessons by herself with a tutor. That's terribly dull for her and she longs for a little playmate. They've been talking about it at my place because of course my family, being relations, are very sorry for her and would like to help her. That's how I heard what they wanted – a simple, unspoilt child to come and stay with her, they said, someone a bit out of the ordinary. I thought of Heidi at once, and I went and saw the lady who keeps house for them. I told her all about

Heidi and she said she thought she would do. Isn't that wonderful? Isn't Heidi a lucky girl? And, if they like her, and anything were to happen to their daughter, which is quite likely, you know, it might well be that . . .'

'Have you nearly finished?' Uncle Alp interrupted her, having listened so far in silence.

Detie tossed her head in exasperation. 'Anyone would think I'd been telling you something quite unimportant,' she said. 'There's no one else in the whole district who wouldn't be thankful to hear such a piece of news.'

'Tell them then,' he said drily, 'it doesn't interest me.'

Detie flew up like a rocket at these words. 'If that's what you think, let me tell you something more. The child will soon be eight and she doesn't know a thing and you won't let her learn. Oh yes, they told me in Dörfli about your not sending her to school or to church. But she's my sister's child and I'm still responsible for her welfare. And when the chance of such good fortune has come her way, only a person who doesn't care what happens to anyone could want to keep her from it. But I shan't let you, I warn you, and everyone in Dörfli's on my side. Also I'd advise you to think twice before taking the matter to court. You might find things being remembered which you'd rather forget. There's no knowing what may come to light in a court of law.'

'That's enough,' thundered the old man, with his eyes ablaze. 'Take her then and spoil her. But don't ever bring her back to me. I don't want to see her with a feather in her hat or hear her talk as you have done today.' And he strode out of the hut.

'You've made Grandfather angry,' said Heidi, giving her aunt a far-from-friendly look.

'He'll get over it,' said Detie. 'Come on now, where are your clothes?'

'I'm not coming,' said Heidi.

'Don't talk nonsense,' snapped her aunt, but continued in a coaxing tone, 'you don't know what a good time you're going to have.' She went to the cupboard and took out Heidi's things and made them into a bundle. 'Put your hat on. It's pretty shabby, but it'll have to do. Hurry now, we must be off.'

'I'm not coming,' Heidi repeated.

'Don't be stupid and obstinate like one of those old goats!' snapped Detie again. 'I suppose it's from them you've learned such behaviour. Just you try to understand now. You saw how angry your grandfather was. You heard him say he didn't want to see us again. He *wants* you to go with me, so you'd better obey if you don't want to make him angrier still. Besides you can't think how nice it is in Frankfurt and how much there is going on there. And if you don't like it you can always come back here. Grandfather will be in a better mood by then.'

'Could I come straight back again this evening?' asked Heidi.

'Well, no. We shall only get as far as Mayenfeld today. Tomorrow we'll go on by train, but you can always get back the same way if you want to come home. It doesn't take long.' Detie caught hold of Heidi with one hand, and tucked the bundle of clothes under the other arm, and so they set off down the mountain.

It was still too early in the year for Peter to be taking the goats up to the pasture, so he was at school in Dörfli – or should have been. But every now and then he played truant, for he thought school a great waste of time and could see no point in trying to learn to read. He liked much better to wander off and gather wood, which was

always needed. On this particular day he was just coming home with an enormous bundle of hazel twigs when he saw Heidi and Detie. 'Where are you going?' he asked, as they came up to him.

'I'm going to Frankfurt on a visit with Auntie,' said Heidi, 'but I'll come in and see Grannie first. She'll be expecting me.'

'No, you won't, there's no time for that,' said Detie firmly, as Heidi tried to pull her hand away. 'You can go and see her when you come back.' And she kept tight hold of her and hurried on. She was afraid Heidi would change her mind again, if she went in there, and the old woman would certainly take her side. Peter rushed into the cottage and flung his sticks on the table as hard as he could. He just had to relieve his feelings somehow. Grannie jumped up in alarm and cried, 'Whatever's that noise?' His mother, who had almost been knocked out of her chair, said in her usual patient voice, 'What's the matter, Peterkin? Why are you so wild?'

'She's taking Heidi away,' he shouted.

'Who is? Where are they going?' asked Grannie anxiously, though she could guess the answer, for her daughter had seen Detie pass on her way up to Uncle Alp's, and had told her about it then. Now she opened the window and called beseechingly, 'Don't take the child away from us, Detie!' But they had hurried on, and though they heard her voice, they couldn't make out the words, but Detie guessed what they were and pulled Heidi along as fast as she could go.

'That was Grannie calling. I want to go and see her,' said Heidi, trying again to free her hand.

'We can't stop for that, we're late as it is,' retorted Detie. 'We don't want to miss the train. Just you think of the wonderful time you'll have in Frankfurt, and when you come back again – if indeed you ever want to, once you're there – you can bring a present for Grannie.'

'Can I really?' Heidi asked, pleased with this idea. 'What could I get for her?'

'Something nice to eat perhaps. I expect she'd like the soft white rolls they have in town. She must find black bread almost too hard to eat now.'

'Yes, she does. I've seen her give her piece to Peter because she couldn't bite it. Let's hurry, Detie. Can we get to Frankfurt today? Then I could come back at once with the rolls.' She started to run so fast that Detie, hampered by the bundle of clothes under her arm, found it hard work to keep up with her. But she was glad to get along so quickly because they were coming to Dörfli where she knew people would start asking questions in a way which might upset the child again.

Sure enough as they went through the village, remarks came from all sides. 'Is she running away from Uncle Alp?' 'Fancy, she's still alive!' 'She looks well enough.' To all questions Detie replied, 'I can't stop to talk. You can see we're in a great hurry and we've a long way to go.' She was thankful when they had left the village behind. Heidi didn't say another word, but ran on as quickly as she could.

From that day Uncle Alp grew more silent and forbidding than ever. On the rare occasions when he passed through Dörfli with his basket of cheeses on his back and a heavy stick in his hand, mothers kept their children well out of the way, for he looked so wild. He never spoke to anyone, but went on down to the valley, where he sold his wares and bought bread and meat with the proceeds. People used to gather in little groups after he had passed, gossiping about his strange looks and behaviour. They all agreed it was a mercy that the child had escaped from him and reminded one another how fast she had been running down the mountain, as if she had been afraid he was coming after them to fetch her back.

But Peter's Grannie always stood up for him. Whenever anyone came to bring her wool to spin or to fetch the finished work, she took care to mention how well he had looked after the child and how kind he had been about repairing their cottage, which might otherwise have fallen down by this time. The villagers found this hard to believe and decided that the old woman did not know what she was talking about, being blind and probably rather deaf as well.

Uncle Alp never went near her cottage again, but he

had done his work well and it was now strong enough to stand up to the stormy weather. Without Heidi's visits, Grannie found the days long and empty and she grew very sad and often used to say, 'I should like to hear that dear child's voice just once again before I die.'

6

A New Life Begins

The house in Frankfurt to which Heidi was being taken belonged to a wealthy man called Mr Sesemann. His only daughter, Clara, was an invalid and spent all her days in a wheel-chair, in which she was pushed wherever she wanted to go. She was a very patient child, with a thin, pale face and mild, blue eyes. Her mother had been dead for a long time, and since then her father had employed as housekeeper a worthy but very disagreeable person called Miss Rottenmeier. She looked after Clara and was in charge of all the servants. As Mr Sesemann was often away from home on business, he left all the household affairs in her hands, on the sole condition that Clara was never to be crossed in any way.

On the evening when Heidi was expected, Clara was sitting, as she usually did, in a pleasant, comfortable room, next to the big dining-room. It was called the study because of the big, glass-fronted bookcase which stood against one wall, and it was here that Clara did her lessons. Now she kept looking at the big clock on the wall, which she felt must be going more slowly than usual, and finally, in a tone of impatience which was rare with her, she asked, 'Isn't it nearly time, Miss Rottenmeier?'

That lady was sitting very stiff and straight at a small work-table, sewing. She wore a jacket with a high collar and had a sort of turban on her head, which made her look very imposing.

'Shouldn't they be here by now?' repeated Clara, still more impatiently.

At that very moment Detie was standing with Heidi at the front door. The coachman, whose name was John, had just brought round the carriage so she asked him whether it would be convenient for her to see Miss Rottenmeier.

'That's not my business,' he replied. 'You'd better ring for Sebastian.'

Detie did so and presently a manservant came hurrying downstairs. He wore a smart coat with big round buttons, and his eyes were as round and big as the buttons.

'Is it convenient, please, for me to see Miss Rottenmeier?' asked Detie.

'That's not my job,' said Sebastian, 'ring that other bell for Tinette,' and he went away.

Detie rang again and this time a smart maid appeared, with a snowy white cap on her head and a very pert look on her face.

'What do you want?' she called saucily from the top of the stairs.

Detie repeated her question, and the maid went away but soon came back to say, 'You are expected.' So Heidi and Detie went up and followed Tinette to the study, where they stood respectfully just inside the door. Detie kept tight hold of Heidi, not being quite certain how she might behave in these strange surroundings. Miss Rottenmeier got up slowly and came over to inspect the companion who had been proposed for the daughter of the house. She did not appear to like what she saw, for Heidi was wearing a shabby cotton frock and a shapeless old hat, and was staring up with undisguised astonishment at the extraordinary head-dress the lady wore.

'What's your name?' asked Miss Rottenmeier, after staring hard at her for some moments. Heidi told her in a nice clear voice.

'That can't be your proper name, surely? What were you christened?'

'I don't remember,' said Heidi.

'That's no way to answer. Is the child halfwitted or impertinent?' Miss Rottenmeier said to Detie.

'If you please, Ma'am, I'll speak for her. She's not used to strangers,' Detie replied, giving Heidi a little push as punishment for her unsuitable reply. 'She's not halfwitted I can assure you, nor impertinent either, but she doesn't know any better. She says the first thing that comes into her head. She's never been in a house like this before and no one's taught her how to behave. But she's bright and quick to

learn if anyone would take a little trouble with her. So please excuse her, Ma'am. She was christened Adelheid after her mother, my dead sister.'

'Well, at least that is a reasonable name, but the child seems to me very young. I told you we wanted someone of Miss Clara's own age, so that they could do lessons together and be real companions. Miss Clara is twelve. How old is this child?'

Detie had expected this question and was prepared with an answer. 'To tell you the truth, Ma'am,' she said glibly, 'I can't remember just how old she is, but about ten I think.'

'I'll soon be eight,' said Heidi. 'Grandfather told me so.'

Detie gave her another cross little push, but Heidi was quite unaware of having said anything wrong.

'Not yet eight!' exclaimed Miss Rottenmeier. 'That's at least four years too young. What's the good of bringing her here?' She turned to Heidi and went on, 'What books have you been using in your lessons?'

'None,' said Heidi.

'What's that you say? How did you learn to read then?'

'I haven't learnt to read,' Heidi replied. 'Nor has Peter.'

'Good gracious me, can't read at your age!' cried Miss Rottenmeier in dismay. 'Impossible! What have you learnt then?'

'Nothing,' said Heidi frankly.

There was a strained silence, while Miss Rottenmeier grasped the situation. 'Really, Detie,' she said at last, 'I don't know what you were thinking about to bring that child here. She won't do at all.'

But Detie was not going to give in easily, and replied with spirit, 'If you please, I thought she would be just what you were looking for, Ma'am. You told me you wanted an unusual sort of child, and there's nothing unusual about the older ones. They are all alike. But Heidi is different. I must go now, if you'll allow me, because my mistress will be expecting me, but I'll leave her here and come back in a few days to see how she's getting on.' With that, Detie dropped a little curtsey, and ran out of the room and downstairs as fast as she could. A moment later Miss Rottenmeier went after her, for there were many things to be discussed if the child was to stay, and apparently Detie was determined to leave her there.

All this time Heidi had not moved, not even when Detie left her. Clara, who had watched everything in silence from her wheel-chair, now called her over.

'Do you want to be called Heidi or Adelheid?' she asked.

'Everyone calls me Heidi, that's my name,' the little girl replied.

'Well, I'll call you that too. It's a queer name, but it suits you. I've never seen anyone quite like you before. Have you always had short, curly hair?'

'Yes, I think so,' replied Heidi cheerfully.

'Are you glad you've come here?' continued Clara.

'No, but I shall be going home again tomorrow, with some nice rolls for Grannie.'

'You are a funny child. As a matter of fact, you've been brought to Frankfurt expressly to keep me company and have lessons with me. We might have some fun too, as you can't even read. Lessons are often very dull. Mr Usher, that's my tutor, comes every day from ten to two, and it's such a long time. Sometimes he puts the book right up to his face, as though he were dreadfully short-sighted, but I know he's only yawning behind it. Then Miss Rottenmeier takes out a handkerchief and holds it up to her face, as though she were crying, but really she's yawning too. That makes me want to yawn, and I have to stifle it because if I yawned she'd be sure to say I must be feeling poorly, and I'd have to take a dose of cod-liver oil, which is the most horrible stuff imaginable. But now I shall be able to listen while you learn to read, and that'll be much more amusing.'

Heidi shook her head doubtfully.

'But of course you will learn to read – everyone has to,' Clara went on quickly. 'And Mr Usher is very kind. He never gets cross and he'll explain everything to you. You probably won't understand what he's talking about at first, but don't ever say so, or he'll go on and on for ever, and you still won't understand any better. Later on, when you've learnt a little, I expect you'll see what he means all right.'

Miss Rottenmeier came back at this point. She had not been quick enough to catch Detie, and was very much put out, for she did not see how to get out of this awkward situation, for which she was really responsible as she had certainly agreed to Heidi's being fetched. She walked about restlessly between the study and the dining-room, and presently came upon Sebastian who had just finished setting the table and was looking it over to make sure he had not forgotten anything.

'Finish your thinking some other time and see about serving the meal,' she snapped, and then called, in a peremptory tone, for Tinette, who minced into the room with a very high and mighty expression on her face which made even Miss Rottenmeier swallow her anger, and she said as coolly as she could, 'See that the room is prepared for the girl who has just come. Everything has been put ready, but it wants dusting.'

'Oh certainly,' retorted Tinette impudently, as she flounced out of the room.

Sebastian too was furious, but had not dared to answer back. He showed it by banging open the double doors leading from the dining-room to the study. Then he slouched over to wheel Clara in to supper, and as he paused to manipulate the handle of the chair, he saw Heidi staring at him. This annoyed him still more, and he growled, 'Well, what are you staring at?'

'You look like Peter the goat boy,' she replied. Miss Rottenmeier came back into the study just then, and held up her hands in disgust.

'What a way to talk to the servants!' she exclaimed. 'She simply hasn't an idea how to behave.'

Clara was wheeled up to the table, and Sebastian lifted her on to an armchair. Miss Rottenmeier sat beside her and motioned to Heidi to take the seat opposite. It was a big table just for the three of them and left plenty of room for Sebastian to stand beside each, as he handed the dishes. Beside Heidi's plate lay a nice white roll, and her eyes lit up at sight of it. She did not take it, however, until Sebastian was offering her the dish of baked fish, then feeling she must be able to trust anyone who looked so like Peter, she said to him, 'May I have this?' and pointed to the roll.

Sebastian nodded and looked out of the corner of his eye to see how Miss Rottenmeier was taking it. When Heidi took up the roll and put it in her pocket, he hardly knew how to keep his face straight, but it would have been more than his place was worth to show amusement. He was not supposed to speak or to move until she had helped herself from the dish, so he continued to stand silently beside her, waiting. At length she looked up at him and said in a tone of surprise, 'Am I to have some of that too?'

He nodded again, making a very odd face in his efforts to stifle his laughter.

'Give me some then,' said Heidi, looking down at her plate.

'You can put the dish on the table and come back later,' said the stern voice of Miss Rottenmeier, and Sebastian made for the door immediately.

'I see I shall have to begin right at the beginning with you, Adelheid,' that lady continued with a pained blink of the eyes. 'Now, this is how you should help yourself at table,' and she proceeded to show how it should be done. 'And understand, you must never speak to Sebastian during a meal, except to give him an order or to ask for something. And you must never speak to any of the servants in that familiar way. You'll address me as Ma'am, as you'll hear everyone else do. As for Clara, it's for her to say what you are to call her.'

'Clara, of course,' put in the invalid.

Miss Rottenmeier then held forth on how Heidi was to behave at every moment of the day, issuing instructions about getting up in the morning, and going to bed at night, about going out and coming in, about shutting doors, and keeping things tidy, and so on and on. In the middle of it all Heidi suddenly dropped off to sleep, for she had been up since five o'clock and travelling all day.

At last Miss Rottenmeier came to the end of her lecture, and said, 'Now, Adelheid, do you understand what I've been saying?'

'Heidi's asleep,' Clara remarked with a smile. It was a long time since she had known a meal pass so agreeably.

'That child's behaviour is really incredible,' exclaimed

Miss Rottenmeier, much annoyed, and she rang the bell so violently that Sebastian and Tinette both came hurrying in, nearly knocking each other over. But the commotion did not wake Heidi, and it was quite difficult to rouse her sufficiently to take her to bed. The room which had been prepared for her was at the other end of the house and, to get to it, she had to go past the study, and past Clara's bedroom and Miss Rottenmeier's sitting-room.

7

A Bad Day for Rottenmeier

Heidi awoke next morning and looked around her, quite forgetting all that had happened to her the day before. She couldn't think where she was. She rubbed her eyes and looked again, but that made no difference. She was in a big room, in a high white bed. There were long white curtains in front of the windows and two big armchairs and a sofa, covered with some beautiful flowery material; there was a round table, and on a washstand in the corner stood a number of things that she had never seen before. All at once she remembered all that had happened to her overnight, particularly the instructions the tall lady had given her, so far, that is, as she had heard them.

She jumped out of bed and dressed quickly. Then she went first to one window, then to the other, and tried to pull back the curtains so that she could see what was outside. They were too heavy to pull so she crept behind them, but then the windows were so high that she could only just peep through them. And wherever she looked there was nothing to be seen but walls and windows. She began to feel rather frightened. At Grandfather's she had always gone out of doors first thing in the morning to have a good look round, to see whether the sky was blue and the sun shining, and to say good morning to the trees and flowers. She ran from window to window frantically, trying to open them, like a wild bird in a cage, seeking a way through the bars to freedom. She felt sure that if she could see what was outside, she would find grass somewhere, green grass with the last snow just melting from it. But though she pushed and tugged and tried to put her little fingers under the frames, the windows stayed tight shut. After a while she gave up. 'Perhaps if I went out of doors and round to the back of the house, I'd find some grass,' she thought. 'I know there were only stones in front.'

Just then there was a tap at the door and Tinette put her head round it, snapped out, 'Breakfast's ready,' and shut it again quickly. Heidi hadn't the least idea what she meant, but she had sounded so fierce that Heidi thought she was being told to stay where she was. She found a little stool under the table and sat down, to see what would happen next. It was not long before Miss Rottenmeier came bustling in, very annoyed, and scolding all the time. 'What's the matter with you, Adelheid? Don't you even know what breakfast is? Come along at once.' This at least Heidi could understand, and she followed her obediently into the dining-room. Clara had been waiting there for some time but gave her a friendly greeting. She looked more cheerful than usual, for she had an idea she was going to have quite an interesting day.

Breakfast passed without further incident. Heidi ate her bread and butter quite nicely, and when the meal was over Clara was wheeled into the study and Heidi was sent with her and told to wait there until Mr Usher arrived. As soon as the two girls were alone, Heidi asked, 'How can I look out of the window and see what's down below?'

'First the window has to be opened,' said Clara, with a smile.

'But they won't open,' Heidi answered.

'Oh yes, they will, but you can't do it yourself and nor can I. But Sebastian will open one for you if you ask him.'

Heidi was relieved to hear that. Then Clara began to ask about her life at home and Heidi was soon chattering away merrily about the mountains and the goats and all the other things she loved so well.

While they talked the tutor arrived, but instead of coming straight to the study as usual, he was waylaid by Miss Rottenmeier who took him into the dining-room to explain the awkward situation in which she found herself.

'Some time ago when Mr Sesemann was in Paris on business,' she began, 'I wrote to tell him that Clara ought to have a companion of her own age. She wanted it, and so did I, for I thought she might work harder at her lessons if she had some competition, and also the companionship would be pleasant and good for her. It would also spare me the necessity to keep her amused all the time, which, believe me, is not easy. Her father agreed, but insisted that the other child should be treated exactly the same as his own daughter. He wrote he would not have any child in his house put upon in any way. A most uncalled-for remark, I must say. No one here would be likely to do any such thing!'

She then told him of Heidi's arrival and how utterly unsuitable she found her, in every way. 'Fancy, she doesn't even know her alphabet, and has no idea how to behave in polite society. There seems to me only one way out of this dreadful situation, and that is for you to say that it is impossible to teach these two children together without holding back Clara quite disastrously. That would surely be reason enough to persuade Mr Sesemann to send this Swiss girl home again.'

Mr Usher was a cautious man, who always tried to look at both sides of any problem, so after several politely consoling remarks, he went on to say that perhaps things might not be as bad as she feared. If the child was backward in some ways, she might be ahead in others, and with regular lessons it might be possible to bring her on quite quickly. Miss Rottenmeier saw that she was not likely to get the support she wanted from this quarter, for obviously the tutor did not at all mind teaching Heidi her ABC from the very beginning. She showed him to the study door, therefore, and watched him go inside, but the thought of having to watch Heidi at her letters was more than she could bear. She walked about the dining-room restlessly, wondering how the servants had better address Adelheid, for Mr Sesemann's instruction that the child was to be treated just like his daughter could only refer to them, she thought. She was not left for long with her thoughts, however. Suddenly there was a tremendous clatter in the study, as though a lot of things had fallen down, and she heard someone call for Sebastian. She hurried into the room and found the floor strewn with books, writing paper, an inkwell, and the table-cloth, from under which a stream of ink was flowing. Heidi was nowhere to be seen.

'This is a fine to-do,' said Miss Rottenmeier, wringing her hands. 'Books, carpet, tablecloth, all covered with ink. Never have I seen such a mess. Of course it's all that wretched child!'

Mr Usher stood looking about him in dismay. Even he could not find anything consoling to say about what had happened, though Clara seemed greatly amused by it.

'Yes, Heidi did it – quite by accident,' she said. 'You must not punish her. She just rushed across the room and caught the tablecloth as she went by, and swept everything on to the floor with it. There were a lot of carriages going by in the street and I expect she wanted to look at them. I daresay she has never seen such a thing in her life before.'

'What did I tell you, Mr Usher? The child is quite impossible. She doesn't even understand that she ought to sit still and listen during a lesson. And where has she got to now? I suppose she's run out of the front door. Whatever would Mr Sesemann say?'

She hurried off downstairs and found Heidi by the open door, looking up and down the street with a puzzled expression.

'What are you thinking of? What do you mean by running away from your lessons like that?' scolded Miss Rottenmeier.

'I heard the fir trees rustling, but I can't see them anywhere. I can't even hear them now,' replied Heidi.

It was the passing of light carriage wheels which she had mistaken for the wind blowing through the trees and which had sent her rushing joyfully downstairs to investigate, but the carriages had gone by before she got there.

'Fir trees indeed! Do you think Frankfurt is in the middle of a wood? Just you come with me and see what a mess you've made,' and Heidi was led back to the study, where she was most surprised to see what havoc she had wrought in her headlong flight from the room.

'Don't you ever do such a thing again,' said Miss Rottenmeier, pointing to the floor. 'You must sit still during lessons and pay attention. If you don't, I shall have to tie you to your chair. Is that understood?'

'Yes. I will sit still,' replied Heidi, accepting this as another rule that she must obey.

Sebastian and Tinette were sent for to clear up the mess and Mr Usher bowed and took his leave, saying there would be no more lessons. Certainly no one had been bored that day!

Clara always had to rest in the afternoons and Miss Rottenmeier told Heidi she could do as she pleased during that time. So after dinner, when the little invalid had settled down to sleep and the housekeeper had gone to her room, Heidi felt the moment had come to carry out something she had been planning. But she needed help, so she waited in the passage outside the dining-room for Sebastian who presently came upstairs from the kitchen with a big tray of silver to be put away in the dining-room cupboard. She stepped forward as he reached the last stair and said, 'You, there,' for she was uncertain how to address him after what Miss Rottenmeier had told her.

'What do you want, Miss?' he asked, rather crossly.

'I only want to ask you something. It's nothing naughty like this morning,' she added, for he seemed in rather a bad mood and she thought that might be because of the ink on the carpet.

'All right,' he said more pleasantly, 'what is it, Miss?'

'My name's not Miss, it's Heidi.'

'Miss Rottenmeier told us to call you that,' he replied.

'Oh, well, I suppose you must then,' she said in a small voice. She was quite aware that that lady's orders had to be obeyed. 'And in that case, I have three names,' she added with a sigh.

'What is it you want to ask, Miss?' asked Sebastian, going into the dining-room with his tray. Heidi followed.

'Can you open a window, Sebastian?'

'Of course,' he said and threw open the big casement. Heidi was too small to see out. Her chin only came up to the sill, but he brought her a high wooden stool and said, 'If you climb on that, Miss, you'll be able to see what's down below.' She got up on it, but after a quick glance, turned back with a very disappointed face.

'There's nothing but stony streets,' she said sadly. 'What should I see on the other side of the house, Sebastian?'

'Nothing different.'

She could not understand what living in a town meant, nor that the train had carried her so far away from the mountains and pastures.

'Then where can I go to see over the whole valley?'

'You'd have to go somewhere high up, a church tower like that one over there with the gold ball on top,' he said, pointing. 'You'd see ever so far from there.'

Heidi climbed down from the stool and ran downstairs and out of the front door. But she did not find the tower just across the road as it had seemed from the window. She

ran right down the street, but couldn't see it anywhere. She turned into a side street and walked on and on. She passed a lot of people, but they all seemed in such a hurry that she did not like to stop one of them to ask the way. Then she saw a boy standing at a corner, with a small hurdy-gurdy on his back and a tortoise in his arms. She went up to him and asked:

'Where's the tower with the gold ball on top?'

'I don't know.'

'Who can I ask then?'

'Don't know.'

'Do you know any church with a high tower?'

'Yes, one.'

'Well, come and show me.'

'What will you give me, if I do?' asked the boy, holding out his hand.

She felt in her pocket and brought out a little card with a wreath of red roses painted on it which Clara had given her that morning. She looked at it for a moment, rather regretfully, but decided it was worth sacrificing to see the view over the valley. 'There, would you like this?' she asked, holding it out to him. He shook his head.

'What do you want then?' she asked, glad to put her treasure back in the pocket.

'Money.'

'I haven't got any money,' said Heidi, 'but Clara has and I expect she'll give me some for you. How much do you want?'

'Two pennies.'

'All right. Now let's go.'

They went off together down a long street. 'What's that on your back?' asked Heidi.

'It's an organ. When I turn the handle, music comes out. Here we are,' he added, for they had reached an old church which had a high tower. The doors were fast shut, however.

'How can I get in?' asked Heidi.

'Don't know.'

Then she caught sight of a bell in the wall.

'Do you think I can ring, like they do for Sebastian?' she asked.

'Don't know,' he said again.

She went up to the wall and pulled with all her might at the bell.

'Wait for me, if I go up, because I don't know the way home, and you will have to show me.'

'What will you give me if I do?'

'What do you want?'

'Another twopence.'

Then they heard the old lock being turned from within, the door opened with a creak, and an old man peered out. He looked very annoyed when he saw the children. 'What do you mean by bringing me all this way down?' he demanded. 'Can't you read what it says under the bell: "For those who wish to climb the tower"?'

The boy jerked his thumb at Heidi, but said nothing.

'I do want to climb the tower,' she said.

'You? What for? Did someone send you?' asked the old keeper.

'No. I want to see what I can see from the top.'

'Be off with you,' he told her, 'and don't try your tricks on me again or it'll be the worse for you,' and he began to shut the door. But Heidi caught hold of his coat.

'Let me go up just this once,' she pleaded.

He looked down at her, and her eagerness softened

him, so that he took her by the hand and said grumblingly, 'Oh well, if it means so much to you, come along.'

The boy made no move to go too, but sat down on the stone doorstep, waiting for her as she had asked him to. The door shut, and she and the old man climbed up and up, the stairs getting narrower, the higher they went. At last they reached the top and the keeper held her up to an open window. 'Now you have a good look round,' he said. But still there was nothing to be seen but a sea of roofs, chimneys, and towers, and after a minute she turned back to him and said, looking very crestfallen, 'It isn't a bit what I expected.'

'I thought as much! What does a little thing like you know about views! Come along now and don't ring any more tower bells.'

He set her on the ground and she followed him down. When they came to the landing at the bottom of the narrowest flight of stairs she noticed a door on the left, which led to the keeper's room. There, in a corner beside it, a fat grey cat sat beside a big basket, and spat as Heidi approached, to warn her that this was the home of her family of kittens and that she would not allow anyone to meddle with them. Heidi stood and stared, for she had never seen such a huge cat before. There were such quantities of mice in the tower that it could catch half a dozen a day without any difficulty, and had grown sleek and fat on them.

'Come and look at the kittens,' said the keeper. 'The mother won't touch you if I'm with you.' Heidi went up to the basket.

'Oh what darlings! Aren't they sweet?' she exclaimed with delight, as she watched seven or eight little kittens tumbling and scrambling over one another.

'Would you like one?' asked the keeper, smiling at her pleasure.

'To keep for myself?' gasped Heidi, hardly able to believe her ears.

'Yes, of course. You can have more than one if you like, or indeed all of them if you've somewhere to keep them,' said the old man, welcoming the opportunity of getting rid of them. Heidi was thrilled. There was plenty of room in the big house and she was sure Clara would love to have them.

'How can I carry them?' she asked, and stooped to pick one up, but the mother cat flew at her so fiercely that she drew back in alarm.

'I'll bring them to you, if you'll tell me where,' said the old man as he stroked the cat soothingly. It had lived alone with him in the tower for many years and they were great friends.

'To Mr Sesemann's house,' Heidi told him, 'where there's a gold dog's head with a ring in its mouth on the front door.'

He recognized the house immediately from that

description for he had lived in the one spot so long that he knew all the houses round about, and besides, Sebastian was a friend of his.

'I know the house,' he said, 'but for whom shall I ask? You don't belong to that family I'm sure.'

'No, I don't, but I know Clara will be pleased to have the kittens.'

The keeper was ready to go down the rest of the way but Heidi couldn't tear herself away. 'Can't I take just two kittens with me now,' she begged, 'one for me and one for Clara?'

'Wait a minute then,' he said, and he picked up the mother cat and carried her into his room where he put her down in front of her food bowl. Then he shut the door and came back to the basket. 'Now you can take them,' he said.

Heidi's eyes were shining. She picked out a white kitten, and a tabby, and put one in each pocket. Then they went on down together and found the boy still sitting on the step, waiting for her.

'Now, which is the way back to Mr Sesemann's house?' Heidi asked him as soon as the keeper had shut the big door behind her.

'Don't know.'

Heidi described the house as well as she could, but the boy only shook his head.

'Well, opposite us, there's a grey house with a roof like

this,' she said, drawing gables in the air with one finger. He thought he recognized that, and ran off at once, with Heidi on his heels. Soon they reached the familiar door with the dog's head knocker. Heidi pulled the bell and almost at once Sebastian answered it. 'Come in quickly,' he cried as soon as he saw her, and he slammed the door without even noticing the boy, who was left outside feeling quite bewildered.

'Hurry, Miss,' urged Sebastian. 'They're already at table and Miss Rottenmeier looks fit to explode. Whatever made you run away like that?'

She went into the dining-room where there was an awful silence. Miss Rottenmeier did not look up as Sebastian pushed Heidi's chair up to the table, and even Clara did not speak. Then, looking very cross and speaking very severely, Miss Rottenmeier said:

'I will speak to you later, Adelheid. Now I will only say that it was extremely naughty of you to leave the house without asking permission or saying a word to anyone, and then to go roaming about until this late hour. I've never heard of such a thing.'

'Miaou,' came the reply, which seemed to be Heidi's, and that was the last straw.

'How dare you mock me in such a fashion, and after such disgraceful behaviour,' said Miss Rottenmeier, her temper rising.

'I didn't,' began Heidi, but got no further before there

was another 'Miaou, Miaou!' Sebastian almost threw what he was holding on to the table, and rushed from the room.

'That will do,' Miss Rottenmeier tried to speak firmly, but she was almost choking with anger and could only whisper. 'Leave the room.'

Heidi got up, feeling quite frightened. She tried again to explain, but the kittens mewed again, 'Miaou, miaou, miaou.'

'Heidi, why do you keep on mewing like that?' asked Clara. 'Can't you see how angry you're making Miss Rottenmeier?'

'But it's not me, it's the *kittens*,' Heidi managed to get out at last.

'What! Kittens! Here?' screamed Miss Rottenmeier. 'Sebastian! Tinette! Come and look for the horrible creatures and get rid of them.' And she rushed off into the study and bolted the door, for she disliked cats so much, she was actually terrified of them!

Sebastian was laughing so much, he had to wait outside the door to compose himself before he could come in. He had seen one of the kittens peeping out of Heidi's pocket as he was handing a plate, and knew there was bound to be trouble. When it started, he could not control his laughter and that was why he had rushed away. When he was in a fit state to come in again, everything had quietened down and Clara had the kittens on her lap.

Heidi was kneeling beside her and they were both admiring the pretty little things.

'Sebastian, you must help us,' said Clara. 'Find a corner for the kittens where Miss Rottenmeier won't see them. She's scared of them and will certainly get rid of them if she finds them, but we want to have them to play with when we're alone. Where can we put them?'

'I'll see to that for you, Miss Clara,' he said obligingly. 'I'll make a cosy bed for them in a basket and put it where the old lady is not likely to look. You can rely on me.' He went off to do as he had promised, chuckling to himself. He could foresee more excitements in the near future and always rather enjoyed watching Miss Rottenmeier in a rage. It was some time before that lady dared to open the study door. Then she called through a mere crack, 'Are those dreadful creatures out of the way?'

'Yes, Ma'am,' replied Sebastian, who was hanging about in the dining-room, expecting that question. Then at once he snatched up the kittens and took them away.

The scolding which Miss Rottenmeier had intended to give Heidi had to be put off until next day, for she felt quite worn out with all she had been through of anxiety and annoyance, anger and fright. Consequently she withdrew very soon to her room, and Clara and Heidi went happily to bed, knowing that the kittens were safe.

8

Strange Goings-On

Next morning, just after Sebastian had opened the door to Mr Usher and shown him into the study, the front door bell rang again, this time so loudly that Sebastian dashed downstairs thinking it must be Mr Sesemann himself, come home unexpectedly. He flung open the door, and found there only a ragged boy with a hurdy-gurdy on his back.

'What's the meaning of this?' snapped Sebastian. 'What do you want? I'll teach you to ring bells like that.'

'I want to see Clara,' said the boy.

'You dirty little brat, don't you even know enough to say "*Miss* Clara"? And what can the likes of you want with her, anyway?'

'She owes me fourpence,' was the reply.

'Rubbish! How do you even know that there is a Miss Clara in this house?'

'I showed her the way yesterday, for twopence, and then the way back for another twopence.'

'You're telling lies,' said Sebastian. 'Miss Clara never

goes out. She can't walk. Be off with you now, before I make you!'

The boy stood his ground, not in the least frightened by this threat. 'I saw her in the street and I can tell you what she looks like,' he said. 'She's got short, curly black hair, black eyes, and she was wearing a brown dress and she doesn't talk like us.'

'Oho,' thought Sebastian with a grin. 'The little miss again! What's she been up to this time? All right,' he said aloud to the boy, 'come with me,' and he led the way to the study door. 'Now wait here until I come back, then, when I let you in, you play a tune. Miss Clara will like that.' He knocked and went in.

'There's a boy here who wants to speak to Miss Clara personally,' he announced. Clara's eyes lit up at this highly unusual occurrence.

'Bring him in at once,' she said. 'He can come, can't he, Mr Usher?'

The boy was in fact already in the room and began to turn the handle of his organ. Miss Rottenmeier had gone to the dining-room to avoid having to listen to a child learning the alphabet. Suddenly she pricked up her ears. Was that noise coming from the street? It sounded nearer but – there could never be a hurdy-gurdy in the study! She ran to the door and there beheld the ragged street urchin calmly playing his organ. The tutor looked as though he wanted to say something, but couldn't make up his mind to, while Clara and Heidi were listening to the music with obvious pleasure.

'Stop, stop that at once!' cried Miss Rottenmeier, but it was difficult to make her voice heard above the noise. She darted towards the boy, and all but tripped over something on the floor. Looking down, she saw, to her horror, a queer dark object at her feet. It was the tortoise. She leaped in the air to avoid it – leaped, and she hadn't done that for years! Then she screamed at the top of her voice for Sebastian, and the boy stopped playing, for this time he heard her in spite of his music. Sebastian was standing just outside the door, doubled up with laughter. When at last he came in Miss Rottenmeier had collapsed on to a chair.

'Get rid of that boy and his animal at once,' she ordered.

The little organ player snatched up his tortoise and Sebastian led him away. On the landing, he put some coins into the boy's hand, saying, 'Here's the money from Miss Clara, and a bit more for playing so nicely.' Then he let him out at the front door.

When quiet had been restored in the study, lessons were resumed, but Miss Rottenmeier remained to prevent any more such unseemly happenings, and as she sat there, she made up her mind to find out what was at the bottom of it and to deal severely with whoever was responsible. Presently Sebastian came back to say that someone had just delivered a big basket which was to be given at once to Miss Clara.

'To me?' asked Clara in surprise, at once feeling most curious to know what it could contain. 'Oh, bring it in at once.' So Sebastian fetched in a closed basket, set it down before her, and went out again quickly.

'You had better finish your lessons before opening it,' remarked Miss Rottenmeier firmly, though Clara looked longingly at it.

Then, in the middle of a declension, she broke off to ask Mr Usher if she couldn't have just a peep inside.

'I could cite good reasons both for and against such a course of action,' he began pompously. 'In its favour is the fact that so long as your attention is entirely engaged ...' He got no further. The lid of the basket was not properly fastened, and suddenly the room seemed to be swarming with kittens. They jumped out one after another and rushed madly about, some biting the tutor's trousers and jumping over his feet, others climbing up Miss Rottenmeier's skirt. One scrambled on to Clara's chair, mewing and scratching as it came. The whole room was in an uproar, and Clara was delighted.

'Oh, aren't they pretty little things! Just look at them jumping about!' she exclaimed to Heidi, who was chasing after them from one end of the room to the other. Mr Usher was standing by the table, trying vainly to shake the kittens off his legs. Miss Rottenmeier, disliking all cats as she did, only found her voice again after an interval, and then called loudly for Sebastian and Tinette. She was afraid that if she moved all the horrid little creatures would jump up at her. The servants came quickly and Sebastian managed to catch the kittens and put them back into the basket. Then he carried them up to the attic where he had already made a bed for those Heidi had brought home the day before.

Once again Clara's lesson-time had been far from boring. That evening, when Miss Rottenmeier had recovered a little from the morning's disturbance, she summoned Sebastian and Tinette to the study to question them about what had happened. Of course it came out that everything was the result of Heidi's escapade the day before. Miss Rottenmeier was so angry she could not at first find words to express herself. She sent the servants away and then turned to Heidi who was standing calmly beside Clara's chair, quite unable to understand what she had done wrong.

'Adelheid,' said Miss Rottenmeier very sternly, 'I can think of only one punishment for such a little savage as you. Perhaps a spell in the dark cellar among the bats and rats will tame you, and stop you having any more such ideas.'

Heidi was very surprised at Miss Rottenmeier's idea of punishment. The only place she knew as a cellar was the little shed in which her grandfather kept their supplies of cheese and milk and where she had always been glad to go. And she had never seen any bats or rats.

Clara, however, protested loudly. 'Oh, Miss Rottenmeier! Wait till Papa comes home! He'll be here quite soon, and I'll tell him everything and he'll decide what's to be done with Heidi.' Miss Rottenmeier could make no objection to this, and besides Clara must never be crossed.

'Very well, Clara,' she said stiffly, 'but I also shall speak to your father.' With that she left the room.

The next few days passed uneventfully, but Miss Rottenmeier's nerves remained on edge. The sight of Heidi kept her reminded how she had been deceived over the child's age, and how she had so upset the household that it seemed as though things would never be the same again. Clara, on the other hand, was very cheerful and no longer found her lessons dull. Heidi always managed to provide some amusement. For one thing, she invariably got the letters of the alphabet so muddled up, it seemed as though she would never learn them, and when Mr Usher tried to make things easier for her by comparing letters to familiar objects such as a horn or a beak, she thought of the goats at home, or the hawk on the mountain and that did not help her at all with her lesson.

In the evenings Heidi used to tell Clara about her life in the hut, but it made her feel so homesick that she often ended by exclaiming, 'Oh I must go home again. I must go tomorrow.' Clara tried to comfort her then by saying, 'Stay at least until Papa arrives and then we'll see what will happen.' Heidi seemed to cheer up at that, but secretly she was consoling herself with the thought that every day she stayed meant two more white rolls for Peter's Grannie. She had been putting them in her pocket at dinner and supper regularly since the day of her arrival and now had quite a pile hidden away. She wouldn't eat a single one herself, because she knew how much Grannie would enjoy them instead of her usual hard black bread.

After dinner Heidi always sat alone in her room for a time. She had been made to realize that she could not simply run out-of-doors in Frankfurt as she had done at home, so she never tried again. Miss Rottenmeier had forbidden her to talk to Sebastian, and she would never have dreamed of starting a conversation with Tinette. Indeed she avoided her as much as possible for Tinette either spoke to her in the most disdainful way, or mimicked her, and Heidi knew quite well that she was being made fun of. So she had plenty of time every day to think how the snow would by now have melted on the mountain and of how beautiful it would be at home with the sun shining on the grass and the flowery slopes and over the valley below. She felt so homesick, she could hardly bear it. Then she remembered that her aunt had said she could go back if she wanted to. So one afternoon she wrapped up the rolls in her big red scarf, put on her old straw hat and went

downstairs. But she had only got as far as the front door when she ran straight into Miss Rottenmeier returning from an outing. That forbidding person stared at Heidi in amazement and her sharp eyes came to rest on the red bundle.

'And what does this mean?' she demanded. 'Why are you dressed up like that? Haven't I forbidden you to go running about the streets alone, or to go out without permission? Yet here I find you trying it again and looking like a beggar's child into the bargain.'

'I wasn't going to run about,' murmured Heidi, a little frightened. 'I only want to go home to see Grandfather and Grannie.'

'What's that? You want to go home?' Miss Rottenmeier threw up her hands in horror. 'You'd simply run off like that? What would Mr Sesemann say? I can only hope he'll never hear of it. What's wrong with this house, pray? Have you ever lived in such a fine place before, or had such a soft bed or such good food? Answer me that.'

'No,' said Heidi.

'You have everything you can want here. You're an ungrateful little girl who doesn't know when she's well off.'

This was too much for Heidi and she burst out, 'I want to go home because while I'm here Snowflake will be crying, and Grannie will be missing me too. And here I can't see the sun saying goodnight to the mountains. And if the hawk came flying over Frankfurt he'd croak louder than ever because there are such a lot of people here being horrid and cross, instead of climbing high up where everything's so much nicer.'

'Merciful heavens! The child's out of her mind!' exclaimed Miss Rottenmeier and ran swiftly upstairs, bumping violently into Sebastian who was going down. 'Bring that wretched child up here at once,' she ordered.

'Very good,' said Sebastian.

Heidi hadn't moved. She was trembling all over and her eyes were blazing. 'Well, what have you done this time?' asked Sebastian cheerfully. Still she didn't stir, so he patted her shoulder and added sympathetically, 'Come now, don't take it so much to heart. Keep smiling, that's the best thing to do. She bumped into me so hard just now she nearly knocked my head off. But don't you worry. Come along. We've got to right-about-turn and upstairs again. She said so.' Heidi went slowly with him, looking so very dejected that Sebastian felt really sorry for her.

'Cheer up,' he said, 'don't be downhearted. I've never seen you cry yet and I know you're a sensible little girl. Later on, when Miss Rottenmeier's out of the way, we'll go and look at the kittens, shall we? They're having a fine time up in the attic and it's fun to watch them playing together.'

Heidi gave a subdued little nod and went to her room, leaving him looking after her with real kindliness.

At supper Miss Rottenmeier hardly spoke, but every now and then she glanced sharply at Heidi as though expecting her to do something unheard-of at any moment. But the little girl sat as quiet as a mouse, eating and drinking nothing, though she managed to put her roll in her pocket as usual.

Next morning, when Mr Usher arrived, Miss Rottenmeier beckoned him mysteriously into the dining-room and told him she feared the change of air and the new way of life, with all its unusual experiences, had affected Heidi's mind. She told him how the child had tried to run away and repeated the extraordinary things she had said. Mr Usher tried to calm her.

'I assure you,' he said, 'that although in some ways Adelheid is rather peculiar, in others she seems quite normal and it should be possible, with careful treatment, to steady her quite satisfactorily in the end. I am really more worried by the fact that she seems to find such difficulty in learning the alphabet. So far we have made no progress at all.'

Miss Rottenmeier felt somehow satisfied by that and let him go to his pupils. Later in the day she remembered the strange garments Heidi had put on to go home in, and decided she ought to give her some of Clara's outgrown clothes before Mr Sesemann came home. She spoke to Clara about it and she agreed at once that Heidi could have several of her dresses, hats, and other garments. So Miss Rottenmeier went off to Heidi's room to look at her clothes and decide what was worth keeping and what should be thrown away. In a few minutes she returned, looking more put out than ever.

'Adelheid' she cried, 'what do I find in your wardrobe? Can I believe my eyes? Just think of it, Clara, at the bottom of the cupboard – a cupboard meant for clothes, Adelheid – I found a great pile of stale dry rolls. Fancy hoarding food away like that!' Then she raised her voice and called Tinette. 'Go to Miss Adelheid's room,' she told her, 'and get rid of the rolls in the cupboard, and throw the old straw hat that's on the table into the dustbin!'

'Oh, no,' Heidi wailed, starting up, 'I must keep my hat, and the rolls are for Grannie.' She tried to run after Tinette but Miss Rottenmeier caught hold of her.

'You'll stay here. That rubbish is going to be thrown away,' she said firmly.

Heidi threw herself down beside Clara's chair and began to cry bitterly. 'Now Grannie won't get any nice white bread,' she sobbed. 'The rolls were all for her and now they're going to be thrown away.' She wept as if her heart would break, and Miss Rottenmeier hurried out of the room. Clara was very upset by all the commotion.

'Heidi, don't cry so,' she begged. 'Listen to me. If you'll only stop, I promise to get you just as many rolls as you had saved, or even more, to take to Grannie when you go home. And they'll be soft, fresh ones. Those you'd saved must have got quite hard already. Come on, Heidi, please don't cry any more.'

It was a long time before Heidi could stop, but she understood what Clara was promising and was comforted at last, though she still wanted to be assured that Clara meant it.

'Will you really give me as many rolls as I had saved?' she asked in a still tearful voice.

'Of course I will. Now do cheer up.'

Heidi came to supper that night with red eyes, and when she saw the roll beside her plate, a lump came in her throat. But she managed not to cry for she knew that would not do at table. Sebastian kept making strange signs whenever he came near her, pointing first to his head, then to hers, nodding and winking as he did so, as though to convey to her something very secret, and when she went to bed she found her battered old straw hat under the quilt. She caught it up and squashed it a little more in her pleasure at seeing it again. Then she wrapped it up in a big old handkerchief and hid it right at the back of the wardrobe.

That was what Sebastian had been trying to tell her at supper. He had heard what Tinette had been told to do, and had heard Heidi's despairing cry. So he had gone after the girl and waited till she came out of Heidi's room carrying the hoard of rolls, with the hat perched on top of them. He had snatched away the hat, saying, 'I'll get rid of this,' and so had been able to save it.

9

A Bad Report to Mr Sesemann

There was a great bustle in the big house and much running up and down stairs a few days later, for the master had returned from his travels, and Sebastian and Tinette had one load of luggage after another to carry up from the carriage, for Mr Sesemann always brought a lot of presents and other nice things home with him.

The first thing he did was to go and find his daughter, and there was Heidi with her, for it was the late afternoon, when they were always together. Father and daughter were very fond of one another and they greeted each other very warmly. Then he put out a hand to Heidi, who had moved quietly away into a corner, and said kindly:

'So this is our little Swiss girl. Come and shake hands. That's right. And tell me, are you and Clara good friends? I hope you don't squabble, so that you have to kiss and make it up and then start the whole performance again.'

'No, Clara is always good to me,' said Heidi.

'And Heidi never quarrels with me,' added Clara.

'I'm glad to hear that,' said her father. 'And now, my dear, you must forgive me if I leave you. I haven't had anything to eat all day. But I'll come back later on and you shall see all that I've brought for you.'

He went along to the dining-room, where Miss Rottenmeier was making sure that everything was in order. There he sat down and she took a seat opposite him, with a face like a thundercloud.

'What's the matter?' he asked. 'Why this gloomy expression to welcome me home, when Clara seems in such good spirits?'

'Mr Sesemann,' she began pompously, 'we have all been dreadfully deceived, Clara not least of us.'

'Indeed?' he returned calmly, sipping his wine.

'You remember we agreed that Clara should have a young companion to live with her? Knowing how careful you are that she should only have about her well behaved, nicely brought up people, I thought a young Swiss girl from the mountains would be suitable. I've often read of these girls, who float through the world like a breath of pure Alpine air; almost, as it were, without touching the ground.'

'I think even Swiss children must put their feet on the ground if they want to get anywhere,' remarked Mr Sesemann drily, 'otherwise they'd have been given wings.'

'Oh, that's not what I meant,' she cried. 'You know a real child of nature, hardly touched by this world at all.'

'I don't quite see what use that would be to Clara,' observed Clara's father.

'I'm serious, Mr Sesemann. I have been disgracefully imposed upon!'

'What's disgraceful about it? I see nothing in the child herself to be so upset about.'

'You should see the sort of people and animals she has been bringing into the house. Mr Usher will bear me out about that. And that's not all.'

'I don't understand you,' he said. But now Miss Rotten-meier saw that she had his attention.

'I don't wonder. Her conduct in general has been almost past belief. I can only think she's not quite right in the head.'

Mr Sesemann had not taken her earlier complaints seriously, but this was another matter and, if true, Clara might come to some harm. He looked at the woman as though wondering whether she herself was quite right in the head, and at that moment the door opened and Mr Usher was announced.

'Just the man we want,' declared Mr Sesemann. 'Come and sit down, and have a cup of coffee. You'll be able to clear things up for me, I'm sure. Tell me plainly what you think of my daughter's little companion. What's all this about her bringing animals into the house? Do you think she's at all odd?'

The tutor began to explain in his roundabout fashion

that he had only come to say how glad he was that Mr Sesemann had returned safely, but the compliments were waved aside. Mr Sesemann wanted a quick answer to his questions. But still Mr Usher began his explanations, as though he was something which had been wound up and had to go on till the works ran down.

'If I am to express an opinion about the young person,' he said, 'I should like first of all to emphasize that, though she may be backward in some respects as a result of a rather neglected – or perhaps I should say late – education, and because of her prolonged sojourn in the mountains, which of course could be beneficial in itself, if not of too long duration ...'

'My dear Mr Usher,' interrupted Mr Sesemann, 'don't bother about such details. Just tell me whether you have been alarmed by her bringing animals into the house and what you think of her in general as a companion for my daughter.'

'I should not like to say anything against the child,' Mr Usher replied carefully, 'for if, on the one hand, her conduct is somewhat unconventional as a result of her primitive way of life before she came to Frankfurt, this change is for her, I make bold to say, undoubtedly important and ...'

Mr Sesemann got up. 'Excuse me, Mr Usher, don't let me disturb you, but I must just get back to my daughter.' He hurried out and did not return, but went to the study and sat down beside Clara. Heidi stood up when he

entered the room and as he wanted her out of the way
for a few minutes, he said:

'My dear, will you go and fetch me – now whatever
was it I wanted? – oh yes, a glass of water.'

'Fresh water?'

'Yes, fresh cold water.' Heidi vanished.

He pulled his chair closer to his daughter and stroked
her hand. 'Now Clara dear, I want you to tell me about
these animals your little playmate has been bringing into
the house, and why does Miss Rottenmeier think she is
not quite right in the head?'

Clara told him just what had happened, about the

tortoise and the kittens, the rolls and everything. When she had finished, her father laughed heartily.

'Well well, then you don't want me to send her home, Clara? You're not tired of her?'

'Oh no, Papa,' she cried. 'Since Heidi's been here, delightful things have happened nearly every day. It's much more amusing, and she tells me all sorts of interesting things.'

'That's all right then. And here comes your little friend. Have you brought me nice cold water, my dear?'

'Straight from the fountain,' said Heidi, handing it to him.

'But you didn't go to the fountain all by yourself?' said Clara.

'Yes I did. And I had to go a long way, because there were so many people round the first two fountains that I had to go on to the next street and fetch it from there. And I met a gentleman with white hair and he sent his kind regards to Mr Sesemann.'

'Well, you've had quite a journey,' said Mr Sesemann with a smile. 'I wonder who the gentleman was.'

'He stopped by the fountain and said, "As you've got a glass, please give me a drink. Who are you fetching the water for?" And I said, "For Mr Sesemann." Then he laughed and said he hoped you would enjoy it.'

'Describe him to us,' said Mr Sesemann.

'He had a nice smile, and wore a thick gold chain with

a gold thing hanging on it which had a red stone in the middle. And he had a stick with a horse's head handle.'

'The doctor,' cried Clara and her father with one voice, and he smiled at the thought of what his old friend would have to say about this unusual search for water to quench his thirst.

That evening, he told Miss Rottenmeier, as they were discussing household matters, that Heidi was to stay. 'The child seems perfectly normal and Clara loves having her here,' he explained. 'You mustn't regard her funny little ways as faults, and I want you, please, to make sure that she's always kindly treated. If you find her too much to manage on your own – well, you'll have some help soon for my mother will be coming for her usual long visit and she can manage anyone, as you know.'

'Yes indeed, Mr Sesemann,' replied Miss Rottenmeier, rather crestfallen, for she did not particularly relish this news.

Mr Sesemann was only at home a fortnight, then had to go to Paris on business. Clara was very disappointed that he could not stay longer, and to cheer her up he told her about her grandmother's promised visit, and almost as soon as he had left, a letter came to say that old Mrs Sesemann was on her way, and would arrive on the following day. She asked for the carriage to be sent to fetch her from the station.

Clara was delighted, and talked so much about

Grandmamma that Heidi began to speak of her as Grand-mamma too. Miss Rottenmeier frowned when she heard her, but the little girl was so used to seeing disapproval on that face that she did not pay much attention to it. But as she was going to bed that night, Miss Rottenmeier called her and told her she was never to address Mrs Sesemann as 'Grandmamma'. 'You must call her "Gracious Madam". Do you understand?' Heidi was puzzled, but encountered such a forbidding look in the lady's eye that she did not like to ask her why.

10

Grandmamma's Visit

Next day everyone was very busy preparing for the expected guest. It was easy to see that she was an important person in that household and was accustomed to being treated as such. Tinette put on a nice new cap in her honour. Sebastian collected all the footstools he could find and put them in convenient places so that she would find one ready wherever she sat down. Miss Rottenmeier fussed about the place, inspecting everything, as though determined to show her authority and that she did not mean to be deprived of any of it by the new arrival.

As the carriage came rolling up to the front door, Sebastian and Tinette ran downstairs. Miss Rottenmeier followed in a more dignified fashion to receive the guest. Heidi had been told to stay in her room until she was sent for, so that Clara and her grandmother could have a little while alone. So Heidi sat there, quietly saying over to herself the words with which she had been told to address the old lady. They sounded so strange to her that she rearranged them, thinking Miss Rottenmeier must surely have made a mistake, and that 'Madam' must come first. Before long Tinette stuck her head round the door, and said sharply, 'You're to go to the study.'

Heidi did as she was told, and as she came into the room, Mrs Sesemann said in a friendly voice, 'Come over here, my dear, and let me have a good look at you.'

Heidi went to her and said clearly and carefully, 'Good evening, Madam Gracious.'

'What was that?' laughed the old lady. 'Is that how you address people up in the mountains?'

'No, no one's called that at home,' said Heidi gravely.

'Nor here either. In the nursery I'm always just "Grand-mamma" and that's what you shall call me too. You'll remember that all right, won't you?'

'Yes, I've used that name.'

'Good,' said Grandmamma, with an understanding nod, patting her cheek. Then she looked closely at her and nodded again, liking what she saw, for the child's eyes were grave and steady as they looked back, and Heidi saw such a kind expression on the old lady's face that she loved her at once. Indeed everything about Grandmamma was delightful to Heidi. She had pretty white hair and wore a dainty lace cap, with two broad ribbons which fluttered behind, as though there was always a gentle breeze blowing round her. Heidi thought that specially attractive.

'And what's your name?' Grandmamma asked.

'My real name's Heidi, but now it's supposed to be Adelheid, so I answer if I'm called that.' At that moment Miss Rottenmeier came into the room and Heidi stopped in confusion, remembering that she was still so unaccustomed to her full name that she frequently did not answer when that lady called her by it.

'I'm sure you'll agree, Mrs Sesemann,' said the disagreeable woman, 'that it is better to call her by a name that can be used without embarrassment, especially to the servants.'

'My good Rottenmeier,' replied Mrs Sesemann, 'if she's always been called Heidi and is used to that name, I shall certainly call her that.'

Miss Rottenmeier did not at all like being addressed by her surname alone, but she always had to put up with it from the old lady who was set in her ways. When she had made up her mind to a thing, there was no changing it. Besides, Mrs Sesemann was still very active, and missed nothing that went on in the house.

The next afternoon Clara went to rest as usual and her grandmother sat beside her in an armchair to have a little nap too. After it, she felt quite refreshed, and went along to the dining-room to find the housekeeper, but the room was empty.

'Perhaps she's having a little sleep too,' she thought, and went on to Miss Rottenmeier's bedroom and knocked sharply on the door. It was opened after a moment by that lady, who looked rather taken aback at sight of her visitor.

'I just want to know where Heidi is, and what she does with herself in the afternoons,' said Mrs Sesemann.

'She sits in her room,' Miss Rottenmeier replied. 'She might be doing something useful if she had the least inclination that way, but instead she makes the most ridiculous plans and even tries to carry them out – things I could really hardly mention in polite society.'

'Depend upon it I should do exactly the same, if I were left alone like that. And probably you wouldn't care to mention my ideas in polite society either. Go and bring her to my room. I want to give her some books I've brought with me.'

'Books!' exclaimed Miss Rottenmeier, clasping her hands together. 'Books are no use to her! In all the time she has been here, she hasn't even learnt her alphabet. It seems quite impossible to teach her, as Mr Usher will tell you. If he hadn't the patience of a saint, he would have given her up long ago.'

'That's strange. The child doesn't look stupid. Go and fetch her anyway. She can at least look at the pictures.' Miss Rottenmeier wanted to say something more, but Mrs Sesemann turned and quickly left her room. She was very surprised to hear that Heidi was so slow to learn and made up her mind to find out why. She had no intention of asking Mr Usher, however. She knew he was quite a good man, and she always made a point of greeting him very politely when they happened to meet, but she took good care not to land herself in conversation with him as she found his pompous way of expressing himself quite unbearable.

Heidi soon came to her, and was delighted to have the beautiful big picture books to look at. Then, all of a sudden, she gave a little cry and burst into tears. Mrs Sesemann glanced at the picture which had upset her, and saw that it was of a green meadow where many animals grazed, watched over by a shepherd leaning on a long staff. The sun was setting and the meadow was bathed in golden light. She patted Heidi's hand and said in a very kind voice:

'Come child, don't cry. I suppose it reminded you of something. But there's a nice story to it, which I'll tell you this evening, and there are lots of other stories in the book to read. Now dry your eyes for I want to talk to you. Sit here where I can see you properly.'

It was some time before Heidi could stop crying, and Mrs Sesemann let her alone while she composed herself. As she grew calmer, the old lady said, 'That's right. Now we can have a nice little talk. First tell me, child, how you are getting on with your lessons. What have you learnt?'

'Nothing,' said Heidi, with a sigh, 'but I knew I should not be able to.'

'What do you mean by that? What is it you don't think you can learn?'

'To read. It's too difficult.'

'What makes you think that?'

'Peter said so, and he ought to know because he's tried and tried but he just can't learn.'

'He must be a very odd boy then. But you mustn't simply take his word for it. You must try hard yourself. I don't think you can have paid proper attention to Mr Usher's lessons.'

'It's no use,' said Heidi in a hopeless tone.

'Now listen to me, Heidi, you've never learnt to read

because you believed what Peter told you. Now you must believe what I say, that in a little while you will be able to read quite well, as most children do, being on the whole like you and not like Peter. And as soon as you can read, you shall have the book with the picture of the shepherd in the meadow for your very own, and then you'll be able to read the story for yourself and find out what happens to him and his animals. You'd like that, wouldn't you?'

Heidi had been listening eagerly, with shining eyes. Then she sighed and exclaimed, 'I wish I could read now!'

'It won't take you long, I'm sure,' Grandmamma told her. 'Now we must go and see Clara. Let us take the books with us.' And hand in hand they went to the study.

A change had come over Heidi since the day she had tried to go home and Miss Rottenmeier had given her such a scolding. She now understood that, in spite of what Detie had told her, she could not go away when she wanted to, and that she would have to stay in Frankfurt for a long time, perhaps for ever. She believed that Mr Sesemann would think her very ungrateful if she said she wanted to go away, and probably Grandmamma and Clara would think the same, if they knew. So she dared not tell anyone how she felt, but went about mournfully, with a heavy heart. She had begun to lose her appetite and grew quite pale. When she was alone in her quiet room at night, she often lay awake for hours, thinking of home and the mountains, and when she fell asleep at last, it was to dream of them so vividly that she woke in the morning expecting to run joyfully down the ladder from the loft – and found herself, after all, still in the big bed in Frankfurt, so far away. The disappointment of that awakening often made her cry miserably, burying her face in her pillow so that no one should hear.

Grandmamma saw her unhappiness but said nothing for a few days, waiting to see if it would pass. When there was no improvement, and she had noticed traces of tears on the little face on several mornings, she took Heidi into her room and asked very kindly what the matter was and why she was so sad.

Heidi was afraid of vexing her if she told her the truth, and answered, 'I can't tell you.'

'Can't? Could you tell Clara then?'

'Oh no, I can't tell anyone,' said Heidi so sadly that the old lady's heart ached for her.

'Listen to me,' she said, 'if we're in trouble and can't tell any ordinary person, why, there is always God whom we can tell, and if we ask Him to help us, He always will. Do you understand? You do pray to God every night, don't you, to thank Him for all the good things and to ask Him to protect you from harm?'

'No, I don't,' was the reply, 'never.'

'Haven't you been taught to pray, Heidi? Don't you know how?'

'I used to pray with my own grandmother, but that's a long, long time ago. I've almost forgotten about it.'

'Ah – and when you are sad, and have no one to turn to for help, can't you see what a comfort it is to tell God all about it, knowing that He will help? Believe me, He always finds some way of making us happy again.'

Heidi's eyes brightened. 'May I tell Him everything, really everything?' she asked.

'Yes, everything.'

Heidi slipped her hand out of the old lady's.

'May I go now?' she asked.

'Of course, child.'

She ran to her own room, sat down on her stool, and folded her hands. Then she poured out all her troubles to God and begged Him to help her to get home to her grandfather.

One morning, about a week later, Mr Usher asked if he might speak to Mrs Sesemann on an important matter. He was invited to her room, where she received him in her usual friendly way.

'Come in and sit down, Mr Usher,' she said. 'I'm pleased to see you. What is it you want to speak to me about? No complaints, I hope?'

'On the contrary, Madam,' he replied. 'Something has come to pass which I had long given up hoping for. Indeed I think no one who knew the facts would have expected it. Yet, there it is – the impossible has happened.'

'Are you going to tell me that little Heidi has learnt to

read at last?' asked Mrs Sesemann. The young man opened his eyes very wide.

'Why, that you should suggest such a possibility, Madam, is almost as surprising as the fact itself. Up till now, in spite of all my efforts, she seemed quite unable to learn even the letters, and I had reluctantly come to the conclusion that she would have to be left to try to learn them in her own way, without any further help from me. Now she has mastered them almost overnight, as it were, and *can read* – and more correctly than most beginners. It's really remarkable.'

'There are many strange things in this life,' agreed Mrs Sesemann, well pleased. 'Perhaps this time there was a new desire to learn. In any case, let us be thankful the child has got thus far, and let us hope she will continue to make progress.'

She then went with the tutor to the door and, as he went downstairs, hurried to the study to find out for herself about this good news. She found Heidi reading aloud to Clara, and quite excited at the new world which had been opened to her, as the black letters on the page came alive and turned into stories about all kinds of people and things.

That evening, at supper, Heidi found the big picture book beside her place. She looked brightly at Grand-mamma, who nodded and said, 'Yes, it's yours now.'

'For ever and ever? Even when I go home?' asked Heidi, flushing with pleasure.

'Yes, of course, and tomorrow we'll start to read it.'

'But you won't be going home, Heidi, not for ages,' put in Clara. 'Grandmamma will be leaving soon and then I shall need you more than ever.'

Before going to sleep that night, Heidi had a good look at her lovely book, and thereafter, reading was her greatest delight. Sometimes in the evening Grandmamma would say, 'Now Heidi shall read to us,' and that made her very proud. She seemed to understand the stories better when she read them aloud, and Grandmamma was always ready with any explanation that was necessary. Her favourite story, which she constantly reread, was about the shepherd whose picture had brought the tears to her eyes when she first saw it. Now she knew it showed him happily tending his father's sheep and goats in sunny meadows, like those on the mountain. In the next picture he had left his good home and was minding a stranger's pigs in a foreign land. Here the sun was not shining and the countryside was grey and misty. The young man looked pale and thin in that picture, for he had nothing but scraps to eat. The last one showed his old father running with outstretched arms to greet him as he returned home sorrowful, and in rags.

With so many nice stories to read and pictures to look at, the days of Grandmamma's visit passed happily, but all too quickly.

11

Homesickness

Every afternoon during Mrs Sesemann's visit, while Clara was resting and Miss Rottenmeier had taken herself off mysteriously, presumably to rest also, the old lady sat with her granddaughter for a few minutes, and then called Heidi to her room, where she talked to her and amused her in a variety of ways. She had some pretty little dolls with her and showed Heidi how to make clothes for them, and in this pleasant fashion the child learnt to sew, almost without realizing it. Mrs Sesemann had a wonderful piece-bag, with materials of all kinds and colours in it, and from these Heidi made dresses, coats, and aprons for the dolls. Sometimes Mrs Sesemann let her read aloud from her book, which of course pleased her very much, and the more often she read the stories the more she liked them. She lived with the characters and got to know them all so well, she was always glad to meet them again. But in spite of these pleasant distractions, she did not look really happy, and her eyes had quite lost their sparkle.

One afternoon during the last week of Grandmamma's stay, Heidi came to her room as usual, with the big book, and the old lady drew her to her side, laid the book down, and said:

'My dear, tell me why you're not happy. Is it still the same trouble?'

Heidi nodded.

'Did you tell God about it?'

'Yes.'

'And do you pray to Him every day to make you happy again?'

'No, not any more.'

'I'm sorry to hear that. Why have you stopped?'

'It's no use,' Heidi told her. 'God didn't hear me and I daresay that if all the people in Frankfurt pray for things at the same time, He can't notice everybody and I'm sure He didn't hear me.'

'Why are you so sure?'

'I prayed the same prayer every day for a long time and nothing happened.'

'It isn't quite like that, Heidi. God is a loving Father to us all and knows what is good for us. If we ask for something it isn't right for us to have, He won't give it to us, but in His own good time, if we go on praying and trust in Him, He'll find us something better. You can be sure it's not that He didn't hear your prayer, for He can listen to everybody at once. That's part of the wonder of it. You must have asked for something He thought you ought not to have at present and probably said to himself, "Heidi's prayer shall be answered but only at the right moment so that she will really be happy. If I answer it now perhaps later on she'll wish she hadn't asked for it, because things may not turn out as she expects." He has been watching over you all this time – never doubt that – but you have stopped praying, and that showed you did not really believe in Him. If you go on like that, God will let you go your own way. Then if things go wrong and you complain that there's no one to help you, you will really have only yourself to blame, because you will have turned your back on the one Person who could really help you. Do you want that to happen, Heidi, or will you go now at once and ask God to forgive you and help you to find more faith, to help you to go on praying every day, and to trust Him to make things come right for you in the end?'

Heidi had listened very carefully to all this. She had great confidence in Grandmamma and wanted to remember everything she said, and at the end she cried, penitently:

'I will go at once and ask God to forgive me and I'll never forget Him again.'

'That's a good girl.'

Heidi went to her own room then, much encouraged, and begged God not to forget her but to give her His blessing.

The day of Grandmamma's departure was a sad one for Clara and Heidi, but she managed to keep them happy right up to the moment when she drove off in the carriage. It was only when the sounds of the wheels died away, and the house was so quiet and empty, that the children felt quite forlorn and did not know what to do with themselves.

Next evening Heidi came into the study carrying her book and said to Clara, 'I'll read to you a lot now, if you'd like me to.' Clara thanked her, and Heidi began the little task she had taken on herself with enthusiasm. But all did not go smoothly, for the story she had chosen proved to be about a dying grandmother. It was too much for Heidi who burst into tears and sobbed, 'Grannie is dead.' Everything she read was so real to her that she was firmly convinced that it was Peter's Grannie in the story.

'Now I shall never see her again,' she wept, 'and she never had one of the nice white rolls.'

Clara had great difficulty in persuading her that the story was about quite another grandmother, and even when she began to understand that, she was not comforted for it had made her realize that Peter's Grannie might really die, and her grandfather too, while she was so far away, and that if she did not go home for a long time, she might arrive to find everything changed and her loved ones gone for ever.

Miss Rottenmeier came into the room during this scene,

and as Heidi went on crying, she looked at her very impatiently and said, 'Adelheid, stop howling like that and listen to me. If I ever hear you making such a to-do again while you're reading to Clara, I'll take the book away from you and you shan't have it again.'

This threat had an immediate effect, for the book was Heidi's greatest treasure. She turned quite pale, quickly dried her eyes, and stifled her sobs. She never wept again after that, no matter what she read, but the effort it cost her sometimes produced such queer grimaces that Clara was quite astonished. 'I've never seen anything like the faces you're making,' she used to say. But at least Miss Rottenmeier did not notice anything, and once Heidi had got over one of her spells of sadness, everything would go smoothly for a time.

Her appetite did not improve, however, and she looked very thin and peaky. It quite upset Sebastian at mealtimes to see her refuse even the most delicious things. As he handed them to her, he would sometimes whisper, 'Just try some of this, Miss, it's so good. That's not enough. Here, take another spoonful.' But all in vain. She ate hardly anything. And when she was in bed and all the well-loved scenes of home came before her eyes, she cried and cried, until her pillows were quite wet.

Time went by, but in the town Heidi scarcely knew whether it was winter or summer. The walls and houses, which were all she could see from the windows, always looked the same, and now she only went out-of-doors when Clara was feeling well enough for a drive. Even then they saw nothing but bricks and mortar, for Clara could not stand a long excursion and they only drove round the neighbouring streets, where they saw plenty of people and beautiful houses, but not a blade of grass or a flower or a tree, and no mountains. Heidi's homesickness grew on her from day to day, till just reading the name of some well-loved object was enough to bring tears to her eyes, though she would not let them fall.

Autumn and winter passed and the bright sunlight shining again on the white walls of the house opposite set Heidi guessing that soon Peter would be taking the goats up to pasture again, and that all the flowers would be in bloom and the mountains ablaze with light each evening. When she was in her own room, she used to sit with her hands over her eyes to shut out the town sunshine, and would stay like that, forcing back her over-whelming homesickness until Clara wanted her again.

12

The House is Haunted!

Strange things began to happen in that house in Frankfurt. Miss Rottenmeier had taken to wandering silently about it, deep in thought; and if she had to go from one room to another or along the passages after dark, she often looked over her shoulder or peered into corners, as if afraid that someone might creep out of the shadow, and pluck at her skirt. If she had to go upstairs to the richly furnished guest-rooms or down to the great drawing-room, in which footsteps echoed at the best of times and where old councillors in stiff white collars stared out from the portraits on the walls, she always made Tinette go with her – in case there should be anything to carry up or down. Strange to say, Tinette behaved in much the same way. If she had to go to those rooms, she got Sebastian to go with her, on the same pretext of helping to carry something. And Sebastian seemed also to feel the same way. If he was sent into any of the unused rooms, he called John the coachman and asked him to go too – in case he could not manage the job alone. And everyone did as they were asked and went along too, without any fuss, though their help was never really needed. It looked as if they all thought that they might want assistance themselves some time. Down in the kitchen things were no better. The old cook, who had been there a long time, stood by her saucepans, shaking her head and muttering, 'That I should live to see such goings on.'

The reason for all this uneasiness was that for some time past the servants had been finding the front door wide open every morning when they came down, but there was never anything to show who had opened it. For the first day or two the house had been thoroughly searched to see whether anything had been stolen, for it was thought a burglar might have hidden himself during the day and made off with his booty during the night. However, nothing was missing. Then they double-locked the front door and bolted it every night, but still they found it wide open in the morning, no matter how early the servants came down.

At last, Miss Rottenmeier persuaded John and Sebastian to spend a night downstairs in the room next to the drawing-room, to see if they could discover the cause of the mystery. They were provided with weapons belonging to Mr Sesemann, and a bottle of wine to fortify them for whatever might happen.

When evening came they settled down and immediately opened the wine which soon made them talkative. Then they grew sleepy and lolled back in their armchairs and fell into a doze. The clock striking twelve brought Sebastian to his senses and he said something to John but John was fast asleep and only settled himself more comfortably into his chair at each effort to rouse him. Sebastian, however, was wide awake now, and listening for unusual sounds. But none came, either from the house or from the street. In fact, the silence was so deep that he grew uneasy. He saw it was no use trying to wake John by calling to him so he shook him, but another hour passed before John was really awake and remembered what he was there for. He got to his feet then, with a fine show of courage, and said:

'We'd better go and see what's going on. Don't be afraid. Just follow me.'

He pushed open the door, which had been left ajar, and went out into the passage. Almost at once the candle in his hand was blown out by a gust of wind from the front door which was standing wide open. He rushed back into the room at that, almost knocking Sebastian over, and slammed the door and locked it. Then he struck a match and lit the candle again. Sebastian did not know what had happened. John was portly enough to block his view completely and he had seen nothing. He had not even felt the draught. But John was white as a sheet and trembling like an aspen leaf.

'What's the matter? What was outside?' Sebastian asked anxiously.

'The front door was wide open,' John told him, 'and there was a white figure on the stairs which suddenly vanished.'

A cold shiver ran down Sebastian's spine. They sat down close together and did not stir thereafter until it was broad daylight and they could hear people going by in the street. Then they went and shut the front door and then reported to Miss Rottenmeier. They found her already up and dressed, for she had been awake most of the night wondering what they would discover. As soon as she had heard their story, she sat down and wrote very emphatically to Mr Sesemann, telling him she was so paralysed with fright she could hardly hold a pen, and must beg him to come home at once as no one in the house could sleep easily in their beds for fear of what might happen next.

The answer, by return of post, said that it was not possible for Mr Sesemann to leave his business and return home so precipitately. He was surprised to hear of a 'ghost' about the house, and hoped it was only some temporary disturbance. However, if the trouble continued, he suggested that Miss Rottenmeier should write and ask his mother to return to Frankfurt. She would certainly know how to deal with any 'ghosts' effectively, so that they did not show themselves again. Miss Rottenmeier was annoyed that he did not take the matter more seriously. She wrote immediately to Mrs Sesemann, but got no satisfaction from this quarter either. The old lady replied somewhat tartly that she had no intention of travelling all the way to Frankfurt again because Rottenmeier imagined she had seen a ghost. There had never been a 'ghost' in the house, and in the old lady's opinion, the present one would prove to be very much alive. If Rottenmeier could not deal with the matter herself, the letter went on, she should send for the police.

Miss Rottenmeier was not inclined to endure much more, and she had a shrewd idea how to make the Sesemanns take notice of her complaint. So far she had not told the children anything, as she was afraid they would be too frightened ever to be left alone – and that would have been most tiresome. Now, however, she went straight to the study and told them in a hoarse whisper about the nightly visitations. Clara at once demanded that she should not be left alone, never, not for a single second.

'Papa must come home. You must sleep in my room,' she cried. 'Heidi mustn't be left alone either, in case the ghost does anything to her. We'd better all stay together in one room and keep the light on all night, and Tinette will have to sleep in the next room and John and Sebastian had better be out in the corridor so that they can frighten the ghost away if it comes upstairs.' Clara was thoroughly worked up by that time, and Miss Rottenmeier had great difficulty in calming her.

'I'll write at once to your papa,' she promised, 'and put my bed in your room so that you're never alone. But we can't all sleep in one room. If Adelheid is frightened

Tinette shall put up a bed in her room.' But Heidi was much more afraid of Tinette than of ghosts, of which indeed she had never heard, so she said she was not frightened and would sleep alone in her own room. Miss Rottenmeier then went to her desk and wrote dutifully to Mr Sesemann to let him know that the mysterious happenings in the house still continued, and were threatening to have a very bad effect on Clara in her delicate state of health. 'Fright might even send her into fits,' she wrote, 'or bring on an attack of St Vitus' dance.'

Her plot was successful. Two days later Mr Sesemann stood at his front door, ringing the bell so vigorously that everyone jumped, thinking the ghost had started playing tricks by daylight. Sebastian peeped through one of the upstairs windows to see what was happening, and at that moment the bell rang again so loudly that there could be no real doubt that a human hand had pulled it. He realized that it was his master and rushed downstairs, almost falling head over heels in his haste. Mr Sesemann hardly noticed him, but went at once to Clara's room. She welcomed him joyfully and he was greatly relieved to find her so cheerful and, to all appearances, much as usual. Clara assured him she was really no worse, and was so pleased to see him that she felt quite grateful to the ghost for bringing him home.

'And how has the "ghost" been behaving, Miss Rottenmeier?' he asked that lady with a smile.

'Oh, it's a serious matter,' she replied stiffly. 'I don't think even you will be laughing about it tomorrow. It seems to me that something terrible must have happened here some time in the past, though it has not come out until now.'

'I must ask you not to cast reflections on my entirely respectable forebears!' said Mr Sesemann. 'Now please send Sebastian to me in the dining-room. I want to talk to him alone.' He had noticed that Sebastian and Miss Rottenmeier were not exactly on the best of terms and that gave him an idea.

'Come here,' he said, as Sebastian entered, 'and tell me the truth. Did you play the ghost to frighten Miss Rottenmeier?'

'Oh, sir, please don't think that. I'm just as frightened as she is,' replied Sebastian, and it was plain that he was speaking the truth.

'Well, if that's the case, I shall have to show you and the worthy John what ghosts look like by daylight. A great strong chap like you ought to be ashamed of running away from such a thing. Now I want you to take a message to Dr Classen. Give him my regards and ask him to come and see me without fail at nine o'clock tonight. Say I've come back from Paris on purpose to consult him, and that the matter is so serious that he'd better come prepared to spend the night. Is that clear?'

'Yes, sir. I'll see to it at once.'

Mr Sesemann then went back to tell his daughter that he hoped to lay the ghost by the next day.

Punctually at nine o'clock, when both children were in bed and Miss Rottenmeier had retired for the night, the doctor arrived. Although his hair was grey, he had a fresh complexion and his eyes were bright and kind. He looked rather worried when he came in, but as soon as he saw his friend, he burst out laughing.

'I must say you look pretty well for a man wanting someone to sit up all night with you!' he said, patting him on the shoulder.

'Not so fast, my friend,' replied Mr Sesemann. 'Your attention is likely to be needed all right, and by someone who won't look as well as I do when we've caught him.'

'So there really is a patient in the house,' returned the doctor, 'and one who has to be caught, eh?'

'Much worse than that! We've a ghost! The house is haunted.'

The doctor laughed outright.

'You're not very sympathetic,' objected Mr Sesemann. 'It's a good thing Miss Rottenmeier can't hear you at the moment. She's firmly convinced one of my ancestors is prowling around, doing penance for his sins.'

'How did she come to meet him?' asked the doctor, still chuckling.

Mr Sesemann told him all he knew, and added, 'To be on the safe side I've put two loaded pistols in the room, where you and I are going to keep watch. I've a feeling it may be a very stupid practical joke which some friend of the servants is playing in order to alarm the household during my absence. In that case a shot fired into the air to frighten him will do no harm. If, on the other hand, burglars are preparing the ground for themselves by making everyone so afraid of the "ghost" that they won't dare to leave their rooms, it may equally be advisable to have a good weapon handy.'

While he was talking, Mr Sesemann led the way to the same room where John and Sebastian had spent the night. On the table were the two guns and a bottle of wine, for if they had to sit up all night, a little refreshment would certainly be welcome. The room was lit by two candelabra, each holding three candles. Mr Sesemann had no intention of waiting for a ghost in the dark, but the door was shut so that no light should penetrate into the corridor to give warning to the ghost. The men settled themselves comfortably in their armchairs, for a good chat and a drink. Time passed quickly and they were quite surprised when the clock struck midnight.

'The ghost's got wind of us and isn't coming,' said the doctor.

'We must wait a while yet,' replied Mr Sesemann. 'It isn't supposed to appear till about one o'clock.'

So they chatted on, for another hour. In the street outside everything was quiet, when suddenly the doctor raised a warning finger. 'Did you hear anything, Sesemann?' he asked.

They listened and heard distinctly the sound of a bolt being pushed back, and a key turned, then the door opened. Mr Sesemann reached for his revolver.

'You're not afraid, are you?' asked the doctor quietly.

'It's better to be careful,' the other whispered back.

They each took a light in one hand and a revolver in the other and went out into the corridor. There they saw a pale streak of moonlight coming through the open door, and shining on a white figure which stood motionless on the threshold.

'Who's there?' shouted the doctor so loudly that his voice echoed down the corridor. They both moved towards the front door. The figure turned and gave a little cry. It was Heidi who stood there, barefooted, in her white night-gown, staring in bewilderment at the weapons and the lights. She began to tremble and her lips quivered. The men looked at each other in astonishment.

'Why I believe it's your little water-carrier!' said the doctor.

'What are you doing here, child?' asked Mr Sesemann. 'Why have you come downstairs?'

Heidi stood before him, white as her nightgown, and answered faintly, 'I don't know.'

'I think this is a case for me,' said the doctor. 'Let me take the child back to her room, while you go and sit

down again.' He put his revolver on the ground, took Heidi gently by the hand, and led her upstairs. She was still shivering and he tried to soothe her by speaking in his friendly way to her. 'Don't be afraid. Nothing terrible is going to happen. You're all right.'

When they reached her room, he set the light down on the table and lifted Heidi back into bed. He covered her up carefully, then sat down in a chair beside her and waited until she was more herself. Then he took her hand and said gently, 'That's better. Now tell me where you were going.'

'Nowhere,' whispered Heidi. 'I didn't know I'd gone downstairs. I just was there.'

Her small hand was cold in the doctor's warm one.

'I see,' he said. 'Can you remember whether you'd had a dream? One perhaps that seemed very real?'

'Oh yes.' Heidi's eyes met his. 'I dream every night that I'm back with Grandfather and can hear the wind whistling through the fir trees. I know in my dream the stars must be shining brightly outside, and I get up quickly and open the door of the hut – and it's so beautiful. But when I wake up I'm always still here in Frankfurt.' A lump came in her throat and she tried to swallow it.

'Have you a pain anywhere?' asked the doctor. 'In your head or your back?'

'No, but I feel as though there's a great stone in my throat.'

'As though you'd taken a large bite of something and can't swallow it?'

Heidi shook her head. 'No, as if I wanted to cry.'

'And do you sometimes have a good cry?'

Her lips quivered again. 'No. I'm not allowed to. Miss Rottenmeier has forbidden it.'

'So you swallow it down, I suppose. You like being in Frankfurt, don't you?'

'Yes,' she said, but it sounded much more as though she meant to say No.

'Where did you live with your grandfather?'

'On the mountain.'

'That wasn't much fun, was it? Didn't you find it rather dull there?'

'Oh no, it's wonderful.' Heidi got no further. The memory of home, added to the shock of all she had been through, overcame the ban which had checked her tears, and they suddenly rained down her cheeks and she sobbed bitterly.

The doctor got up and laid her head gently on the pillow. 'Have a good cry, it won't do you any harm,' he said. 'Then go to sleep, and in the morning everything will be all right.' He left the room and went to find Mr Sesemann, who was anxiously awaiting him.

'Well, in the first place your little foster-child is a sleep-walker,' he began. 'Without knowing anything about it, she has been opening the front door every night and frightening the servants out of their wits. In the second place she's terribly homesick, and appears to have lost a great deal of weight, for she's really not much more than skin and bone. Something must be done at once. She's very, upset and her nerves are in a bad state. There's only one cure for that sort of trouble – to send her back to her native mountains, and immediately. She should leave for home tomorrow – that's my prescription.'

Mr Sesemann got to his feet and paced up and down the room, much disturbed. 'Sleepwalking, homesick, and losing weight – fancy her suffering all this in my house without anyone noticing! She was so rosy and strong when she arrived. Do you think I'm going to send her back to her grandfather looking thin and ill? No, you really mustn't ask me to do that. Cure her first. Order whatever you like to make her well, then I'll send her home, if she wants to go.'

'You don't know what you're talking about,' protested the doctor. 'This is not an illness that can be cured with pills and powders. The child's not robust, but if you send her back to the mountains at once she'll soon be herself again. If not . . . you might find you have to send her back ill, incurable, or even not at all.'

Mr Sesemann was greatly upset. 'If that's how things are, doctor, of course I'll do as you say,' he promised.

When at last the doctor took his leave, it was the light of dawn which flooded through the front door.

13

Home Again

Mr Sesemann went upstairs feeling both anxious and annoyed, and he knocked loudly on Miss Rotten-meier's door. She awoke with a start to hear him say, 'Please get up quickly and come to the dining-room. We have to make preparations for a journey.' She looked at her clock: its hands pointed to only half past four. She had never got up so early in her life. What could have happened? She was in such a state of curiosity and excitement that she hardly knew what she was doing, and kept looking for garments which she had already put on.

Mr Sesemann then went along the passage and pulled vigorously at the bells which communicated with the rooms where the servants slept. Sebastian, John, and Tinette all leapt out of bed and threw on their clothes just any how, thinking the ghost must have attacked their master and that he was calling for help. They sped to the dining-room one after the other, all rather dishevelled, and were taken aback to find Mr Sesemann looking as brisk and cheerful as usual, and not at all as though he had seen a ghost. John was dispatched to fetch the carriage and horses at once, Tinette to waken Heidi and get her ready for a journey. Sebastian was sent to fetch Detie from the house where she worked.

Meanwhile Miss Rottenmeier completed her toilet, though she had put on her cap the wrong way round, so that from a distance it looked as though she were walking backwards, but Mr Sesemann rightly attributed this to her having been disturbed so early. He wasted no time on explanations, but told her to find a trunk immediately, and pack all Heidi's belongings in it. 'Put some of Clara's things in as well,' he added. 'The child must be well provided for. Hurry, now, there's no time to lose.'

Miss Rottenmeier was so astonished that she just stood and stared at him. She had been expecting him to tell her some terrible story about the ghost (which she would not have minded hearing by daylight). Instead she was met with these extremely businesslike (if rather inconvenient) orders. She could not understand it, and simply waited blankly for some sort of explanation. But Mr Sesemann left her, without saying anything further, and went to Clara's bedroom. As he expected, she had been awakened by all the commotion and was most anxious to know what had happened, so he sat down at her bedside and told her the whole story, ending up, 'Dr Classen is afraid Heidi's health has suffered, and says she might even go up on the roof in her sleep. You can understand how dangerous that would be. So I've made up my mind that she must go home at once. We can't risk anything happening to her, can we?'

Clara was very distressed at this news and tried hard to make her father change his mind, but he stood firm, only promising that if she was sensible and did not make a fuss, he would take her to Switzerland the following year. Then, seeing there were no two ways about it, she gave in, but she begged that, as a small consolation, Heidi's trunk should be brought to her room to be packed, so that she could put in some nice things which Heidi would like. To this her father willingly agreed.

By this time Detie had arrived and was wondering uneasily why she had been sent for at such an unearthly hour. Mr Sesemann repeated to her what he had learnt about Heidi's condition. 'I want you to take her home at once, this very day,' he said. Detie was very upset, remembering how Uncle Alp had told her never to show her face again upon the mountain. To have to take Heidi back to him like this, after the way she had carried her off, was asking too much of her.

'Please do excuse me,' she said glibly, 'but it is not possible for me to go today, nor yet tomorrow. We're very busy, and I really couldn't even ask for the day off just now. Indeed, I don't quite know when I could manage it.'

Mr Sesemann saw through her excuses, and sent her away without another word. He told Sebastian instead to prepare himself at once for a journey.

'You'll take the child as far as Basle today,' he said, 'and go on with her to her home tomorrow. I'll give you a letter for her grandfather so there will be no need for you to explain anything and you can come straight back here. When you get to Basle, go to the hotel whose name I've written on this visiting card. I'm well known there, and when you show it you'll be given a good room for the child, and they'll find a room for you too. And now listen to me,' he went on, 'this is very important. You must make sure all the windows in her room are shut securely so that she can't open them. Then, once she's in bed, you are to lock her bedroom door on the outside for she walks in her sleep, and in a strange house it might be very dangerous if she wandered downstairs and tried to open the front door. Do you understand?'

'So that's what it was,' exclaimed Sebastian, as the truth suddenly dawned upon him.

'Yes, that was it. You're a great coward and you can tell John he's another. You made fine fools of yourselves, all of you!' And with that Mr Sesemann went to his study to write to Uncle Alp. Somewhat shamefaced, Sebastian muttered to himself, 'I wish I hadn't let that idiot of a John push me back into the room, when he saw the figure in white! If only I'd gone after it. I certainly would if I saw it now.' But of course by that time the sun was lighting up every corner of the room.

Meanwhile Heidi was waiting in her bedroom, dressed

in her Sunday frock and wondering what was going to happen. Tinette considered her so far beneath her notice that she never threw her two words where one would do, and she had simply wakened her, told her to dress, and had taken her clothes out of the wardrobe.

When Mr Sesemann came back to the dining-room with his letter, breakfast was on the table. 'Where's the child?' he asked, and Heidi was at once fetched, and came in, giving him her usual 'Good morning.'

'Well, child, is that all you have to say?' he inquired.

She looked at him questioningly.

'I do believe nobody's told you,' he said with a smile. 'You're going home today.'

'Home,' she gasped, so overwhelmed that for the moment she could hardly breathe.

'Well? Aren't you pleased?'

'Oh yes, I am,' she said fervently, and the colour came into her cheeks.

'That's right. Now you must eat a good breakfast,' and he took his place at the table and signed to her to join him. She tried hard but couldn't swallow even a morsel of bread. She was not sure whether she was awake or still dreaming, and might not find herself presently standing at the front door again in her nightgown.

'Tell Sebastian to take plenty of food with him,' Mr Sesemann said to Miss Rottenmeier, as that lady came into the room. 'The child is not eating anything at all – and that is not to be wondered at.' He turned to Heidi. 'Now go to Clara, my child, and stay with her until the carriage arrives.' That was just what Heidi wanted to do, and she found Clara with a big trunk open beside her.

'Come and look at the things I've had put in for you,' Clara cried. 'I hope you'll like them. Look, there are frocks and aprons and hankies and some sewing things. Oh, and this!' Clara held up a basket. Heidi peeped and jumped for joy, for inside were twelve beautiful rolls for Grannie. In their delight the children quite forgot that they were so soon to part, and when they heard someone call, 'The carriage is here,' there was no time to be sad. Heidi ran to the room which had been hers, to fetch the book which Grandmamma had given her. She always kept it under her pillow, for she could never bear to be parted from it, so she felt sure no one would have packed it. She put it in the basket. Then she looked in the cupboard and fetched out her precious old hat. Her red scarf was there too, for Miss Rottenmeier had not thought it worth putting in the trunk. Heidi wrapped it round her other treasure and put it on top of the basket where it was very conspicuous. Then she put on a pretty little hat which she had been given, and left the room.

She and Clara had to say goodbye quickly, for Mr Sesemann was waiting to put Heidi in the carriage, and Miss Rottenmeier was standing at the top of the stairs to say goodbye too. She saw the funny-looking red bundle at once, and snatched it out of the basket and threw it on the floor. 'Really, Adelheid,' she scolded, 'you can't leave this house carrying a thing like that, and you won't need it any more. Goodbye.' After that Heidi did not dare to pick it up again, but she gave Mr Sesemann an imploring look.

'Let the child take what she likes with her,' he said sharply. 'If she wanted kittens and tortoises too, there would be no reason to get so excited, Miss Rottenmeier.'

Heidi took up her precious bundle, her eyes shining with gratitude and happiness. 'Goodbye,' said Mr Sesemann, shaking hands before she got into the carriage. 'Clara and I will often think of you. I hope you'll have a good journey.'

'Thank you for everything,' said Heidi, 'and please thank the doctor too, and give him my love.' She remembered that the doctor had said that everything would be all right the next day, so she was sure he must have helped to make this come true. She was lifted into the carriage, the basket and a bag of provisions were handed up, then Sebastian got in.

'Goodbye and a pleasant journey,' Mr Sesemann called after them, as the carriage drove off.

Soon Heidi was sitting in the train, with the basket on her lap. She would not let go of it for an instant, because of the precious rolls inside. Every now and then she peeped at them and sighed with satisfaction. For a long time she spoke never a word, for she was only beginning to realize that she was really on her way home to Grandfather, and would see the mountains and Peter and Grannie. As she thought about them all, she suddenly grew anxious, and asked, 'Sebastian, Peter's Grannie won't be dead, will she?'

'Let's hope not,' he replied. 'She'll be alive all right, I expect.'

Heidi fell silent again, looking forward to the moment when she would actually give the rolls to her kind old friend. Presently she said again, 'I wish I knew for certain that Grannie's still alive.'

'Oh, she'll be alive all right. Why shouldn't she be?' said Sebastian, who was nearly asleep. Soon Heidi's eyes closed too. She was so tired after her disturbed night and early rising that she dozed off, and slept soundly till Sebastian shook her by the arm, crying, 'Wake up. We have to get out here. We're at Basle.'

For several hours more next day they continued their journey by train, and Heidi still sat with the basket on her lap. She would not let Sebastian take it, even for a moment. She was very silent, but inside she grew more and more excited. Then, just when she was least expecting it, she heard a voice calling, 'Mayenfeld, Mayenfeld.' She and Sebastian jumped up in surprise, and scrambled out on the platform with the trunk. Then the train went puffing on down the valley and Sebastian looked after it with regret. He preferred travelling comfortably and without effort, and did not look forward to climbing a mountain. He felt sure it would be very dangerous, and the country seemed to him only half-civilized. He looked about for someone to tell them the safest way to Dörfli, and near the station entrance he noticed a small cart to which a skinny pony was harnessed. A big man was carrying out to it some heavy sacks which had come off the train, and to him Sebastian put his question.

'All the paths here are safe,' was the answer. That did not satisfy Sebastian, who went on to ask how they could best avoid falling down precipices, and how to get a trunk up to Dörfli. The man glanced at it, then said, 'If it's not too heavy, I'll take it on my cart. I'm going to Dörfli myself.'

After that it was a short step to persuade him to take Heidi, as well as her trunk, with him and to send her on the last part of the journey up the mountain with someone from the village.

'I can go alone. I know the way all right from there,' Heidi put in, after listening attentively to the conversation. Sebastian was delighted at having got out of the climb. He took Heidi to one side and gave her a fat packet and a letter for her grandfather. 'The packet's for you, a present from Mr Sesemann,' he said. 'Put it at the bottom of the basket and see you don't lose it. He'd be very angry if you did.'

'I won't lose it,' said Heidi, tucking both letter and packet away. She and her basket were then lifted on to the driver's seat, while the trunk was placed in the back of the cart. Sebastian felt rather guilty as he knew he was meant to take her all the way home. He shook hands with her and reminded her with warning signs to remember what he had just given her. He was careful not to mention it out loud in the hearing of the driver. Then the man swung himself up beside Heidi, and the cart rolled off towards the mountain, while Sebastian returned to the little station to wait for a train to take him home.

The man on the cart was the baker from Dörfli, who had been to collect some flour. He had never seen Heidi, but like everyone in the village he had heard of her. He had known her parents and realized at once who she was. He was surprised to see her back again and was naturally curious to find out what had happened, so he began to talk to her.

'You must be the little girl who used to live with Uncle Alp, your grandfather, aren't you?' he inquired.

'Yes,' said Heidi.

'Did they treat you badly down there, that you're coming so soon?'

'Oh no,' Heidi cried. 'Everyone was very kind to me in Frankfurt.'

'Then why are you coming back?'

'Mr Sesemann said I could come.'

'I'd have thought you would rather have stayed if you were so well off there.'

'I'd a million times rather be with Grandfather on the mountain than anywhere else in the world,' she told him.

'Perhaps you'll change your mind when you get there,' muttered the baker, thinking to himself, 'It's a rum business, but she must know what it's like.'

He began to whistle then, and said no more. Heidi looked around with growing delight at the mountain peaks she knew so well and which seemed to greet her like old friends. She wanted to jump down from the cart and run the rest of the way, but she managed to sit still, though she was shivering with excitement. They reached Dörfli just as the clock struck five, and there was soon a little crowd of villagers round the cart, curious to find out about the child and the trunk which had come in on it.

The baker lifted Heidi down. 'Thank you,' she said hastily. 'Grandfather will come and fetch the trunk,' and she turned to run off home at once, but the villagers crowded round her, with a string of questions. She struggled through them, looking so pale and anxious that they murmured among themselves, as they let her go, 'You can see how frightened she looks, and no wonder,' and they added, 'If the poor child had anywhere else in the world to go, she'd never come running back to that old dragon.' The baker, aware that he was the only person who knew anything on that subject, now spoke up. 'A gentleman brought her to

Mayenfeld and said goodbye to her in a very friendly way, and he gave me what I asked for bringing her up here without any haggling, and something over as well. She has been well treated, wherever she's been, and has come home of her own accord.' These little bits of news spread so rapidly that before nightfall every house in the village knew that Heidi had left a good home in Frankfurt to come back, of her own accord, to her grandfather.

As soon as she got away from the people, Heidi rushed uphill as fast as she could go. She had to stop every now and then to get her breath, for her basket was heavy and the mountain slope steep, but she had only one thought: 'Will Grannie still be sitting in the corner by her spinning-wheel? Oh, I hope she hasn't died.' Then she saw the little house in the hollow, and her heart beat faster than ever. She raced up to the door but could hardly open it, she was trembling so much, but she managed it, and flew into the little room quite out of breath and unable to say a word.

'Goodness me,' someone said from the corner of the room, 'that was how Heidi used to come in! How I wish she would come and see me again. Who is it?'

'It's Heidi, Grannie,' she cried, and threw herself on to the old woman's lap and hugged her, too overcome with happiness to say anything more. And at first Grannie was so surprised, she could not speak either, but just stroked Heidi's head. Then she murmured, 'Yes, it's Heidi's curly

hair and her voice. Praise God she's come back to us.' A few big tears fell from her old blind eyes on to Heidi's hand. 'It's really you, child.'

'Yes, really and truly, Grannie. Don't cry,' said Heidi. 'I'm here and I'll never go away again. I'll come and see you every day. And you won't have to eat hard bread for a few days, Grannie,' she added, and she brought out the rolls one by one and laid them on Grannie's lap.

'Child, what a present to bring me!' exclaimed the old woman, as her hands moved over the load on her lap. 'But you're the best present of all.' And she stroked Heidi's hot cheeks. 'Say something, anything at all, just to let me hear your voice.'

'I was so afraid you might have died while I was away,' said Heidi, 'then I would never have seen you again, and you wouldn't have had the rolls.'

Peter's mother came in at this moment and stared in amazement when she saw Heidi. 'Fancy you here,' she said at last, 'and she's wearing such a pretty dress, Grannie. She looks so fine I hardly recognized her. And a little hat with a feather – I suppose that is yours too. Put it on and let me see you in it.'

'No, I won't,' said Heidi very decidedly. 'You can have that. I don't want it any more. I've got my old one.' And she opened her red bundle and there it was, more battered than ever after the journey, but that didn't worry her. She had never forgotten her grandfather saying that he would not like to see her in a hat with a feather, and that was why she had taken such care of the old one, for she had always counted on going back to him.

'That's silly,' said Bridget. 'I can't possibly take it from you. It's a very smart hat, and if you really don't want it, perhaps the schoolmaster's daughter would buy it from you.' Heidi said no more, but put the hat away in a corner out of sight. Then she took off her pretty dress, and put the old red scarf on over her petticoat.

'Goodbye, Grannie. I must go on to Grandfather now, but I'll come and see you again tomorrow.'

Grannie hugged her as if she could not bear to let her go.

'Why have you taken off your pretty frock?' asked Bridget.

'I'd rather go to Grandfather like this, otherwise he might not recognize me. You hardly knew me in it.'

Bridget went outside with her. 'You could have kept it on,' she said, 'he'd have known you all right. But you be careful. Peter says Uncle Alp is so bad-tempered now, and never speaks to him.'

Heidi said goodbye and went on her way. The evening sun shone rosily on the mountains, and she kept turning round to look at them, for they lay behind her as she climbed. Everything seemed even more beautiful than she had expected. The twin peaks of Falkniss, snow-covered Scesaplana, the pasture land, and the valley below were all red and gold, and there were little pink clouds floating in the sky. It was so lovely, Heidi stood with tears pouring down her cheeks, and thanked God for letting her come home to it again. She could find no words to express her feelings, but lingered until the light began to fade and then ran on. Soon she could see the tops of the fir trees, then the roof, then the whole hut and last Grandfather himself, sitting on the bench outside and smoking his pipe, just as he used to do. Before he had time to see who it was, she had dropped her basket on the ground and flung her arms around him, crying, 'Grandfather, Grandfather.' She could say no more, and he couldn't speak at all. For the first time in years, his eyes were wet with tears and he had to brush his hand over them. Then he loosened her arms from his neck and set her on his knee.

'So you've come back, Heidi,' he said. 'Why's that, eh? And you don't look so very grand either. Did they send you away?'

'Oh no, Grandfather, don't think that. Clara and her father and Grandmamma were all very kind to me. But I was very homesick. I used to get a lump in my throat, as if I was choking. But I didn't say anything, because they would have thought I was not grateful. Then suddenly Mr Sesemann called me very early one morning – but I think the doctor had something to do with it. Oh, I expect it's all in the letter.' She jumped down and ran to fetch the letter and the fat packet.

'The packet is for you,' he said, laying it on the bench. Then he read the letter and put it in his pocket without a word.

'Do you think you could drink some milk, Heidi?' he asked, preparing to go indoors with her. 'Bring the packet with you. There's money in it for you to buy a bed and any clothes you may need.'

'I don't want it,' said Heidi gaily. 'I've got a bed already, and Clara gave me so many clothes I'm sure I shall never want any more.'

'Bring it in all the same, and put it in the cupboard,' said Uncle Alp. 'You'll find a use for it one day.'

Heidi brought it indoors. She looked round eagerly at everything, then climbed up to the loft. 'Oh, my bed's gone,' she cried, very disappointed.

'We can soon make it again,' he called up. 'I didn't know you'd be coming back. Now come and have some milk.'

She sat down on her old high chair and drained her mug as though she had never tasted anything so delicious in her life. Then she drew a deep breath and said, 'There's nothing as good as our milk anywhere in the world.'

There came a shrill whistle then, and Heidi shot out of the door to see Peter coming down the path, surrounded by his lively goats. When he caught sight of her, he stopped dead and stared in astonishment.

'Hullo, Peter,' she called and ran towards him. 'Oh, there's Daisy and Dusky. Do you remember me?' They did indeed seem to recognize her voice, and rubbed their heads against her, bleating. She called the other goats by name and they all came crowding round her. Impatient Finch jumped clean over two other animals to reach her, and even shy Snowflake pressed forward and butted big Turk to one side. Turk was very surprised and tossed his head as if to say, 'Look what you're doing!' Heidi was delighted to see them all again. She put an arm round one and patted another. The animals pushed her this way and that with their affectionate nudgings, but at last she came to Peter's side.

'Aren't you going to say hallo to me?' she asked.

He recovered himself then and said, 'So you're back again,' adding, as he always used to in the old days, 'Coming up with me tomorrow?'

'Not tomorrow, but perhaps the day after. I must go and see Grannie tomorrow.'

'I'm glad you're back,' he said, with a wide grin, and prepared to move on, but he found it very difficult to get the goats together again. He called and scolded, but as soon as he had gathered them round him, they all turned to follow Heidi who was taking Daisy and Dusky towards their stall, with an arm thrown round each. She had to go right inside with them and shut the door, before Peter could get the rest of the herd on the move.

When she went indoors again she found her grand-father had made her a lovely sweet-smelling bed, with hay which had not long been gathered in, and had covered it comfortably with clean linen sheets. When she lay down in it a little later, she slept as she had not done all the time she had been away.

During the night Uncle Alp went up to the loft at least ten times to make sure she was all right, and to see that the round hole in the wall was still stopped with hay to prevent the moonlight shining on her face. But Heidi did not stir. She slept soundly all night long, satisfied through and through. She was home again. She had seen the sun setting on the mountains. She had heard the wind whistling through the fir trees.

14

When the Church Bells Ring

Heidi stood under the swaying trees, waiting for her grandfather to go down the mountain with her. He was going to fetch her trunk from Dörfli while she visited Grannie. She was eager to get there, to hear how she had enjoyed the rolls but, listening to the familiar rustling of the trees with her eyes resting on the distant green pastures, she did not grow impatient.

Presently he came out of the hut and took a last look round. It was Saturday, the day when he always cleaned the whole place, inside and out, and tidied up generally. He had worked hard all the morning so that he would be free to go with Heidi in the afternoon, and now everything looked spick and span so he could leave it with a clear conscience. 'Now we can go,' he said.

They parted company outside the little house where Peter lived, and Heidi went in there. Grannie heard her step at once, and called affectionately, 'Is that you, child?' She took Heidi's hand and held it tightly as if she was afraid of losing her again.

'How did you like the rolls?' asked Heidi at once.

'Oh, they taste good! I feel better already.'

'Grannie's so anxious to make them last that she would only eat one last night and another this morning,' put in Bridget. 'If she has one every day for the next ten days, I'm sure she'll get back her strength.'

Heidi listened thoughtfully and an idea came to her. 'I know what I'll do, Grannie,' she cried. 'I'll write to Clara. I'm sure she'll send me more rolls. I'd saved lots and lots for you, but they were all thrown away, and then Clara promised she'd give me as many as I wanted. She'll keep her word, I know.'

'That's a kind thought,' said Bridget, 'but I'm afraid they'd be quite stale and hard by the time they got here. If I had a spare copper or two I'd get some from the baker in Dörfli, but it's as much as I can do to buy the black bread.'

A beaming smile spread over Heidi's face. 'But I've got lots of money, Grannie,' she exclaimed, 'and now I know what I can do with it. You shall have a fresh roll every day and two on Sundays, and Peter can bring them up with him from the village.'

'No, no,' protested Grannie, 'you mustn't spend your money on me. You give it to Grandfather, and he'll tell you what to do with it.'

Heidi paid no attention but pranced round the room, singing, 'Now Grannie can have a fresh roll every day and will soon be strong again! And oh, Grannie, when you're quite well, surely you'll be able to see too. It's probably only because you're so weak that you can't see.'

Grannie just smiled. She would not spoil the child's happiness. As she danced around, Heidi caught sight of Grannie's old hymn-book, and that gave her another idea. 'I can read now, Grannie,' she said. 'Would you like me to read you something out of your old book?'

'Oh, yes,' exclaimed Grannie, delighted. 'Can you really read?'

Heidi climbed on a stool and took down the book, which had lain on the shelf so long that it was thick with dust. She wiped it clean and took the stool close beside the old woman. 'What shall I read?' she asked.

'What you like, child,' Grannie said, pushing her spinning-wheel to one side and waiting eagerly for her to begin.

Heidi turned the pages, reading a line here and a line there. 'Here's one about the sun,' she said at last. 'I'll read that.' And she began with great enthusiasm.

> 'The golden sun
> His course doth run,
> And spreads his light,
> So warm and bright,
> Upon us all.

'We see God's power
From hour to hour.
His love is sure,
And will endure
For evermore.

'Sorrow and grief
Are only brief.
True joy we'll find,
And peace of mind,
In God's good time.'

Grannie sat through it with her hands folded. Heidi had never seen her look so happy, though tears were running down her cheeks. And at the end she said, 'Read it again, Heidi. Please read it again.'

Heidi was delighted to do so for she liked the hymn very much herself.

'Oh, that's done me so much good,' Grannie sighed at last. 'It makes my old heart rejoice.'

Heidi had never seen such a peaceful expression before on Grannie's careworn face. It looked as though she had indeed found 'true joy and peace of mind'.

Then there came a knock on the window and Heidi saw her grandfather outside, beckoning to her. She said goodbye and promised to come again the next day. 'I may go to the pasture with Peter and the goats in the morning,' she added, 'but I'll be here in the afternoon.' It had been pleasant to be able to give so much happiness, and Heidi wanted to do that even more than running on the mountain among the flowers with the goats.

As she was going Bridget brought out the dress and hat which Heidi had taken off and left behind the day before. Now she thought she might as well take the dress, for she was sure it would not make any difference to Grandfather, but the hat she absolutely refused. 'You keep that,' she told Bridget. 'I'll never wear it again.'

Heidi had so much to tell her grandfather that she began at once. 'And I'd like to buy rolls for Grannie with my money,' she told him. 'She doesn't want me to, but it'll be all right, won't it? Peter can get them in Dörfli, if I give him a penny every day, and two on Sunday.'

'What about your bed, Heidi? It would be nice for you to have a proper one, and there would still be enough money to buy the rolls.'

'But I sleep much better on my hay mattress than I did in that great big bed in Frankfurt. Please, please let me spend the money on rolls.'

'Well,' he agreed at last, 'the money is yours. Do what you like with it. There'll be enough to buy Grannie rolls for many a long year.'

'Good, good! She needn't ever eat the hard black bread again. Oh, we are having good times, Grandfather, aren't we?' and she skipped gaily along beside him. Then all at once she grew serious and said, 'If God had let me come back to you at once, like I asked in my prayers, none of this would have happened. I should have brought Grannie a few rolls I had saved, but they would soon have been gone, and I wouldn't have been able to read. God knew what was best, just as Clara's Grandmamma said He did, and see how perfectly He arranged everything. I'll always say my prayers after this, as Grandmamma told me to, and if God doesn't answer them at once I shall know it's because He's planning something better for me, just as He did in Frankfurt. We'll pray every day, won't we Grandfather, and we'll never forget God again, and He won't forget us.'

'And when someone does forget?' he said softly.

'That's very bad,' Heidi told him earnestly, 'because then God lets him go his own way and then, when everything has gone wrong, no one will feel sorry for him. They'll only say, "You didn't bother about God, and now God has left you to yourself."'

'That's true, Heidi. How did you find out?'

'Grandmamma explained it all to me.'

The old man walked on in silence. After a while he said, half to himself, 'If God forsakes a man, that's final. There's no going back then.'

'Oh, but there is. Grandmamma said so, and everything will come right in the end, like it does in the lovely story in my book. You haven't heard it yet, but we'll soon be home now, and then I'll read it to you.' Heidi hurried as fast as she could go up the last steep slope, and when they reached the hut, she let go his hand and ran indoors. He took the basket off his back. He had packed half the contents of her trunk in it, for the whole thing would have been too heavy for him to carry so far uphill. Then he sat down on the bench outside, lost in thought, until Heidi reappeared with the book under her arm. 'That's good, you're all ready,' she said, climbing on to the seat beside him.

She had read the story so often that the book opened at the right place by itself, and she began straightaway to read about the young man with the shepherd's crook and the fine cloak, who looked after his father's sheep and goats in the fields. 'One day,' she continued, 'he asked for his share of his father's fortune so that he might go away and be his own master. As soon as he got it, he left home and wasted it all. When it was gone, he had to go and work for his living, and he got a job with a farmer, who had no flocks nor pastures as his father had, but only pigs. This young man had to look after them. His fine clothes were gone, and he had only rags to cover him, and only the pigs' swill to eat, and he was very sad when he remembered how well he had been treated at home, and realized how ungrateful he had been to his father. Alone with the pigs, he wept with remorse and homesickness and thought, "I will rise up and go to my father and ask him to forgive me. I will say to him that I am no longer worthy to be treated as his son, but ask if he will let me be one of his servants." So he set out, and when he was still a long way off, his father saw him and came running towards him.' Heidi broke off to ask, 'What do you suppose happens now? I expect you think his father would be angry and say, "I told you so." Just you listen though. When his father saw him, his heart was filled with compassion for him, and he ran and met him and put his arms round him and kissed him; and his son said, "Father, I have done wrong against Heaven and against you and am no longer worthy to be your son." But his father called to the servants, "Bring me the good robe and put it on him, and a ring for his finger and shoes for his feet. Fetch the calf we have fattened and kill it for a feast, and we will eat and be merry, for my son was dead to me and is alive again, he was lost and is found." And they began to be merry.'

Instead of looking pleased and surprised as she had expected, the old man sat very still, without speaking, until she said, 'Isn't that a lovely story, Grandfather?'

'It is indeed,' he replied, but he looked so grave that she too fell silent, and sat looking at the pictures. Presently she pushed the book gently in front of him. 'You can see how happy he is,' she said, pointing to the picture of the return of the prodigal son.

Some hours later, when Heidi was in bed and asleep, the old man climbed up to the loft and put his lamp on the ground so that its light fell on her. She lay with her hands folded, as if she had fallen asleep saying her prayers. There was a peaceful, very trusting expression on her face, which moved him deeply and he stood gazing down at her for a long time. Then he too folded his hands, bowed his head, and, in a low voice, said, 'Father, I have sinned against Heaven and before Thee and am no longer worthy to be called Thy son,' and down his wrinkled cheeks rolled two large tears.

He rose early next morning and went out of doors. It was a beautiful day – a Sunday. The sound of bells floated up from the valley and the birds in the fir trees were singing their morning chorus. Then he stepped back into the hut and called up to Heidi, 'Time to get up. The sun is shining. Put on your best dress and we'll go to church together.'

She had never heard him suggest such a thing before, and she soon came hurrying down, wearing one of the pretty Frankfurt dresses. At sight of him, she stopped in astonishment.

'I've never seen you dressed like that before, Grandfather,' she exclaimed. 'Silver buttons on your jacket. You do look fine in your Sunday clothes.'

He smiled at her. 'And so do you,' he said. 'Now let's go.' He took her hand and together they set off down the steep path. Bells from many churches were ringing, getting louder and clearer as grandfather and child went on, and the joyful clanging delighted Heidi.

'Oh, Grandfather, this must be a very special day,' she cried.

The people of Dörfli were already in church and the

singing had started as Heidi and Uncle Alp went in and sat down at the back. The hymn was hardly over before people were nudging one another and whispering that Uncle Alp was in church. Women kept turning round to look and so lost the place in their hymn-books, and the leader of the choir simply could not keep the voices together. But when the pastor began to preach, everyone gave him their attention, for he spoke of praise and thanksgiving, and with such warmth that his listeners were truly moved.

At the end of the service the old man took Heidi by the hand again, and they went towards the pastor's house. The congregation watched them with interest. Several people followed to see whether they would actually go inside and, when they did so, hung around in little groups, asking what it could possibly mean and speculating whether Uncle Alp would come out again angry or friendly. There were those who said, 'He can't be as bad as people make out. Did you see how gently he held the child by the hand?' or 'I've always said they were wrong! He wouldn't be going to see the pastor at all if he was such a bad lot.'

'What did I tell you?' demanded the baker. 'Would the child have left that place where she was so well looked after, with plenty to eat and drink, and have come back, of her own accord, to him if he was as hard and bad as people said?' Gradually they all changed their minds about old Uncle Alp and began to feel quite friendly towards him. Then some women joined in the talk, and they had heard from Bridget and Grannie how Uncle Alp had come down and patched up their cottage for them and stopped the shutters rattling; and in no time, they were looking eagerly at the house door, like old friends waiting to welcome home a traveller who had been long away, and greatly missed.

Now when Uncle Alp had gone inside the pastor's house, he knocked on the study door and the pastor came out, looking quite as though he had expected the visit – for of course he had seen them in church. He shook hands with Uncle Alp so warmly that at first the lonely old man could hardly speak. He had not expected such kindness. When he had collected himself, he said:

'I've come to ask you to forget what I said when you called on me that time, and not to hold it against me that I wouldn't take your friendly advice. You were quite right and I was wrong. I shall do as you suggested and move down to Dörfli for the winter. The weather is too severe then for the child to be up in the hut. And if the people down here do regard me with suspicion, that's no more than I deserve; and I know *you* won't do so.'

The pastor's face showed how pleased he was. He pressed Uncle Alp's hand again, and said, 'Neighbour, your mountains have been a good church to you, and brought you to mine in the right frame of mind. You've made me very happy. You'll never regret coming back to live among us, I'm sure. And as for myself, I shall always welcome you as

a dear friend and neighbour, and I look forward to our
spending many pleasant winter evenings together. And we'll
find friends for Heidi too,' he added, putting his hand on
her curly head. He went with them to the door, and all the
people outside saw them part like old friends. As soon as
the door was closed everybody crowded round Uncle Alp
with outstretched hands, each wishing to be the first to greet
him, so that he didn't know where to begin. 'We're so pleased

to see you among us again,' they said; or 'I've long been wanting to have a chat with you, Uncle.' Such greetings were heard on every side, and when he told them that he intended to come back to his old home in Dörfli for the winter, there was such a chorus of delight and enthusiasm that he might have been the most beloved person in the village, whose absence had been keenly felt by everyone.

When he and Heidi started for home at last, many people went part of the way with them, and when they finally said goodbye, they begged him to visit them in their homes before long. As he watched them go, Heidi saw such a kind light in his eye, that she said, 'Grandfather, you look quite different – nicer and nicer. I've never seen you so before.'

'No,' he replied. 'You see, today I am happy, as I had never thought to be again. Much happier than I deserve. It's good to feel at peace with God and man. It was a good day when God sent you to me.'

When they reached Peter's cottage, he opened the door and went in. 'Good day, Grannie,' he called. 'I can see I must get busy with some more repairs before the autumn winds begin to blow.'

'Goodness me, is it Uncle Alp?' cried the old woman. 'What a fine surprise. Now I can thank you for all you did for us before. May God reward you.' She held out her hand, which trembled a little, and he shook it heartily. 'I've some-thing in my heart, I'd like to say to you,' she went on. 'If I've ever done you any harm, don't punish me by letting

Heidi go away again, while I'm still above ground. You don't know what she means to me,' and she hugged Heidi, whose arms were already round her neck.

'Don't worry, Grannie,' Uncle replied reassuringly, 'I won't punish either of us in that way. We'll all be together now, and for some time yet, please God.'

Bridget took Uncle aside then to show him the hat with the feather, and told him that Heidi had said she could keep it, but that she really couldn't take it from the child. Uncle Alp gave Heidi an approving look. 'That hat is hers, and if she doesn't want to wear it, she's right. You should certainly keep it since she's given it to you.'

Bridget was delighted. Holding the hat up, she exclaimed, 'Just fancy, it must be worth quite a lot of money. How well Heidi got on in Frankfurt. I wonder if it would be any good sending Peter there for a while. What do you think, Uncle?'

His eyes twinkled. 'It certainly wouldn't do him any harm, but opportunity's a great thing.'

At that moment Peter himself came charging in, out of breath, and banged his head against the door in his haste. He held out a letter for Heidi which he had been given at the post office. No one had letters in his home, and Heidi had certainly never had one before. Everybody sat down and listened while she opened it, and read it aloud. It was from Clara, who wrote:

'It's been so dreadfully dull here since you went away,

that I can hardly bear it. But Papa has promised me that I can go to Ragaz in the autumn. Grandmamma will come with me. After that she says we may come to visit you and your grandfather. I told her about you wanting to take some rolls to Grannie, and she was pleased, and said I was to tell you you were quite right. She is sending some coffee for her to have with them, and says she would like to see Grannie as well when we come to the mountains.'

Everyone was interested in Clara's news, and they talked about it so long that not even Uncle noticed how late it was getting. Then again, they had had much to say about the pleasure of Uncle's visit, and the promise of more to come.

'It feels good to have you here again, old friend, after such a long time,' Grannie said. 'It gives me faith that one day we'll all be together with those we love. Do come again soon, and Heidi, you'll be here tomorrow?'

They both assured her that they would, and then said goodbye. All the church bells around were ringing for evening prayer as they went back up the mountain, and they found the hut bathed in the glow of the setting sun.

The prospect of Clara's Grandmamma coming there in the autumn gave Heidi plenty to think about. She had seen, at Frankfurt, that when that lady came upon the scene, she had a way of making everything run happily and smoothly.

15

Preparation for a Journey

One sunny September morning, the kind doctor who had been responsible for Heidi being sent home walked along the street to the Sesemanns' house. It was the sort of day on which everyone should have been happy, but he went along with eyes downcast, and did not once lift them to the blue sky above. His hair had grown whiter since the spring and he wore an air of great sadness. His only daughter had died recently and he had never recovered his spirits, for she had been the great joy of his life since his wife's death some time before.

Sebastian opened the door to him and showed him in with something more than respect, for besides being a close friend of the family, the doctor always treated the servants too with kindness and courtesy, and they looked on him as a friend.

'Everything all right, Sebastian?' he asked, as he was taken upstairs, and as he entered the study, Mr Sesemann rose to greet him, saying:

'I'm glad to see you, doctor. I want to talk to you again

about the Swiss trip. Haven't you changed your mind, now that Clara seems so much better?'

'My dear Sesemann, I never knew such a man!' exclaimed the doctor as he sat down. 'This is the third time that you've sent for me to tell you the same thing. But there's no convincing you. I wish your mother was here. She'd see my point of view.'

'I know. You must be almost at the end of your patience with me. But I'm sure you realize how I dislike refusing the child something I have actually promised her; and to which she has been looking forward so eagerly for months. She was so patient all through her last bad attack, believing that she would soon be in Switzerland and able to visit her little friend in the mountains. And now you want me to tell her she can't go. She's missed so much in life already, I can't bear to disappoint her over this.'

'I'm afraid you must,' said the doctor very decidedly. His friend sat in silence, looking very depressed, so he continued, 'Just consider. This has been the worst summer Clara has had for many years. The fatigue of such a journey as you propose is out of the question for her. We're already into September, and although there may still be some fine weather in the mountains, it may also be quite cold. The days are getting shorter and there could be no question of Clara spending the night up there with Heidi, so she could only be there for an hour or so. It's a long way from Ragaz, as you know, and of course she'd have to be carried up the mountain. Surely you see it's not practicable. But I'll go in with you and talk to Clara. She's a reasonable child, so I'm sure she'll understand, and agree to what I am going to propose. Let her go to Ragaz next May and have some treatment there until the weather gets really warm. Then she can be carried up the mountain occasionally, and she will certainly be able to enjoy the visits far more when she's feeling stronger, than she would now. You understand, Sesemann, that she must have the greatest care if she is to recover.'

Mr Sesemann listened at first with a resigned expression on his face, then got to his feet, saying anxiously, 'Doctor, tell me the truth. Have you any real hope of a full recovery?'

The doctor shrugged his shoulders, with a thoughtful air. 'Not a great deal,' he admitted, 'but think, my friend. At least you still have your child. She loves you and looks forward to your return when you go away. You don't come back to an empty house and sit down alone to your meals. And your child is happy at home. Even if she does miss much, she's still better off than many children. Count your blessings. Remember how lucky you are to have each other.'

Mr Sesemann paced up and down the room, as he always did when he was thinking hard. Then he stopped abruptly in front of his friend and patted his shoulder. 'Doctor, I've an idea. I can't bear to see you look so unlike your old self. You ought to have a change. How would it be if *you* were to go to Switzerland and visit Heidi on our behalf?'

This suggestion took the doctor quite by surprise, but he was not allowed to speak, for Mr Sesemann was so pleased with the idea that he seized him by the arm immediately and hurried him off to his daughter's room. Clara was as usual very pleased to see her nice friendly doctor, who nearly always had something amusing to tell her when he came, in spite of his own sorrow. She understood about that and would gladly have helped to make him his old cheerful self again.

They sat down beside her, and her father took her hand and began to talk about the trip to Switzerland and how much he had been looking forward to it. He told her briefly that it would have to be postponed and, dreading to see her upset as he feared she would be, he passed quickly on to his plan for the doctor to go, stressing how good it would be for him to get away.

Clara could not keep the tears from her eyes though she knew her father hated to see her cry, but it was very hard to have to give up the visit to Heidi, for she had counted on it all through the long and lonely hours of her illness. But her father would never have disappointed her unless he thought it important for her good, she knew that, so she blinked back the tears and turned to the doctor.

'Oh, please,' she begged softly, 'please go and see Heidi

for me. Then, when you come back, you will be able to tell me all about it – how she is, and about her grandfather and Peter and the goats. I almost feel I know them all already! And you'll be able to take presents to Heidi and to Grannie. I had them all planned. You will go, won't you? And I promise I'll take as much cod-liver oil as you like!'

It may or may not have been the cod-liver oil which decided him, but the offer certainly made him smile and he said, 'Then of course I must go, for then you'll grow fat and rosy as Papa and I would like to see you. Have you decided when I am to start?'

'Tomorrow morning, if possible,' Clara replied.

'She's right,' said her father. 'It's a pity to lose a single day of this beautiful weather when you might be up in the mountains.'

The doctor laughed a little wryly. 'You'll be telling me next that I ought to be there already! I see I'll have to start getting ready at once.'

But Clara had still a great deal to tell him about what he was to look at specially for her, and the many messages he was to take to Heidi. She would have to send the presents round to his house as soon as Miss Rottenmeier had helped her pack them. The doctor then promised to set out, if not tomorrow, at least within the next few days and to bring her back a full account of everything he saw and heard.

Servants have a remarkable faculty of knowing what is going on in a house, long before they are actually told, and Sebastian and Tinette were particularly good at it. As Sebastian accompanied the doctor downstairs, Tinette went to answer Clara's bell.

'Go out and buy enough of those little cakes I like, to fill this,' said Clara, holding out a large box. Tinette took it disdainfully by one corner and let it dangle from her hand.

'Such a fuss,' she muttered pertly, as she went out.

And as he showed the doctor out, Sebastian said, 'Will you please give my regards to the little miss?'

'What, Sebastian,' said the doctor in his friendly way, 'you already know I'm going away, then.'

Sebastian coughed. 'I am – er – I have – er – I hardly know how ... Oh yes, I remember. I was in the dining-room and heard the name mentioned and you know how one thought leads to another ...'

'I do indeed,' said the doctor with a smile. 'And the more one thinks, the more one knows. I will certainly deliver your message. Goodbye.' He turned to go, but was prevented by the arrival of Miss Rottenmeier, her shawl blown out like a sail by the strong wind. The doctor took a step back to let her pass, and she did likewise, being accustomed to treat him with respect and consideration. So they stood, each holding back for the other to pass, until an extra strong gust of wind blew her indoors with all sails set! The doctor just got out of the way in time as she was carried past him. Her temper had been somewhat ruffled by the wind's unruliness, but as she came back to greet him with due decorum, the doctor smoothed her down as he knew very well how to do. He told her about the plans for his holiday, and, in the most flattering way, asked her to pack the parcel for Heidi as only she could. Then he took his leave.

Clara quite expected to have a tussle with Miss Rottenmeier about sending Heidi all the things she had collected for her, but all went well. That difficult woman was in an exceptionally good mood. She cleared the big table so that everything could be spread out for Clara's inspection. The packing was no easy task for there were so many different things. First there was a thick coat with a hood, so that Heidi could go and visit Grannie during the winter whenever she wanted to, without having to wait until her grandfather was free to take her down, wrapped in the old sack. Next came a thick, warm shawl for Grannie to wrap herself in when cold winds howled round the hut. Then there was the box of little cakes for her to eat sometimes with her coffee as a change from the rolls. There was an enormous sausage, which Clara had originally intended to send to Peter, because he never had anything but bread and cheese to eat. On second thoughts, however, she decided to send it to Bridget to share out among all three of them, lest he might eat it all up at once. There was a pouch of tobacco for Grandfather, who enjoyed a pipe when he sat outside his hut in the evening, and finally, there were a lot of little surprise packets, which Clara had specially enjoyed getting for Heidi. Miss Rottenmeier surveyed the collection of articles thoughtfully, considering how best to pack them, and Clara looked on, imagining Heidi dancing and shouting with excitement when the great parcel arrived. The packing was soon done, and well done, and the parcel was ready for Sebastian to carry at once to the doctor's house.

16

A Visitor for Heidi

Dawn was breaking over the mountains and a fresh breeze blew through the branches of the old fir trees, making the rustling sound Heidi loved so well. It woke her, and she jumped out of bed, so impatient to get to the trees that she could hardly wait to dress. But she had learnt now to like being neat and tidy, so she took the time to put her clothes on properly before she climbed down the ladder. Her grandfather's bed was already empty, for he was outside, looking round as he did every morning to see what kind of day it was going to be. Rosy clouds were floating by in the clear blue morning sky, and the sun was just coming over the tops of the mountains, bringing a wash of gold to the rocky peaks and pastures.

'Oh how beautiful!' exclaimed Heidi, as she ran out into it. 'Good morning, Grandfather. Isn't everything lovely today?'

'What, you awake already?' he replied.

She ran over to the trees and skipped delightedly about under the waving branches, giving an extra little jump with each gust of wind which blew through them. Uncle Alp went into the stall and milked the goats. Then he washed them, and brushed them, and brought them outside ready for their daily journey. As soon as Heidi saw them she ran and put her arms round their necks and patted them. They bleated a greeting, and rubbed their heads against her shoulder as a sign of their affection.

They pressed so close she was almost squashed between them but she did not mind that a bit. Only when the brown goat got too boisterous, she cried, 'Really, Dusky, you're as bad as Turk,' and Dusky immediately drew back. Daisy stood a little aloof, looking as though she hoped no one could accuse her of behaving like Turk. She was always the more sedate of the two.

Peter was whistling as he came up the path, and soon the whole herd appeared, led by frisky Finch. They immediately bounded up to Heidi, pushing her from one side to the other as they greeted her in their own obstreperous fashion. She made her way through them to Snowflake who, being timid, had not been able to get near Heidi. Peter wanted to talk to Heidi himself, so he gave a particularly piercing whistle, which drove the animals off for the moment.

'You might come up with me today,' he said to her.

'I can't, Peter. My nice people from Frankfurt might come any minute now, and I must be here when they do.'

'You keep saying that,' he grumbled.

'I shall go on saying it until they arrive,' she answered. 'I daresay you don't think it's necessary, but how could I not?'

'Uncle would be here,' he persisted.

At that moment, Uncle Alp called loudly from the hut, 'What's the delay? Is it the Field-Marshal or his troops?'

At that Peter turned and slashed his stick through the air. The goats recognized the signal and ran off at full tilt to their high pasture and he followed them.

Heidi had brought several new ideas back with her from Frankfurt. She made her bed every morning now, tucking in the clothes so that it looked smooth and trim. Then she tidied up the hut, setting each chair in its proper place and putting anything which might be lying about back in the cupboard. After that she fetched a duster, climbed on a stool and polished the table till it shone. When her grandfather came in, he used to look round at her work, well pleased, and say to himself, 'We look like Sunday every day now! Heidi didn't go away for nothing.'

They had breakfast together as soon as Peter had gone that day, and then Heidi started the housework. But she did not get on with it very fast. First one thing, then another, distracted her. A sunbeam shone straight through the open window and seemed to be calling to her to come out. Out she ran, and found everything so beautiful and the ground so warm and dry that she could not resist sitting down for a while, just to look at the meadows and the trees and the mountains. Then she remembered she had left the three-legged stool standing in the middle of the hut and that she had not polished the table, so up she jumped and ran in. But before long the rustling fir trees called her outside again. Grandfather was busy in the shed, but every now and then he came out to watch her dancing about in rhythm with the swaying branches. He had just gone in again when he heard her call, 'Grandfather, Grandfather! Come quickly!' He hurried out, afraid that something must be wrong, and saw her running away from him, down the slope.

'They're coming! They're coming!' she shouted over her shoulder. 'That's the doctor in front.' She rushed on and greeted him affectionately. 'Doctor, Doctor! Thank you again a thousand times!'

'Bless you, child,' cried the doctor. 'What are you thanking me for?'

'Why, for sending me home to Grandfather.'

The doctor's face brightened. He had not expected a reception like this. Indeed he had felt rather gloomy as he climbed the mountain, and had not even noticed the beautiful surroundings. He had imagined that Heidi would scarcely remember him, for she had seen very little of him, and he was sure she would be disappointed to see him instead of her dear friends. But apparently she was overjoyed, for she held his arm tightly and lovingly.

'Come, Heidi,' he said, taking her hand in a fatherly way. 'Take me to your grandfather and show me where you live.'

But she did not move. She was looking down the mountain path, puzzled. 'Where are Clara and Grandmamma?' she asked at last.

'I'm afraid I'm going to disappoint you, Heidi,' he replied. 'I've come alone. Clara has been very ill and wasn't fit to travel, and so of course Grandmamma stayed with her. But they'll come in the spring, as soon as the days begin to get longer and warmer.'

Heidi was very upset then, and found it difficult to believe that what she had looked forward to so long was not going to happen after all. For a minute or two she could not speak, and the doctor gazed in silence about him. Then the pleasure she had felt as she ran to meet him came back to her, and she remembered that he, at least, had come to visit her.

She looked up at him and saw the lonely look in his eyes which she did not remember seeing there when she was in Frankfurt. She could not bear to see anyone unhappy, least of all the good doctor, and thinking his sadness must be because Clara and her grandmother had not been able to accompany him, she tried to comfort him.

'Oh, it will soon be spring,' she reminded him, and herself. 'Time goes quickly up here. They'll be able to stay longer then, and Clara will like that. Now come and see Grandfather.'

They went towards the hut hand in hand. In her anxiety to chase the shadow from his eyes, she told him again and again how soon summer would come, and almost convinced herself of it, so that when they reached her grandfather, she called out, 'They haven't come yet, but they will quite soon.'

The doctor seemed no stranger to Uncle Alp, for Heidi had talked a great deal about him, and the old man put out his hand and welcomed him warmly. They sat down together on the seat outside, and the doctor made room for Heidi beside him. Sitting there in the September sunshine, he told them how Mr Sesemann had suggested he should come, and that it had seemed to him a good idea because he hadn't been feeling well lately. Then he whispered to Heidi that there was something being brought up the mountain for her, something from Frankfurt, which would give her much more pleasure than he could. This news, of course, excited all her curiosity.

'I hope you'll spend as many of these beautiful autumn days as you can on the mountain,' said Uncle Alp, explaining that unfortunately they could offer him no lodging in the hut, but that there was a good little inn at Dörfli. 'There is no need to go all the way back to Ragaz,' he assured him. 'Ours is a simple little place, but clean. Then you could come up to us every day, which I know will do you good, and if you would like it, I will be your guide over any part of the mountains you wish to see.'

This suited the doctor very well and he accepted the suggestion with pleasure.

The sun by now was overhead, for it was midday, and the fir trees stood motionless. Uncle Alp went indoors and brought out the table which he placed in front of the seat. 'Heidi,' he said, 'bring out what we need. The doctor must take us as he finds us. Our food is simple, but he will agree that the dining-room is fine!'

'I do indeed,' said the doctor, looking down on the valley, which was gleaming in the sunlight. 'I shall be glad to accept your invitation. Everything will taste extra good up here.'

Heidi ran back and forth, bringing out everything she

could find in the cupboard. She felt very proud to be helping to entertain the doctor. Grandfather was preparing the food, and came out presently with a steaming jug of milk and a piece of golden toasted cheese. Then he cut thin slices of the delicious meat which he had dried in the open air during the summer, and the doctor enjoyed his meal more than any he had eaten that year.

'This is certainly the place for Clara to come to,' he declared. 'She would soon become a different person if she could eat as I have today, and get quite plump and rosy.'

There was a man coming towards them with a huge bundle on his back, and as he reached the hut, he lowered it on to the ground and filled his lungs with great draughts of mountain air.

'Ah, here's what came with me from Frankfurt,' said the doctor. He went over and began to undo the parcel, then he said, 'Now, my dear, you can unpack it for yourself.'

Heidi, speechless with excitement, began at once and when all the things had been spread out, she just stared at them in amazement. It was only when the doctor opened the box of cakes, and showed her that they were for Grannie to have with her coffee, that she found her tongue again. She wanted to hurry down with them at once, but her grandfather suggested they would go down together later on, when it was time for the doctor to leave. Then she found the pouch of tobacco, and how pleased the old man was! He filled his pipe at once, and after that the two men sat together on the bench, smoking and talking, while Heidi went on opening all her lovely presents. After a while she came across to them and waited for a pause in the conversation to say, 'What you said was not right, Doctor. All these nice things put together aren't as nice as seeing you!' They both laughed at this pronouncement, which the doctor said he certainly had not expected.

As the sun began to go down, the doctor rose, thinking it time to go to the village and see about quarters. He took Heidi by the hand, and her grandfather carried the box of cakes, the shawl, and the sausage, and thus they went off together as far as Peter's home. There Heidi said goodbye to the doctor and asked him:

'Would you like to go up to the pasture with the goats tomorrow?' for this was the greatest treat she could offer him.

'That'll be fine,' he replied. 'We'll go together.' The two men went on to Dörfli, and Heidi ran in to Grannie. Uncle Alp had put the presents down in front of the door, and Heidi fetched them in, one by one, first the cakes (and the box was so big she staggered under the weight), then the sausage and lastly the shawl. She brought them close up so that Grannie could put her hands on them and know what they were.

'They've come all the way from Frankfurt, from Clara and Grandmamma,' she explained, and both Grannie and Bridget were duly impressed. Indeed Peter's mother had been too surprised to lend a hand and had simply stared while Heidi lugged the heavy things into the cottage.

'Grannie, aren't you pleased with the cakes? Feel how soft they are for you to eat.'

'Yes, child. What kind people they are.' The old woman stroked the warm, soft shawl. 'This will be wonderful in the winter. I've never looked to have anything as fine as that.'

Heidi was surprised that she seemed to like the grey shawl even better than the cakes; but Bridget stood looking almost reverently at the sausage on the table. She had never seen such an enormous one before, and could hardly believe that it was all for her and Grannie and Peter. 'I must ask Uncle what to do with it,' she said, shaking her head doubtfully.

'You're to eat it, that's all,' declared Heidi.

And then Peter came tumbling in, calling out, 'Uncle Alp's just coming and Heidi's to . . .' He got no further for his eyes fell on the sausage, and the sight quite robbed him of speech. However Heidi guessed what he had been going to say and quickly kissed Grannie goodbye.

As a rule now, Uncle Alp never passed the hut without a cheery word for Grannie, and she always listened for his step. But this time it was late, more than time for Heidi to be in bed after getting up so early, for he was very particular about her having plenty of sleep. So he just called a greeting through the open door, took Heidi's hand, and together they went on, up the path under the starry sky to their peaceful little home.

17

Happy Days

Early next morning the doctor climbed up from Dörfli with Peter and the goats. He tried several times to start a conversation, but without success. It was not easy to get Peter to talk, and he hardly got a word in answer to his questions. So they tramped along in silence most of the way, and when they reached the hut Heidi was waiting for them with Daisy and Dusky, all three in high spirits.

'Coming up today?' asked Peter as usual.

'Yes, of course. The doctor is coming too,' she replied.

Peter glanced sideways at the visitor. Then Uncle Alp came out, greeted the doctor warmly, and hung a bag of food over Peter's shoulder. The bag was heavier than usual, for he had put in a good-sized piece of dried meat, thinking the doctor might like to stay and eat his midday meal with the children. Peter grinned from ear to ear when he felt its weight, guessing that there was something special inside.

So they set off, Heidi surrounded by the goats who were pushing and shoving each other as usual in their efforts to get near her. She went a little way with them, then stood still. 'Run along now,' she said, 'and don't come back to bother me. I want to walk with the doctor today.' Then she patted Snowflake and told her to be good.

The doctor had no difficulty in talking to Heidi. She chattered away all the time about the goats and their strange little ways, or the mountain peaks and the flowers and birds they would find up above. Several times on the way, Peter glanced sourly at the doctor, but no one noticed him. It seemed no time at all before they reached the pasture.

Heidi led the way to her favourite spot from which she could look down on the distant valley, so green below them, and up to the great mountains where the eternal snows sparkled in the sunlight. The grey rock of the two towering peaks rose majestic against the strong blue of the sky. The grass underfoot was dry and warm, and Heidi invited the doctor to sit down there and rest. They listened to the pleasant tinkling of the goat-bells, as the herd moved about to graze. A few harebells remained of all the summer flowers and swung airily on their slender stalks in the morning breeze. The hawk was soaring overhead in ever-widening circles, making no sound. Heidi's eyes were happy as she gazed out at the beautiful things she loved so well, and she glanced at the doctor to see if he was enjoying them too. He caught her look and replied to it, though his eyes had not lost their sadness.

'Yes, Heidi, it's very beautiful here,' he agreed, 'but

can a heart forget its sorrow and rejoice, even here?'

'No one is sad here,' she told him, 'only in Frankfurt.'

A fleeting smile crossed his face. 'But supposing the sorrow could not be left in Frankfurt, but dogged one up here too. What then?'

'When you can do no more yourself,' said Heidi confidently, 'tell God.'

'Those are good words, my dear,' said the doctor, 'but suppose it was God Himself who sent the sorrow.'

Heidi sat pondering for a while. She was sure God could always help, but was trying to find the answer out of her own experiences. 'I think you have to wait,' she said at last, 'and keep on thinking that God has something good which He's going to give you out of the sad thing, but you have to be patient. You see, when something's awfully bad, you don't know about the good bit coming, and you think it's going on for ever.'

'I hope you will always feel like that, Heidi,' he said, and fell silent, drinking in the scene before him. Presently he went on, 'Can you understand that even up here it is possible for sorrow to cast a shadow over the eyes so that one can't really enjoy the beauty, and that adds to the sadness? Do you know what I mean?'

His words sobered her for a time, for they brought home to her afresh that Grannie's eyes were always veiled so that she could never see the sunlight, nor any of the beauties of the mountains. 'Yes, I understand,' she replied then. 'Perhaps it would help to hear one of Grannie's hymns. She says they bring her back the light.'

'What hymns do you know?'

'I only remember the one about the sun, and part of another long one, which Grannie likes very much. I always have to read the verses three times over to her.'

'Let me hear them now,' said the doctor, settling himself against a boulder and preparing to listen.

Heidi clasped her hands and asked, 'Shall I begin with the verse Grannie likes so much because it gives her fresh hope?' He nodded, and she began,

> 'To God confide thy cares,
> On Him thy burden cast,
> He heareth all thy prayers
> And sends relief at last.

> 'His never-failing love,
> His wisdom sure and true,
> Bring comfort from above
> And all thy hopes renew.'

Heidi stopped for she was not sure that the doctor was listening. He had covered his eyes with his hand and sat very still. She half thought he might have fallen asleep, and decided that if he wanted to hear any more, he would ask her to go on when he woke up. He was not asleep, however, only lost in thought. The hymn had taken him right back to when he was a little boy and stood beside his mother's chair, listening to those same words, and he saw again how fondly her eyes rested on him, and he heard her voice, speaking so gently. These pleasant memories held him for a long time, and when at last he looked up, there were Heidi's big eyes watching him thoughtfully. He patted her hand and said quite cheerfully:

'That was very nice, Heidi. We'll come up here again and you shall tell me some more.'

All this had not been at all to Peter's liking. This was the first time for weeks that Heidi had come up with him, and now she went and sat all the time with the doctor, and never even looked his way. He kicked the turf and scowled, but neither of them saw him. He even went and shook his fists close behind the doctor's back, but that went unseen also. As the sun came round to midday and the time for eating, he shouted loudly at them, 'Dinner time!'

Heidi stood up then, meaning to bring the doctor's share over to him, but he told her he was not hungry and would like only a little milk, and then he was going a little higher up the mountain. At that Heidi decided that she was not hungry either, and would also have only milk. She thought she would like to show the doctor the place where Finch had nearly fallen down the ravine and where there were so many tasty herbs for the goats. So she asked Peter just to get milk from Daisy for the doctor and herself.

'Only milk? What about all the food in the bag?' he asked in astonishment.

'You can have it, as soon as you've got the milk.'

He had rarely done as he was asked so promptly. He was longing to know what had made the bag so heavy that morning, and as soon as Heidi had taken the milk, he opened it and peeped inside. When he saw the meat he could hardly believe his eyes. He was just taking hold of it, when he remembered how angrily he had shaken his fists at the doctor, for whom this treat had really been provided. He felt sorry about that, and it somehow held him back. So after a moment he jumped up and ran over to the place where he had stood before, stretched up his arms with hands open to show that he did not want to fight anyone any more, and he kept them like that until he felt he had made amends. Then back he went to his feast and began to eat with a clear conscience.

Heidi and the doctor went on up the mountain, talking as they went. After a while he told her that he was going back, but that she no doubt would like to stay a little longer with the goats. This she would not hear of, but insisted on accompanying him at least as far as the hut, perhaps even farther. So down they went, hand in hand, and on the way she showed him all the goats' favourite grazing places and where the best flowers grew in summer. She could tell him the names of many, for her grandfather had taught her them. At last the doctor said she must go back, so they said

goodbye and he went on alone. He looked back from time to time, and found her watching and waving to him, as his own dear daughter used to do when he went out.

The weather was fine and sunny all that month, and the doctor came up to the hut every morning, and from there went off on long walks, often with Uncle Alp as his companion. Together they climbed high up where the grand old fir trees were storm-tossed, and higher still to where the hawk nested. They saw the great bird rise up, protesting, at their intrusion. The doctor found great pleasure in Uncle Alp's society, and was constantly surprised at his wide knowledge of mountain plants and their uses. Uncle Alp showed him little crevices where, even at those heights, tiny plants grew and blossomed. He also knew a great deal about the wild life up there and had many good stories to tell about the creatures which lived in caves or holes in the ground or even in the branches of the trees. As the doctor took his leave after one of these expeditions, he said, 'My friend, I learn something new every time I am with you.'

Several times, when the weather was particularly fine, the doctor went up to the pasture with Heidi, and they always rested at the same spot, while she chattered away or recited the verses she had learnt by heart. Peter never joined them, but he was quite resigned now to the loss of her company and no longer bore the doctor any ill will.

With the last day of September, the holiday came to an end. On the day before his return to Frankfurt, the doctor appeared at the hut looking rather sad. He was very sorry to go for he had felt at home on the mountains. Uncle Alp was going to miss him too, and Heidi had grown so accustomed to seeing him every day that she could hardly believe that those pleasant times were nearly over. After he and Uncle Alp had said goodbye, she went a little way down the mountain with him, but when he thought she had come far enough, the doctor stopped and gently stroked her hair.

'Now I have to go, Heidi,' he said, 'but I wish I could take you back with me to Frankfurt.'

Heidi suddenly beheld, in her mind's eye, that town with its many tall houses and cobbled streets, and thought of Miss Rottenmeier and Tinette. 'It would be nicer if you came back to us,' she said hesitantly.

'Yes, you are right,' he agreed, 'quite right. Goodbye, my dear.'

As she gave him her hand, she thought there were tears in his kind eyes, then he turned quickly and hurried away. Heidi stood looking after him, feeling very miserable, and after a few moments ran pell-mell after him, crying, 'Doctor, doctor.' He turned as he heard her, and when she reached him, she sobbed out:

'I will come with you to Frankfurt and stay with you as long as you like, but I must go and tell Grandfather first.'

The doctor laid his hand on her shoulder to calm her. 'No, no,' he said, 'you must stay here among the fir trees for the present, or I might have you ill again. But I tell you what, perhaps you'll come and take care of me if I'm ever ill and lonely. I should like to think I could have someone who loves me to look after me then.'

'Oh, yes, I'll come at once, the moment you send for me,' Heidi promised eagerly. 'And I love you nearly as much as Grandfather.'

He thanked her and went on his way again, while she stood and waved till all she could see was a speck in the distance. As he turned for the last time to wave back, he thought to himself. 'This is certainly a wonderful place for sick minds as well as bodies. Life seems really worth living again!'

18

Winter in Dörfli

The snow lay so deep on the mountain that winter, that Peter's hut was buried in it up to the window sills. Fresh snow fell almost every night, so on most mornings he had to jump out of the living-room window. If the frost in the night had not been enough to harden the surface, he stepped deep into soft snow and then had to battle his way out with feet and hands and even head. Then his mother handed him out a big broom, with which he cleared a path to the door. This had to be done skilfully, piling the snow well away from the entrance, so that there was no likelihood of a great mass of soft snow falling into the house when the door was opened. There was also the danger that hard frost might turn soft snow into a solid wall, and so barricade the door – and only Peter was small and agile enough to squeeze through the window.

But when it froze in the night, Peter had a grand time, for his mother used to hand him out his little sleigh, and on this he almost flew down to Dörfli – or wherever he had to go – for the whole mountainside became one wide, unbroken sleigh run.

Uncle Alp would have had to clear the snow from his hut just as carefully, but he had kept his promise and, as soon as the first snow fell, he took Heidi and the goats down to the village for the rest of the winter.

Near the church and the parsonage in Dörfli, there was a great rambling, ramshackle place, almost in ruins. It had once belonged to a soldier, who had fought bravely in Spain and acquired a considerable fortune. He had come back to Dörfli, meaning to settle down there for the rest of his life, and had built this great house, but alas, he had lost the taste for quiet living and soon went away and never returned. The house stood empty and uncared for. When he died many years later, it came into the hands of a distant relative in the valley, but by then it was in such a bad state that the new owner was not inclined to spend money on it. He let it to poor people for very little rent, but made no attempt to repair it. That was years before Uncle Alp had come to Dörfli with his son, and they had lived in it for a time. Then it stood empty again, with great holes and cracks in roof and walls, and in winter (always long and severe up there), the icy winds blew right through the place. Now, after Uncle Alp had made up his mind to pass the winter in Dörfli, he rented the old house again. Being handy with his tools, he knew he could make it habitable, and he went down often during the autumn to work on it, and in the middle of October he and Heidi went to live there.

At the back of the house there was a high vaulted building which had once been a chapel, though it had gone to rack and ruin. One whole wall and most of another had fallen down, ivy was growing through a window which had lost all its glass, and the roof looked as though it might collapse any day. The door was missing between this and the room next to it, which was also very dilapidated. Grass was growing between the stones of its paved floor, the walls were crumbling and part of the ceiling was down. The rest only held because strong pillars supported it. Uncle Alp put up some wooden partitions here and laid straw on the floor to make winter quarters for the goats. Beyond this room was a passage half in ruins, and with cracks in the outer wall so wide you could see the sky and the fields through them. But at the end of all this was a solid oak door, still fixed on its hinges, leading to a fine room, in quite good condition. It had panelled walls, and in one corner was an enormous white tiled stove, reaching nearly to the ceiling. It was decorated in blue with pictures of a huntsman with his dogs in a wood surrounding an old castle, and a fisherman dangling his rod in a calm lake beneath some oak trees. A seat was built on conveniently all round the stove, and as soon as Heidi came into the room with her grandfather, she ran straight over to it and sat down to look at the pictures.

She slid along it until she reached the back of the stove, and came to a space between it and the wall, which might have been intended for storing apples, but which now held her bed. It had been brought from the loft, just as it was, with its mattress of hay, the sheet, and the heavy linen cover. Heidi was delighted to find it there.

'Oh, Grandfather,' she exclaimed happily, 'my room! Isn't it lovely? Where are you going to sleep?'

'I thought you ought to sleep close to the stove, so that you won't freeze,' he told her. 'Now come and see my room.' She followed him into a smaller one, where he had set up his bed. There was a second door beside it, which Heidi opened and saw a huge kitchen, bigger than any she had ever seen. There was still much to be done to it, though Grandfather had patched it till the walls looked as though they were made up of a lot of little cupboards. He had mended the heavy old outer door too, with nails and screws so that it was possible now to shut it, and that was a comfort for outside lay ruins, hidden in tall weeds where beetles and spiders lurked.

Heidi liked their new home very much, and she had explored every nook and corner of it by the time Peter came to visit her next day. She took him over it, and would not let him go until he had seen all its surprises. She slept very well in her cosy corner, though at first she still thought herself back in the hayloft when she awoke in the mornings, and started up to see if the fir trees were so quiet

because snow had fallen in the night. Then, remembering she was not in the hut, she used to feel almost stifled for a moment, though that went as soon as she heard her grandfather talking to the goats next door, and the goats bleating as though calling her to get up. Then, knowing that, whatever the place, she was still at home, she would jump out of bed and hurry out to the goats as quickly as she could.

On the fourth morning there, she said, 'Today I must go and see Grannie. She'll be missing me.'

But grandfather would not hear of it. 'You can't go today nor tomorrow,' he told her. 'The snow is deep on the mountain and still falling. It will be as much as Peter can do to get through, and a little thing like you would be buried in no time and no one would be able to find you. You'll have to wait until the snow freezes hard, then you'll be able to walk over it easily.'

She did not like having to wait, but there was much to do and she hardly noticed how the days flew by. She went to school, for one thing, and worked hard to learn all she could. Peter, on the other hand, was hardly ever there, but the teacher was a kind-hearted man, who only said, 'So Peter's away again. School would do him good, but I expect the snow is too deep for him to get here.' But Peter came down easily enough in the evening to visit Heidi.

After a few days of snow the sun shone again, glistening

on the white ground, but soon disappearing again behind the mountains as though it did not like the winter scene nearly as well as the grass and flowers of summer. But when it was dark, the moon shone down on the cold snow and the frost came, so that next morning the air was crisp and the whole mountainside sparkled like crystal. Then Peter, expecting to sink into soft snow as usual, jumped out of his window and found himself spinning over the frozen surface like a riderless sleigh, but he picked himself up and went stamping about to see if the snow was really hard everywhere. He was delighted to find he could not kick up more than a tiny fragment of ice here and there. The hillside was frozen hard, and at last Heidi would be able to come up to see them. He went indoors and gulped down some milk, put a piece of bread in his pocket and announced, 'I'm going to school.'

'That's a good boy,' said his mother. 'Learn all you can.'

He got out of the window again, for the door was of course quite frozen up, pulled his little sleigh after him, and shot off on it like a streak of lightning. Right through Dörfli he sped for he could not stop, but flew on down to the valley right past Mayenfeld, before the sleigh came to a standstill. He knew where he was, and decided happily that it was too late for school. It would take him a good hour to climb up to the village again, and lessons would already have started. There was no point in hurrying, so he took his time, and reached Dörfli just as Heidi and her grandfather were sitting down to dinner. He could not wait to tell them his great news, but burst in upon them, and announced, 'It's happened.'

'You sound very fierce, General! What do you mean?' asked Uncle Alp.

'The frost,' said Peter.

'Oh, now I can go and see Grannie,' cried Heidi, understanding this cryptic remark perfectly, and added, 'Why weren't you at school then, Peter? You could easily have come down on your sleigh.' It seemed to her all wrong to stay away from school without good reason.

'I got carried too far down, and then it was too late,' he replied.

'That's desertion,' said Uncle Alp, 'and deserters get punished.'

Peter looked slightly alarmed and stood twiddling his cap, for he had a great respect for Uncle Alp.

'And for a commander like you, it's even worse,' went on the old man. 'What would you do to your goats if they were to take it into their heads to run away and disobey your orders?'

'Beat them.'

'What would you say, then, if a boy who behaved like a disobedient goat got beaten for it?'

'Serve him right.'

'Then listen to me, General. If you ever again let your

sleigh carry you off when you ought to be at school, you can come to me afterwards to get what you deserve.'

Light dawned on Peter with that last remark, and he looked cautiously round the room to see if there was a stick anywhere about that might be used for such a purpose. But Uncle Alp continued in a friendly voice:

'Now come and have something to eat, and then Heidi can go home with you. Bring her back in the evening and you can stay and have supper with us.'

Peter grinned widely at this unexpected change of tune, and sat down. Heidi was so excited at the thought of seeing Grannie again that she couldn't eat any more and passed him the rest of her potatoes and cheese. Uncle Alp had already given him a plate piled high with food and he attacked it all with gusto. Heidi went to the cupboard, and put on the coat which Clara had sent her. She pulled the hood over her head, and stood beside Peter, ready and impatient for him to finish eating. 'Come on now,' she urged, as he reached the last mouthful, and off they went. She chattered away to Peter, telling him how miserable Daisy and Dusky had been on the first day in their new stall, refusing to eat, just standing quietly, with drooping heads.

'Grandfather said they were feeling like I did in Frankfurt,' she told him, 'because they'd never left the high pasture before, and you don't know what that's like, Peter.'

Peter hadn't been listening properly. He was deep in

thought and he didn't say a word until they reached the cottage, then he announced gloomily, 'I'd rather go to school than have Uncle do what he said.' Heidi thought he was quite right, and said so.

They found Bridget alone, mending. 'Grannie's in bed,' she told them. 'She isn't very well, and feels the cold badly.'

This was something new in Heidi's experience. She had always before found Grannie in her corner seat. She ran quickly into the next room, where the old woman lay on her narrow bed, covered with only a single thin blanket, but wrapped in her warm grey shawl.

'Thank God,' said Grannie, as she heard Heidi's step. All through the autumn she had been worrying secretly during the time when Heidi had not been able to visit her, for Peter had told her all about the visitor from Frankfurt, who had spent so much time with Heidi, and she had been sure he must be going to take her away. Even after he had gone back, she still expected to see someone come from Frankfurt and carry her off.

'Are you very ill, Grannie?' asked Heidi, standing close beside her.

'No, no,' said the old woman, stroking her fondly. 'It's only the frost which has got into my old bones.'

'Will you be well when it turns warm again?' Heidi persisted anxiously.

'Oh, I'll be back at my spinning-wheel long before that,

God willing,' Grannie assured her. 'I really meant to get up today, and I'll be all right again tomorrow I'm sure.'

Heidi looked relieved, and as her bright eyes took more in, she remarked, 'In Frankfurt, people put on a shawl when they go for a walk. Did you think it was meant to wear in bed, Grannie?'

'I put it on to keep me warm,' Grannie replied. 'My blanket's rather thin, and I'm thankful to have it.'

'Your bed slopes down at the head instead of up,' Heidi next observed. 'That's not right.'

'I know, child,' said Grannie. 'It's not very comfortable,' and she tried to find a soft place for her head on the pillow, which was not much better than a piece of wood. 'It was never very thick, and my old head, resting on it for so many years, has worn it thinner still.'

'I wish I'd asked Clara if I could bring the bed I had at Frankfurt with me. It had three fat pillows, one on top of the other, and I kept slipping down the bed, away from them – but I had to get back on them again before morning because that was the proper way to go to sleep in. Would you be able to sleep like that?'

'Yes, indeed, it would be very cosy. It's easier to breathe, well propped up with pillows,' Grannie sighed, trying to raise her head a little. 'But we won't talk about that. I've so much to be thankful for, more than many old sick people – the lovely rolls every day, this fine warm shawl, and now you to visit me. Will you read to me today?'

Heidi fetched the old book and read her several hymns. They were all familiar ones, and she enjoyed the sound of them afresh after the long interval. Grannie lay with her hands folded, and a happy look spread over her thin old face. Suddenly Heidi stopped reading to ask, 'Are you better now, Grannie?'

'Yes, that's done me a lot of good, my dear. Please go on.'

Heidi did so and when she came to the last verse of the hymn, Grannie repeated it several times.

> 'My heart is sad, my eyes grow dim,
> Yet do I put my trust in Him,
> And in due time, all sorrow past,
> In safety home I'll come at last.'

She found the words very comforting, and Heidi liked them too, for they made her think of that sunny day when she had come back to the mountains. 'I know how lovely it is to get home,' she exclaimed.

Soon after that she got up to go, for it was getting dark. 'I'm so glad you're better,' she said, as Grannie took her hand and held it tight.

'Yes, I'm happier now. Even if I have to go on lying here, I shan't worry any more. You don't know what it means to lie for days on end in darkness, and most of the time in silence. Sometimes I'm ready to give up, knowing

I shall never see the sunshine again. But when you come and read me these wonderful words, my heart looks up again, and I'm comforted.'

Heidi said goodnight then and went outside with Peter. The moon shining on the snow made it as light as day. Peter got on his sleigh, with Heidi behind him, and they skimmed down the hill like a couple of birds.

Lying in her comfortable bed behind the stove that night, Heidi thought about Grannie's poor thin pillow, and how much good the hymns had done her. If she could go and read to her every day, Grannie might get better, but it would probably be a week or even longer before she could go up again. She wondered what could be done about it, then suddenly had an idea which pleased her so much she could hardly wait for morning, to carry it out. She had been so occupied with these things that she had forgotten her prayers, and now she never finished a day without them. So she sat up and prayed for Grannie and Grandfather, as well as for herself. After that she lay back on the soft hay and slept soundly till morning.

19

Peter Surprises Everyone

Next day Peter went to school, and arrived punctually, bringing his midday meal with him in his little satchel. The Dörfli children went home in the middle of the day for dinner, but those who lived too far away used to sit on the desks, with their feet on the benches, holding what they had brought with them on their laps. Afterwards they could do as they liked until one o'clock, when lessons started again.

Peter always went over to Uncle Alp's to see Heidi after he had been to school and that day she had been looking out for him eagerly, and ran to him as soon as he came inside the door.

'I've thought of something,' she cried in great excitement.

'What?' he asked.

'You must learn to read.'

'I have learned,' Peter replied.

'I mean learn properly, so that you can read anything,' she insisted.

'Can't be done,' Peter replied promptly.

'I don't believe that any more,' she told him squarely, 'and nor does anyone else. Clara's Grandmamma told me it wasn't so and she was right.'

Peter looked rather taken aback at the Frankfurt lady being brought into it.

'I'll teach you,' Heidi went on, 'I know how. Then you can read a hymn to Grannie every day.'

'Not me,' growled Peter.

This refusal to help her to carry out the plan on which she had set her heart annoyed Heidi. Her black eyes flashed as she said threateningly, 'I'll tell you what will happen to you if you won't learn. You'll have to go to Frankfurt, like your mother said, and I know what the school there is like. Clara pointed out the great big building one day when we were out for a drive. And the boys stay there until they're grown up. I've seen them myself. And you needn't expect just one kind teacher there, like we have here. There are lots of teachers, all dressed in black as if they were going to church, and they wear tall black hats like this,' and she measured their height from the ground with her hand. Peter felt as though a cold wind had blown down his back.

'You'd be there with all those gentlemen,' she continued, quite carried away, 'and when it came to your turn, you wouldn't be able to read, nor even say your letters properly. Then they'd all make fun of you, and that would be worse than Tinette, and she was bad enough.'

'Oh all right, I'll do it,' said Peter grumpily.

At once Heidi was all smiles again. 'That's good. We'll start at once,' and she pulled him over to the table, on which a book lay ready. It was a rhyming A B C, which had come in the big parcel from Clara. Heidi liked it very much and thought it just the thing for teaching Peter. They sat down side by side, bent their heads over the book, and the lesson began. Peter had to spell out the first rhyme over and over again, for Heidi was determined he should know it thoroughly.

'You still don't get it right,' she said after some time. 'I'll read it all through to you. If you know what it says, perhaps you'll find it easier.' And she read out:

'If A B C you do not know
Before the judge you'll have to go.'

'I won't go,' mumbled Peter.

'Won't go where?'

'Before the judge.'

'Then hurry up and learn those three letters, so that you don't have to,' Heidi urged. So Peter set to and repeated them until she was satisfied.

She saw what an effect the little rhyme had had on him, and thought it would be a good idea to prepare the way for the next lessons. 'Wait a minute,' she said, 'and I'll read you the rest of the rhymes, then you'll know what to expect.

'If D E F you cannot say
Bad luck is sure to come your way.

'If you forget your H J K
You'll have misfortune all the day.

'If L and M you can't say clear
You'll have to pay a fine, I fear.

'Trouble will be in store for you
If you can't say N O P Q.

'If you get stuck at R S T
A dunce's cap your lot will be.'

Peter was listening so quietly that she stopped to look at him and found him staring at her with dismay, bewildered by all these threats of trouble. Heidi's tender heart melted at sight of him, and she hastened to reassure him.

'Don't worry. Just come every evening, and if you go on as you've done today, you'll soon know all your letters and then nothing will happen to you. But you must come every day, and not stay away, as you do from school. Even if it's snowing, it won't hurt you to come.'

Peter promised, for Heidi's picture of the school at Frankfurt had taken the fight out of him. After that he did what Heidi told him and came regularly for his lessons, and soon made quite good progress with his letters, though he always found it difficult to learn the rhymes by heart. Uncle Alp often sat in the room with them, smoking his pipe and listening to the lessons, much amused by all that went on. After his exertions, Peter was usually invited to stay to supper, which quite made up for all he went through. At length they reached the letter U, and Heidi read:

> 'If you confuse a V with U,
> You'll find yourself in Timbuctoo.'

'No I won't,' growled Peter, but he made haste to learn the letters all the same, as if he was afraid someone might carry him off by the scruff of his neck. Next evening Heidi read:

> 'If over W you fall,
> Beware the rod upon the wall.'

Peter glanced round the room and said scornfully, 'Isn't one.'

'No, but do you know what Grandfather has in the cupboard?' she asked. 'A stick almost as thick as my arm. You can just pretend that's hanging on the wall when you say this rhyme.'

Peter knew Uncle Alp's stout hazel stick, and he bent

over his book again at once, determined to master W. Next day the rhyme went:

> 'If letter X you can't recall,
> You'll get no food today at all.'

Peter looked towards the cupboard where the bread and cheese were kept and remarked crossly, 'I never said I was going to forget X.'

'Good, then we can learn another letter at once, and there'll be only one left for tomorrow.' Peter was not keen on learning any more that day, but Heidi had already begun to read.

> 'If you find Y is hard to say,
> They'll laugh at you at school today.'

Peter remembered about the gentlemen in Frankfurt with their tall black hats, and he made himself study Y till he knew it with his eyes shut.

When he came again, he was inclined to be cocky, knowing he had only one more letter to learn. As usual Heidi read the couplet aloud.

> 'If Z should tie you up in knots,
> They'll send you to the Hottentots.'

'Nobody knows where they live,' he commented scornfully.

'Grandfather will know,' Heidi returned quickly, 'and I'll just run and ask him. He's over with the pastor.' She jumped up and was really starting off when Peter caught hold of her.

'No, wait,' he cried, for he could quite see Uncle Alp and the pastor coming over together to pack him off to the Hottentots forthwith, if he had not yet learnt Z. Of course Heidi stopped then.

'What's the matter?' she asked.

'Nothing. Come back. I'll learn it,' he muttered.

But Heidi was now eager on her own account to know where the Hottentots lived, and said again that she must run and ask her grandfather about it. It was only when she saw that Peter was really worried that she gave up and came back to the table. She made Peter pay for it though, by repeating the letter Z till she felt sure he could never forget it. And then she started immediately to teach him to read whole words, which was a great step forward.

It was just about this time that it began snowing again, and continued for several days, so that the ground was covered with soft snow once more, and Heidi could not get up to Grannie's. For nearly three weeks she did not see her, and that made her all the more anxious for Peter to be able to read to Grannie in her place. Sure enough, one evening he came up from Dörfli, and announced to his mother, 'I can do it.'

'Do what, Peter?' she asked.

'Read.'

'Can you really? Do you hear that, Grannie?' exclaimed Bridget.

Grannie had indeed heard, and was wondering how it could possibly have come about.

'I am to read a hymn to you now,' he said. 'Heidi told me to.'

His mother fetched the book, and Grannie composed herself to listen. Peter sat down at the table and really began to read. At the end of each verse, his mother exclaimed, 'Well, would you believe it!' Grannie did not speak, but listened closely.

At school in the village next day Peter's class had a reading lesson as usual, and when it came to his turn, the teacher said:

'I suppose we must pass you over again, Peter, or will you just try, not perhaps to read, but just to pick out a word or two?'

Peter took the book and read three lines without a mistake. The teacher stared at him in silent amazement. Finally he said:

'Is this a miracle? I have spent hours, weeks, years, trying to teach you, and you've never even been able to say your letters. Now, when I'd practically given you up as hopeless, you suddenly get up and read quite fluently. How has this come to pass?'

'It was Heidi,' Peter replied.

The teacher glanced across at Heidi, sitting quietly in her place and looking very innocent.

'Well, I have noticed a great improvement in you lately, Peter. You used to stay away from school for weeks on end, now you never miss a day. Who is responsible for that?'

'Uncle Alp,' was the answer.

This surprised the teacher even more. 'Just let me hear you read again,' he said cautiously, and Peter continued for another three lines. There was no mistake about it. He could read.

As soon as school was over, the teacher went across to the pastor to tell him the news, and they talked about the good influence that Heidi and her grandfather were having in the village.

After that when he got home each evening, Peter read one hymn aloud – one only. He could not be persuaded to try a second, nor did Grannie press him. It was a never failing source of wonder to Bridget, and sometimes after he had gone to bed, she would say to Grannie, 'Now Peter has learnt to read, there's no knowing what he may do!'

Once Grannie replied to her, 'Yes, I'm glad for his sake that he has learnt something. But I shall be thankful when the spring is here, and Heidi can come again. They are somehow not the same hymns when Peter reads them, and I keep trying to fill in the gaps, and so I miss what comes next. So they don't do me as much good as when Heidi reads them.'

The truth was that Peter made things as easy as possible for himself. When he came to a difficult word, he just left it out, thinking that a few words less among so many would make no difference to Grannie. Consequently there was sometimes little sense in what he read.

20

More Visitors

The winter passed, and it was May again. The last snows had disappeared, and the little mountain streams raced in full flood down to the valley. The mountainsides were green again, and bathed in warm, clear sunlight. The flowers were opening their petals among the fresh green grass. The gay young winds of spring blew over the tops of the fir trees, carrying off showers of old needles to make room for the new growth. High in the blue sky the old hawk hovered and circled once more, while the golden sunshine played round the hut, and made the ground warm and dry, and fit to sit upon.

Heidi was back on the mountain, running hither and thither to all her old haunts, unable as ever to decide which she liked best. She listened entranced to the sound of the wind blowing down from the heights, gathering strength as it came nearer, till it came up with the fir trees, and spent itself on their branches. She lay on the ground and watched the beetles in the grass. She listened to the hum and buzz of insects. It seemed to her that all those tiny creatures were singing 'We're on the mountain! We're on the mountain!' in tune with her own heart. Her lips parted and she drew in great draughts of the fine sparkling air, and thought that spring had never been so beautiful before.

The familiar sound of hammering and sawing also reached her ears, and presently she ran to the shed to see what Grandfather was doing there. In front of it stood a chair, quite finished, and he was busy making another.

'Oh, I know what these are for!' she cried gleefully. 'We shall want them when they all come up from Frankfurt. This will be for Grandmamma, and the one you're making for Clara. I suppose you'll have to make a third,' she added reluctantly, '– or do you think Miss Rottenmeier might not come?'

'I really don't know,' he told her, 'but it would be better to have a chair ready so that we can ask her to sit down if she does come.' Heidi looked thoughtfully at the straight wooden chair, without arms, and tried to imagine Miss Rottenmeier sitting on it.

'I don't believe she would ever sit on a chair like this, Grandfather,' she said at last.

'Then we'll invite her to sit outside on the turf feather-bed,' he replied quietly.

Heidi was not sure what this strange article of furniture might be, but Peter's familiar whistling and shouting above distracted her, and a few moments later she was surrounded by her old friends, the goats, who leaped about her as eagerly as ever, bleating for joy. Peter pushed his way through them and handed her a letter.

'Here you are,' he said, with no other explanation.

'Did you find a letter for me up on the pasture?' she inquired in surprise.

'No.'

'Where did you get it, then?'

'Out of my satchel.'

The fact was that the postman in Dörfli had given him the letter the evening before, and he had put it in his empty bag. In the morning his bread and cheese had gone in on top of it, and he had forgotten about it when he called at the hut that morning for Uncle's two goats. He only found it when he was shaking out the last crumbs of food at dinner time. Heidi looked at the envelope carefully, and then ran to her grandfather.

'Look,' she cried, 'I've got a letter from Clara. Shall I read it aloud?'

He at once prepared himself to listen, and Peter, who also wanted to hear it, propped himself up against the door post, as he found it easier to attend in that position.

'Dear Heidi,

'We are all packed up and hope to leave in two or three days – as soon as Father is ready – though he is not coming with us. He has to go to Paris. Dr Classen comes every day and keeps telling us to hurry up and get off. He is really impatient for us to start. He enjoyed the happy days he spent with you and your grandfather, and during the winter, when he came to see me so often, he used to tell me about them, and how peaceful it was up where you live. He used to say no one could help getting well in that wonderful mountain air, and he has certainly been much better since he came back, and Father says he looks younger than he has done for a long time.

'You can't think how much I am looking forward to being with you and seeing everything, and meeting Peter and the goats. We have to go to Ragaz first for me to have some treatment, and I shall be there about six weeks. Then we shall come to Dörfli, and on every fine day I shall be brought up to the hut. Grandmamma will be with me, and is looking forward to seeing you. But Miss Rottenmeier won't come! Grandmamma keeps saying to her, "Now what about this trip to Switzerland, my good Rottenmeier? You must not hesitate to say if you would like to come with us." But she always declines very politely and says she doesn't wish to intrude. But the real reason is that when Sebastian got back from taking you to Dörfli, he told such awful stories about the mountains, fearful peaks and ravines and gorges,

overhanging rocks, and mountain slopes so steep
that anyone trying to climb them would almost
fall over backwards. They might be all right for
goats, he said, but certainly not for people! So
Miss Rottenmeier is not at all keen on going to
Switzerland. Tinette too is afraid to come. So
it will be just Grandmamma and me, though
Sebastian is to come with us as far as Ragaz,
and then go home again.

    'I can hardly wait to see you!

    'Grandmamma sends you her love.

    'Goodbye for the present,

    'Your affectionate friend,

    'Clara.'

When Heidi came to the end of the letter, Peter leapt away
from the wall and began to swish his stick in the air furi-
ously. The goats were so frightened that they bounded
down the mountain at a great rate, and Peter went after
them brandishing the stick as though he were challenging
someone unseen. The prospect of more visitors from
Frankfurt had made him very angry indeed.

    Heidi, on the contrary, was overjoyed and felt she must
go down next day and tell Grannie all about it. She was sure
to be interested in who was coming and, almost more important, who was not, for the old woman knew all the members
of the Sesemann household very well now by hearsay.

Now that the weather was so fine, she could go alone, and set out early the following afternoon. It was delightful to go running down the mountainside in the bright sunshine, with the wind at her back, and she was soon there. Grannie was back in her usual corner, spinning, but she looked sad and worried. Peter had come home the evening before in such a bad temper, and had told them that so many people were coming from Frankfurt to visit Heidi, and he didn't know what might happen after that. All night Grannie had lain awake worrying about it. Heidi went at once to the little stool which was always kept ready for her, and began to tell her great news, getting more and more excited as she talked about it. Then all of a sudden she stopped short in the middle of a sentence, and asked:

'What's the matter, Grannie? Aren't you pleased about it?'

'Yes, yes,' Grannie replied, trying to smile. 'I'm glad for your sake, because it makes you so happy.'

'But something's troubling you,' Heidi insisted. 'Are you afraid Miss Rottenmeier may come after all?' and she began to feel worried herself at this idea.

'No, no, it's nothing. Give me your hand so that I know you're really here,' said Grannie. 'It will be best for you, I'm sure, even if I don't survive it.'

'I don't want what's best for me, if you're not going to survive it,' declared Heidi.

This convinced Grannie that the friends from Frankfurt

were really coming to take Heidi away. No doubt they wanted to have her back, now that she was quite well again. That was what was troubling her, but she wished she had not let Heidi notice it. The child was so tender-hearted, she might refuse to go away and leave them, and that would not be right. To change the subject, Grannie now said:

'I know what would do me good, and make me happy again. Please read me the hymn that begins, "Though the storm clouds gather".'

By now Heidi knew the old hymn-book very well, and she soon found the one Grannie wanted and read in her clear voice:

'Though the storm clouds gather,
God thy Heav'nly Father
Gives thee peace within.
Nothing shall distress thee,
If God keep and bless thee,
Lasting joy thou'lt win.'

'I needed to be reminded of that,' said Grannie, and the troubled look left her face.

It was dusk when Heidi went home, and the stars came twinkling out one by one as she climbed up to the hut, sending her a greeting out of the sky. She stopped sometimes to gaze up at them, feeling a deep peacefulness in her heart, and said a little prayer of thanks. She found her grandfather also looking at the stars spangling the heavens so brilliantly.

All through that month the sun shone down every day from a cloudless sky, and morning after morning Uncle Alp looked out, remarking in wonder, 'This is indeed a year of sun! It will bring the grass and flowers on quickly and the pasture will be so rich that Peter will have to watch his army or they'll get out of hand from over-feeding.' And Peter, when he heard him, swung his stick with an 'I'll see about that' air.

So May passed, and June came with longer days and hotter sun, which brought the flowers out all over the mountain, filling the air with their sweet scents. One morning towards the end of the month, Heidi came out of the hut after doing her little round of housework. She intended to climb up behind the fir trees to see a big clump of centaury, which was in full flower and looked very beautiful with the sun shining through its petals. She only reached the corner of the hut, however, when she gave a shout which brought her grandfather out of the shed to see what had happened. 'Grandfather, come and look! Come and look!' she cried, beside herself with excitement.

When he looked in the direction she was pointing, he saw quite a remarkable procession was coming up the mountain. First came two men, carrying between them a chair on poles, and in it sat a girl, very carefully wrapped up. A stately looking lady rode on horseback behind them,

gazing about her with interest and chatting to a young man who was holding the bridle. Then came two more men, one pushing an empty wheel-chair and the other carrying an enormous bundle of rugs and wraps in a basket on his back.

'They've come! They've come!' Heidi shouted, jumping up and down with delight. And sure enough, it was the long expected party from Frankfurt. As they came near the hut, the chair-carriers put their burden down. Heidi sped over the grass to welcome Clara and hug her. Mrs Sesemann dismounted too, and Heidi ran to greet her also. Then the old lady turned to Uncle Alp, who had come forward with outstretched hand. They had heard so much about each other that they met as old friends and greeted one another without formality.

'My dear Uncle,' Mrs Sesemann exclaimed, 'what a magnificent place to live! I can't imagine anything more beautiful. A king might envy you. And my little friend Heidi looks so well, like a June rose,' and she drew the child to her, stroking her fresh pink cheeks lovingly. 'It's so fine, I don't know where to look first. What do you think of it, Clara?'

Clara had never seen or dreamed of anything like it. 'It's heavenly,' she sighed, 'simply heavenly. Oh Grandmamma, I wish I could stay here for ever!'

Uncle Alp brought the wheel-chair forward and spread some rugs in it. Then he went over to Clara and said,

'Supposing I carry you to your usual chair? That would be more comfortable, I'm sure. This one you're in must be a trifle hard.' Without more ado he lifted her in his strong arms and settled her gently into it. Then he wrapped the rugs round her as tenderly as though he had spent the whole of his life looking after invalids. Mrs Sesemann watched him with astonishment.

'My dear Uncle,' she exclaimed, 'if I knew where you had learnt to care like that for the sick, I would send all the nurses of my acquaintance to study there. How did you come by it?'

'From experience and not training,' he replied, a shadow falling across his face, for his thoughts had travelled swiftly back to the time when he was a soldier, and had brought his captain off the battlefield so badly wounded that he spent the rest of his days on a couch, hardly able to move. No one but Uncle Alp was allowed near him, and he had looked after him till he died. He had quite naturally handled Clara as he used to deal with that other sufferer, and he understood without telling the little services which would make her comfortable.

Clara could not drag her eyes away from the scene which stretched before her, the fir trees, the mountains with great grey peaks, glistening in the sun. 'Oh Heidi!' she cried, 'if only I could run about with you, and look at all the things I know so well from what you have told me!'

Heidi took hold of the chair handle and, pushing with

all her might, managed to get it as far as the firs. Clara had never in her life seen anything like these tall old trees, with their straight trunks, and long thick branches sweeping almost to the ground. Even Grandmamma, who had followed them, had never seen such trees before. She stood admiring them, thinking how long they must have stood there looking down on the valley below, while generation after generation of men came and went, were born and died, and they stood fast, for ever stretching upwards to the sky.

Heidi wheeled Clara on to the goat-stall and opened the door wide so that she could have a good look inside, though as the goats were not at home, there was nothing particular to see.

'Oh Grandmamma,' said Clara regretfully, 'I wish I could stay till Daisy and Dusky get back with Peter, and the rest of the goats.'

'Let's enjoy the beautiful things we can see, my dear, and not think about those we cannot,' said Mrs Sesemann who was following the chair in its progress.

'Just look at those clumps of pretty red flowers and all the harebells,' exclaimed Clara. 'I wish I could pick some.'

That was enough for Heidi who immediately dashed off and came back with a beautiful bunch, which she laid on Clara's lap. 'Wait till you see the flowers up on the pasture, though,' she said. 'There the meadows are absolutely covered

with them. There's centaury, and many, many more harebells than here and thousands of yellow rock-roses. Then
there are things with big leaves which Grandfather calls
Bright Eyes, and little brown flowers with round heads
which smell delicious. I could stay there for hours – it's all
so lovely!' Heidi's eyes danced as she tried to make Clara
see it all, and soon Clara caught her excitement too.

'Do you think I could ever get up as high as that,
Grandmamma?' she asked anxiously. 'If only I could walk
and clamber about with you, Heidi.'

'I'll push you up,' promised Heidi, 'I'm sure I could,
for the chair goes very easily,' and as if to show how easily,
she went running off with it at such a rate that they might
have gone right over the edge if Uncle Alp hadn't caught
the handle in the nick of time.

During the tour of inspection, he had been fetching
out the table and chairs, and had laid everything ready
for their meal. Milk and cheese were warming on the
stove, and before long the company sat down to dinner.
Mrs Sesemann was delighted with this unusual 'dining-
room', with its views right down the valley and away, over
the peaks, to the blue sky beyond. A gentle breeze fanned
them as they sat at table, and rustled in the trees, making
agreeable music.

'I've never enjoyed anything so much,' declared Grandmamma, 'it's quite magnificent,' and then 'What's this I
see? A second piece of toasted cheese for Clara?'

'Oh, it is so good, Grandmamma. Better than anything they give me at Ragaz,' said Clara, and she took another bite with obvious enjoyment.

'Just keep on like that,' said Uncle Alp. 'It's our mountain air – it makes up for any deficiencies in the cooking.'

Mrs Sesemann and Uncle Alp got on famously together, and found they had many ideas in common. They might have been friends for years, and time passed quickly, but at last she looked towards the west and said, 'We shall have to go very soon, Clara. The sun's going down, and the men will be back any moment with the horse and your chair.'

Clara's face fell at that. 'Can't we stay?' she implored. 'Another hour, or two? I haven't even been inside the hut yet, or seen Heidi's bed. Oh, I wish there were another ten hours of this day!'

'I am afraid that's not possible,' said her grandmother. But she too wanted to see inside the hut, so they all got up and Uncle Alp wheeled Clara over to the doorway. The chair was too wide to go through it, but he picked her up and carried her. Mrs Sesemann looked at everything with great interest, and was delighted with the orderliness and the cunning arrangements of the place.

'And is your bed up here, Heidi?' she asked, beginning without more ado to mount the ladder to the hayloft. 'Oh, how sweet it smells – a fine healthy place to sleep.' She peeped through the hole in the wall which was Heidi's window. Then Uncle Alp came up the ladder with Clara in his arms and Heidi hopped up after them, and they all crowded together, admiring the bed.

'Oh Heidi, what a lovely place to sleep!' cried Clara in delight. 'Fancy being able to lie in bed and look right out into the sky and hear the fir trees, and smell such nice scents. I've never imagined such a heavenly bedroom.'

Uncle Alp glanced then at Mrs Sesemann. 'I've been thinking,' he began, 'and I hope you'll not object to the suggestion. Suppose you leave your little girl here for a time. I'm sure she'd soon get stronger. You brought so many rugs and wraps with you that we could easily make her a comfortable bed up here, and I promise to look after her and give her all the attention she needs. You need not worry about that.'

Clara and Heidi were overjoyed at his words, and Grandmamma turned a beaming smile on him.

'What a kind fellow you are,' she said. 'You must have read what was in my own mind. I was actually thinking how much good it would do Clara to stay here – but I feared it would be too much to ask of you. Then you come out with an offer which solves the whole problem, and as though it were the easiest thing in the world. I can't thank you enough.' And she shook him warmly by the hand.

Immediately he set to work. First he carried Clara back to her chair outside the hut, with Heidi skipping round them in a great state of excitement. Then he took up an armful of the rugs saying, 'What a good thing you came up equipped for a winter campaign! We shall make good use of these.'

'Foresight is a virtue and averts many a misfortune,' said Mrs Sesemann cheerfully. 'For a journey to the mountains we should have been foolish not to prepare for storms. We've been lucky enough to escape them, but you see my precautions are proving useful.'

As they talked, they climbed up to the loft again and began to prepare Clara's bed, piling one thing on top of another till the erection began to look like a fortress. 'Just let a single stalk of hay poke its way through that,' said Grandmamma, as she tucked the ends well in and patted the surface to make sure it was smooth and even. Then down she came, well satisfied, and went out to the children, who were eagerly discussing how they would spend their precious days together.

'How long can I stay?' Clara asked as soon as her grandmother reappeared.

'We must ask Uncle that,' was the reply, and as he arrived at that moment, he told them gravely that, in his opinion, they would be able to judge in about four weeks whether the mountain air was really doing Clara good. The children clapped their hands at this, for they had not expected half as much.

The men with Clara's chair were now sent off and Mrs Sesemann got ready to leave. 'I won't say goodbye, Grandmamma,' said Clara, 'because you'll come up sometimes to see how we're getting on, won't you? We shall love that, won't we, Heidi?' But Heidi's reply was simply to jump up and down, and clap her hands.

Mrs Sesemann then mounted her horse, and Uncle Alp took the bridle, to lead them down the steep slope. She begged him not to trouble himself, but he declared his attention of seeing her safely back to Dörfli, for the steep path could be dangerous to anyone on horseback. Mrs Sesemann did not care to stay on in quiet little Dörfli alone, but decided to go back to Ragaz and make an occasional trip to the mountains from there.

Peter arrived with the goats before Uncle Alp got back, and Heidi was immediately surrounded by them, and Clara too. Heidi called each one by name so that Clara could make their acquaintance at last and see Snowflake, Finch, Daisy and Dusky, and all the others for herself, as she had longed to do – not forgetting big Turk. Peter stood a little to one side, glaring at the newcomer, and made no reply to their friendly greetings. Instead, he slashed out violently with his stick, as his habit was when he was out of humour, swishing it to and fro as though he wanted to break it. Then he ran off with his herd.

Perhaps the loveliest moment of all that exciting day for Clara came when she and Heidi were in bed in the hayloft, and she found herself looking straight out to the starry sky. 'Oh, Heidi,' she cried, 'it feels as if we were riding in a high sort of carriage right into heaven.'

'Why do you think the stars twinkle so brightly at us?' asked Heidi.

'I don't know. Tell me,' Clara replied.

'Because they are up in heaven and know that God looks after us all on earth so that we oughtn't really ever to be afraid, because everything is bound to come right in the end. That's why they nod to us and twinkle like that. Let's say our prayers now, Clara, and ask God to take care of us.'

They both sat up in bed then, and said their prayers, and after that Heidi laid her head on her arm and was asleep in no time. But Clara lay awake looking out at the sky, hardly able to close her eyes on those wonderful stars, which she had scarcely ever seen before, for she never went out at night in the ordinary way, and at home the curtains were drawn tight before they appeared in the sky. Even when she became drowsy, she kept opening her eyes again to make sure that two particularly bright stars were still shining into the room, nodding and twinkling to her, as Heidi had said. And when she could keep awake no longer, the stars seemed to be there still in her dreams.

21

Clara Begins to Enjoy Life

As the sun rose next morning Uncle Alp was outside as usual, quietly watching the mists disperse over the mountains and the light clouds grow pink as day broke. Soon the valley was flooded with gold and the whole countryside awoke to another glorious day. Then he went indoors and softly climbed the ladder. Clara had just opened her eyes and was gazing with astonishment at the sunbeams, dancing on her bed, not remembering at first where she was. Then she saw Heidi beside her, and heard Uncle Alp's friendly voice ask, 'Well, have you had a good sleep? Do you feel rested this morning?'

'Oh yes,' she replied. 'I didn't wake up once during the night.'

Uncle nodded in a satisfied way, and began to get her up in the same gentle, understanding way that he had arranged things for her overnight. Heidi woke up to find Clara already dressed and in his arms, ready to be carried down. She did not want to miss a single moment, so she leapt out of bed, threw on her clothes, and was down the ladder after them in a flash.

The evening before, Uncle Alp had thought of a way of putting the wheel-chair under cover. It was too wide to go through the door of the hut, but he removed two boards from the entrance to the shed and pushed it in there, and then propped the boards back afterwards so that they could easily be moved when necessary. Heidi came down just as he brought it out of the shed, with Clara in it, and wheeled her into the sunshine. He left her in front of the hut and went off to see to the goats, while Heidi came to say good morning. It was the very first time in all her life that Clara had been out in the open

country so early, and she sniffed the cool mountain air, so fragrant with the scent of the fir trees, and drew in deep, long breaths of it. She felt the warm sunshine on her face and hands. Though she had thought so much about it, she had never dreamed that life on the mountain would be like this.

'I wish I could stay here for ever,' she told Heidi.

'You see now what I told you was true. Isn't it heavenly up here with Grandfather?' said Heidi.

At that moment Grandfather came out with two mugs full of foaming milk, one for each of them. 'This will do the little one good,' he said in his gentle way to Clara. 'It's from Daisy. It will help to make you strong, so drink it up. Good health to you!'

Clara had never tasted goat's milk, and she sniffed at it uncertainly, but when she saw how quickly Heidi was emptying her mug, she began to drink too, and thought the milk tasted as sweet and spicy as if it had sugar and cinnamon in it.

'Tomorrow we shall drink two mugfuls,' said Uncle Alp, pleased to see how she had followed Heidi's good example.

Peter appeared then with the goats, and the animals rushed up to Heidi as usual, bleating so loudly that Uncle Alp, who had something to say to Peter, had to take him aside to make him hear.

'Now attend to me. From now on let Daisy go where

she likes. I want her to give extra good milk, and she will know where to find the best grass. If she wants to go higher up than usual, you go too, and the other goats as well. She's wiser than you in such matters, and it won't hurt you to scramble about a bit. Now why are you staring over there, as if you wanted to eat somebody? They won't interfere with you. Now be off and remember what I've told you.'

Peter was accustomed to do what Uncle Alp told him promptly and he went on his way at once, but not without turning and rolling his eyes at the girls, as though he had something on his mind. The goats swept Heidi along with them a little way and this was just what Peter wanted.

'You'd better come too, because I've got to be after Daisy all the time,' he shouted to her.

'I can't,' she called back. 'I shan't be able to as long as Clara is here. But Grandfather's promised we shall all come up together one day.' By this time she had managed to extricate herself from the goats, and ran back to Clara. Peter shook both fists in the direction of the wheel-chair, then turned and ran till he was out of sight, afraid Uncle Alp might have seen him, and he preferred not to hear what the old man might have to say about such behaviour.

Clara and Heidi had so many plans that they did not know where to begin, but Heidi thought they should first write to Grandmamma as they had promised to do every day. Grandmamma had been first a little worried as to whether Clara would really be comfortable at the hut for any length of time, and how she would stand the life, and she needed to have regular news of her. If she had a daily letter telling of Clara's doings, she would be content to stay quietly at Ragaz, knowing she could get up to the hut quite quickly if she was needed.

'Must we go indoors to write?' asked Clara, quite ready to fall in with Heidi's ideas, but not wanting to be moved. Heidi ran and fetched some of her school books and a three-legged stool. She put the books on Clara's knee for her to write on, and used the bench herself, sitting in front of it on the little stool. They both began to write letters, but Clara's eyes kept straying. It was all so wonderful. The wind had dropped, and only a gentle breeze fanned her cheeks and whispered through the trees. Thousands of tiny insects were dancing in the clear air, but everything else was very still. Only an occasional shout from some goatherd came echoing down the rocky crags.

The morning passed in a flash, and Uncle Alp appeared with two steaming bowls, saying that Clara should stay out of doors as long as it was light. So they had another pleasant meal in the open air. Afterwards Heidi wheeled Clara under the shade of the fir trees, where they spent the afternoon telling each other everything that had happened since Heidi left Frankfurt. Though nothing very remarkable had occurred, there was still plenty for Clara to tell about the household which Heidi had come to know so well. So they chattered away gaily, and in the branches over their heads the birds twittered and sang, as though they were enjoying the conversation too and wanted to join in.

Time passed very quickly, the light changed, and Peter, still scowling, was back with the goats. 'Good night, Peter,' called Heidi, seeing that he did not mean to stop, and Clara too called a friendly goodnight, but he made no reply, only drove the goats straight on.

Clara saw Uncle Alp taking Daisy to her stall, and found herself actually looking forward to the milk she knew he would presently bring her. 'Isn't it queer,' she said to Heidi. 'As long as I can remember I've only eaten because I had to. Everything always tasted so of cod-liver oil, and I used to wish I didn't have to eat at all. And here, I can hardly wait for your grandfather to bring my milk.'

'I know what you mean,' replied Heidi, remembering very well the days in Frankfurt when the good food seemed to stick in her throat.

Clara was surprised at herself. But she had never in her life spent a whole day out of doors anywhere, and did not know what strength was in this high mountain air. So when Uncle Alp brought over the milk, she took hers and drank it up before Heidi finished, and asked for more. Delighted, he took the mugs indoors and when he returned, each was covered with a slice of bread, thickly spread with butter – and that was a special treat. During the afternoon he had been to another hut a little way over the mountain, where they made delicious butter, and had brought back a fine big ball of it. As he stood and watched them, he was pleased to see how the children enjoyed it.

Clara meant to keep awake again that night, to watch the stars, but simply couldn't keep her eyes open and fell at once into the soundest sleep she had ever known.

The next day or two passed as happily, then came a great surprise for the children. Two strong carriers arrived, each with a bed and bedding in a basket on his back. There was also a letter from Mrs Sesemann to say that the beds were for Clara and Heidi. From now on, instead of her couch of hay, Heidi was to have a proper bed, and when she went down to Dörfli in the winter, one was to be taken there, while the other remained at the hut, so that Clara would know there was always a bed for her whenever she could go to see Heidi. She thanked them for their daily letters, which she hoped would continue, so that she would know all that was going on as though she were there with them.

Uncle Alp went up to the loft and threw the hay back where it belonged, and folded the rugs away. Then he helped the two men to carry up the beds, and he put them close together so that the children could still look out of the window from their pillows.

Clara's letters to her grandmother showed that she was

enjoying life at the hut more and more every day. Uncle Alp was so kind and thoughtful, Heidi so gay and amusing – far more so than she had seemed in Frankfurt. So every morning Clara's first thought was, 'Oh, how lovely! I'm still here at Heidi's!' Mrs Sesemann was quite reassured by these promising accounts of her granddaughter, and felt there was no real need for her to make the journey up to the hut again at present, and she was not sorry for that as the steep slopes had made it rather tiring for her.

Uncle Alp grew very attached to his little guest and tried to find something new every day to make her better. He took to going off in the afternoons high up on the mountain top to look for special plants and herbs, and he hung bunches of them in the goat-stall, where they scented the air with their fragrance. When Peter's goats came down in the evening, they sniffed and wrinkled their noses, and tried to get into the stall, but the door was firmly shut against them. Uncle Alp had not gone scrambling about up there just to give the herd a treat. His herbs were only for Daisy, to improve her milk still more. It was easy to see that this diet agreed with her. She became very lively and tossed her head, and her eyes were very bright.

When Clara had been there a fortnight. Uncle Alp began trying to get her on her feet each morning, before putting her in her chair. 'Won't the little one try to stand for a minute?' he asked gently, and to please him, she did try, but gave up very quickly because it hurt her, and she clung to him for support. But each day he persuaded her to try for a little longer.

There had not been such a beautiful summer as that on the mountain for many years. Day after day the sun shone from a cloudless sky, and the flowers had never been so gay nor so sweet before. And when evening came, snow-fields and rocky peaks were a blaze of colour, purple, pink, and gold, but the full glory was only to be seen higher up than Uncle's hut. Heidi told Clara all about it, and how specially lovely everything was up on the high pasture which she loved so much. One evening, as she was talking about it, she suddenly longed to see it so passionately that she ran to her grandfather, who was busy at his bench in the shed, and cried, 'Oh Grandfather, will you take us up to the pasture tomorrow? It'll be so lovely there now.'

'Very well,' he agreed, 'if the little one will first do something for me, and try her best to stand alone this evening.' Heidi ran back, delighted, to tell Clara the news, and Clara promised to try hard for Uncle Alp, as she too was excited at the thought of such an expedition.

Heidi was so thrilled that she called out as soon as she caught sight of Peter, 'We're coming up with you tomorrow, to spend the whole day on the pasture.'

In reply Peter only growled like a bear that has been teased, and hit out with his stick at Finch, who was trotting peaceably beside him. But Finch avoided it by leaping right over Snowflake's back, and the stick fell on empty air.

Clara and Heidi went to bed so full of the plans for next day that they agreed to stay awake all night talking about them. However their heads had hardly touched the pillows, when all their chatter ceased. Clara dreamed of a great stretch of turf, covered with harebells, and Heidi of the hawk croaking away on the heights, as if he were calling, 'Come, come, come!'

22

The Unexpected Happens

Uncle Alp was out before sunrise next morning to look at the sky and see what kind of day it was going to be. He stood watching the light come over the mountain tops, till the sun itself appeared and the shadows died away, and even the valley came to life again. Then he fetched the wheel-chair from the shed and put it ready in front of the hut, before going to waken the children.

Peter arrived just then, and the goats were shifting rather nervously about him, for he had been hitting out at them without the slightest cause all the way up. He was feeling very sore and cross. For weeks now he had not once had Heidi to himself, for she was always with the girl in the wheel-chair, and they stayed by the hut or just under the trees. She had not been up to the pasture with him once that summer, and she was only coming now to show it to that stranger. Peter knew just how it would be, and his resentment got too much for him. There stood the empty wheel-chair and he glared at it, as if it were his worst enemy, and the cause of all his troubles. He looked round, and saw there was no one at hand, and no sound of anyone came from the hut. In a sudden burst of rage, he rushed at the chair, and gave it a spiteful shove which sent it rolling down the steep slope. It moved easily, gathered speed, and then plunged headlong out of sight.

He flew up the mountain as though he had wings and hid behind a big blackberry bush. He wanted to see what

happened to the chair, but had no desire for Uncle Alp to catch him. With wicked glee he watched it, far below, bouncing off the rocks and leaping on until it crashed to its final destruction. He leaped for joy at the sight and laughed aloud. He told himself that now that horrid girl would go away and everything would be as before. Heidi would be free to go with him up to the pasture often, every day perhaps. The real badness of what he had done had not yet occurred to him, nor any idea of what consequences it might have.

Heidi came out almost at once, followed by her grandfather carrying Clara. The shed door was wide open and she could see that the place was empty. She ran round to the back of the hut, and came back looking puzzled.

'What's the matter, Heidi?' asked her grandfather. 'What have you done with the chair?'

'You said it was in front of the door, but I can't see it anywhere,' she replied.

A strong gust of wind just at that moment sent the shed door slamming back against the wall.

'Perhaps the wind has blown it away,' Heidi cried, looking anxiously about. 'Oh dear, if it has rolled right down to Dörfli, we shan't get it back in time to go.'

'If it has fallen as far as that, we shan't get it back at all,' said her grandfather. 'It will be broken in a hundred pieces.' He went to look over the edge, and murmured to himself, 'That's curious.' He saw the chair, and realized that to fall where it had, it would have had to turn a corner on its way from the shed!

'Oh, how dreadful!' Clara wailed. She was really upset. 'Now we shan't be able to go today – I shan't ever be able to go – because I shan't be able to stay here without my chair. Oh, what shall I do?'

'We'll go up to the pasture today anyway, as we planned,' Grandfather told her kindly. 'After that, we'll see.'

That satisfied them both. He went indoors and returned with an armful of rugs, which he spread out in the sunniest spot he could find, then he settled Clara on them. He fetched their milk, and brought out Daisy and Dusky from their stall.

'I wonder where that boy's got to,' he remarked thoughtfully. 'He's very late.' Peter had not given his usual whistle.

When the girls had finished their breakfast, he picked Clara up and the rugs and said, 'Now we can go, and we'll take the goats with us.'

Heidi went happily ahead, with a hand on each animal's neck. They were so pleased to be with her again that they pressed against her on either side so that they almost crushed her between them. When they reached the pasture, they saw the other goats grazing peacefully in little groups and Peter stretched full length on the ground.

'Hi, I'll teach you to pass us by, you lazy rascal,' cried Grandfather. 'What do you mean by it?'

Peter shot up at the sound of that voice. 'No one was up,' he replied.

'Did you see anything of Clara's chair?' asked Uncle Alp.

'What chair?' Peter mumbled sourly.

Uncle said no more. He found a sunny place for Clara and settled her there.

'How's that?' he asked, and she replied, 'As comfortable as if I was in my chair, thank you. And oh, isn't it lovely here?'

'Now enjoy yourselves,' said Uncle Alp, as he prepared to leave them. 'Your dinner is in the bag over there in the shade. Get Peter to give you as much milk as you want, but see he takes it from Daisy. I'll come back for you in the evening, but I must go down now to see what's become of the chair.'

There was not one cloud in the deep blue sky. The great snowfield sparkled, and the massive bare peaks stood out clearly against the unbroken blue. The two girls sat side by side, as happy and contented as could be. From time to time one of the goats came and lay down beside them. Snowflake came most often, and nestled against Heidi until one of the others came and drove her away. So Clara learnt to recognize each one. Some came right up to her and rubbed against her shoulders, a sure sign that they trusted her. Presently Heidi thought of the meadow where all the flowers grew, and wished she could go and see if they were as beautiful as last year, but Clara could not go till Grandfather returned in the evening, and by then the flowers would probably have closed their petals for the night. She wanted to go so badly that after a little she said hesitantly:

'Would you mind if I left you alone for a few minutes, Clara? I want to go and look at the flowers. Wait a minute, though,' she went on, as an idea came to her. She picked some handfuls of grass and spread it on Clara's lap. Then she brought Snowflake over and gave her a little push to make her lie down. 'There, you won't be alone, now,' she said.

'Go and look at the flowers for as long as you like,' said Clara. 'I shall be quite happy here with Snowflake. It'll be fun to feed her.' So Heidi ran off, and Clara gave the grass to the little goat blade by blade. Snowflake took it gently from her hand, already quite at home with this new friend. To Clara this strange new experience was very exciting. To be here, all by herself, and out of doors in such a beautiful place, with this little goat eating so trustfully out of her hand – was all so delightful. She had never expected to know such happiness, and it gave her a new idea of what it must mean to be like other girls, well and free, to run about and to help people, instead of always having to be the one who sat still and was waited on. The thought seemed to add an extra radiance to the scene, and a deeper glow to her own happiness. She put an arm round Snowflake's neck. 'I should like to stay here for ever and ever,' she murmured aloud.

Heidi meanwhile had reached the flowery meadow, and was gazing ecstatically at the yellow carpet of rock-roses, and the blue gleam of harebells, the sweet-scented primulas, and dozens of other flowers. Suddenly she raced back to Clara, arriving beside her quite breathless.

'Oh, you simply must come too,' she exclaimed. 'The flowers are so beautiful, and they might not be the same later on. Don't you think I could carry you?'

Clara shook her head. 'You couldn't possibly, Heidi. You're smaller than I am. Oh, if only I could walk!'

Heidi looked round for inspiration. Peter was sitting higher up the slope, staring down at them, as he had been doing for an hour or more, as though unable to understand how it had happened. He had destroyed the hateful chair, so that Clara could not be moved about, and yet here she was, where he least wanted to see her and, of course, Heidi was with her. He could hardly believe his eyes.

'Come down here, Peter,' called Heidi.

'Shan't,' he replied.

'Oh, you must. I want you. Quick!'

'Shan't.'

Heidi got angry and ran a few steps towards him, her eyes flashing. 'If you don't come at once,' she stormed at him, 'I'll do something you won't like. I mean it!'

Her words disturbed him. He had done a dreadful

thing, but up till now he had not cared because he thought no one knew about it. But Heidi sounded as though she might and, if she did, she would be sure to tell her grandfather, and Peter did not like that prospect at all. Reluctantly he got up and said, 'All right, I'll come, if you don't do what you said.' He sounded so anxious that Heidi forgave him.

'Of course I won't,' she cried. 'Come on. There's nothing to be afraid of.'

When they got back to Clara, she told Peter to prop her at one side, while she took the other, and together they helped her to her feet. So far, so good, but Clara could not keep upright without support.

'Put your arm round my neck,' Heidi told her, 'and Peter, give her your arm, and then we'll be able to help her along.' Peter had never done anything like this before, and though Clara took hold of his arm, he kept it stiffly down at his side which did not help her much.

'No, not like that, Peter,' said Heidi. 'Make a crook with your arm, so that Clara can lean on it. And for goodness' sake don't let it give way. That's better. Now we shall manage it.'

But still they were not very successful. Clara flopped heavily between them, and Peter was taller than Heidi, so that Clara was all up one side and down the other. However she tried to put one foot in front of the other, though she drew it back very quickly.

'Try just putting one foot down firmly,' Heidi advised her. 'I'm sure that would hurt less.'

'Do you think so?' asked Clara, rather doubtfully, but she tried it, and cried joyfully, 'You're right. That didn't hurt nearly so much.'

'Try again,' urged Heidi, and Clara did so, taking several more steps.

'Oh Heidi,' she cried then, 'look at me. I'm walking! I'm walking!'

'Yes, you are, you are! All by yourself! Oh, I wish Grandfather was here!'

Clara still kept hold of Heidi and Peter, but with each step they could feel her getting steadier on her feet. Heidi was quite wild with excitement.

'Now we can come up to the pasture every day, and wander about wherever we like,' she exclaimed, 'and you'll never have to be pushed about in a wheel-chair again. Oh, isn't it wonderful?' And Clara agreed from the bottom of her heart. Nothing could be more wonderful to her than to be strong and able to get about like other people.

It was not much farther to Heidi's special spot, where Clara was able to sit down on the warm grass among all the profusion of beautiful flowers. She was so affected by all that had happened to her that she was silent as she gazed at all their lovely colours and smelt their delicious scents. Peter lay down in the long grass and was soon fast asleep, but Heidi could not keep still. She wandered away over the meadow, then the exciting memory of what had happened to Clara sent her flying back again.

Some time later a few of the goats, led by Finch, came slowly towards them. As a rule they avoided this meadow, for they did not like grazing among the flowers, but now they came with deliberate steps as though to remind the herdsboy that he had left them alone too long. Then Finch saw the girls, and gave a loud bleat. The others took up the cry and all came trotting up to them. Peter woke with a start and rubbed his eyes. He had been dreaming of the wheel-chair, still undamaged, standing outside the hut, and when he first opened his eyes, he thought he saw its brass studs gleaming in the sun. But it was only the yellow of the flowers which his sleepy eyes had caught, and the horrid memory of what he had done returned to him. Even if Heidi said nothing, he was afraid it would be found out sooner or later. In that state of misery he behaved with unusual meekness, and let Heidi order him about as she liked.

After a while they took Clara back to the pasture, and Heidi fetched the lunch bag. She had seen the good things her grandfather had put in it, and when she had threatened Peter earlier on, she had meant that he wouldn't get his share of the food. But she had forgiven him, and now divided it equally into three. They were all hungry as it was long past noon, but neither Clara nor Heidi could eat all that had been provided for them, and after they were satisfied, Peter found himself with a second portion as big as his first. He ate it all, to the last crumb, but somehow did not enjoy it as much as usual. He felt as though something was gnawing at his inside, and the food lay heavily on his stomach.

They had eaten so late that they had not long finished their meal when Uncle Alp arrived to fetch them home. Heidi saw him coming, and ran to meet him, eager to be the first to tell him the great news. She was so excited that she could hardly get the words out, but he gathered what she meant very quickly, and his face lit up. He went on to where Clara was sitting, and gave her an understanding smile, as he said, 'Something attempted, something won.'

He helped her up and made her walk a few steps, putting one arm round her waist, and holding the other before her to hold on to. With this firm support, she walked with much more confidence than before. Heidi skipped joyfully beside them, and the old man looked as though a great happiness had come to him. After a little, he picked Clara up in his arms, and carried her. 'We mustn't overdo things,' he told her. 'It's time to go home now,' and he set off with her down the path, for he could see she had had quite enough for one day and needed rest.

When Peter went down into Dörfli that evening, he saw a knot of people staring at something, talking and elbowing each other aside to get a better view of it. Peter wormed his way through them to see what it was all about – and saw the remains of Clara's chair. There was enough of it left still to show how fine it had been.

'I saw it when the carriers brought it,' said the baker. 'It must have cost a lot of money, I'll be bound. I can't think how such a thing could have happened.'

'Uncle Alp said the wind might have blown it down,' a woman said, looking at the quality of the red leather.

'Let's hope he's right,' remarked the baker, '– or someone will smart for it. The gentleman in Frankfurt is sure to want the matter looked into, and then there'll be trouble. But no one can say I had a hand in it. I haven't been near the hut these two years or more.'

There was more talk of the same kind, but Peter had heard enough. He slunk away and ran home as if he thought someone was after him. The baker's words frightened him, and he was afraid that a policeman might arrive from Frankfurt any moment, and that everything would come out and he would be sent to prison. His hair stood on end with horror at the mere idea, and he reached home in such a state, he could neither speak nor eat, but went straight to bed and hid under the bedclothes, groaning aloud in his misery.

'Peter must have been eating sorrel again, and given himself stomach-ache,' said his mother. 'Just listen to him.'

'Give him a little more food to take with him tomorrow,' Grannie suggested kindly. 'Give him some of my bread.'

As Clara and Heidi lay in bed that night, looking at the stars, Heidi said suddenly, 'I've been thinking. Isn't it a good thing God doesn't always give us just what we're asking for, even though we pray ever so hard? Of course, it's because He knows something else will be better for us.'

'What makes you say that now?' asked Clara.

'When I was in Frankfurt I prayed so hard to be allowed to go home at once, but God didn't let me, and I thought He had forgotten me. But if I had gone home then, you would never have come here and got well.'

Clara considered this, then she said, 'But in that case, perhaps we ought not to pray for anything, because God knows – as we don't – what is best for us.'

'I don't think that's quite right either,' Heidi replied quickly. 'We ought to pray to Him every day to show our trust, and that we know that everything comes from God. If we forget Him, then sometimes He lets us go our own way, and then things go very wrong with us. Your grandmamma told me that, and everything turned out as she said it would. So now we ought to thank Him for making you walk.'

'I'm glad you reminded me,' Clara agreed. 'I was so happy, I'd almost forgotten my prayers.'

Next morning Uncle Alp suggested they should write and invite Mrs Sesemann to pay them a visit as they had something special to show her. But the children had planned a better surprise still for Grandmamma. They wanted Clara to practise until she could really walk alone before Grandmamma heard about it, and they asked Uncle Alp how long he thought it would take. He said about a week, so their next letter to Ragaz contained a pressing invitation for her to come up the mountain in about a week's time, but they did not tell her why.

The next days were the happiest Clara had known on the mountain. Her waking thought each morning was, 'I am well! I can walk!' Each day she went a little farther alone, and the exercise gave her such an appetite that Uncle Alp cut her bread and butter thicker each day, and filled the mugs again and again with milk, and nodded and smiled to see it all disappear so rapidly. In this pleasant fashion the week passed.

23

Goodbye for the Present!

Mrs Sesemann wrote the day before she intended to travel, telling them that she would come for certain, and Peter brought the letter up with him in the morning. The children were already out of doors with Uncle Alp, and the goats were waiting for him impatiently. Uncle was watching the girls with a very satisfied smile playing about his lips. Peter's steps lagged at sight of them, but he brought them the letter, and ran off quickly, glancing back over his shoulder uneasily as if afraid someone might come after him.

Heidi was puzzled by his behaviour and asked, 'Grandfather, why does Peter always behave now as big Turk does when he expects a beating?'

'Perhaps he thinks he deserves a beating,' Uncle replied.

Peter ran until he was out of sight. Then he stopped and looked about him again. He had grown more and more worried as the days passed. At any moment he expected to see the policeman from Frankfurt jump out from behind a bush and seize him by the scruff of the neck, and the suspense was weighing on him.

Heidi spent the morning cleaning out the hut thoroughly, so that everything would be spick and span when Grandmamma arrived. Clara sat and watched her. Then they tidied themselves and sat down outside to wait for her in a state of great excitement. Uncle Alp had been out already to gather some blue gentians on the mountain, and brought back a big bunch which he showed to the children, and then carried indoors. Heidi kept getting up to see if there was any sign of their visitor, and at last the little procession came in sight. In front was a guide, leading Mrs Sesemann's horse, and a man with a laden basket brought up the rear. When they reached the little plateau on which the hut stood, and the old lady really saw the children, she cried out in some concern:

'Why Clara, where's your chair? What does this mean?' But as she dismounted and came towards them, astonishment took the place of anxiety, and she exclaimed, 'How well you look, my dear. I hardly recognize you.'

Then Heidi got up – and so did Clara, and they walked before her, Clara quite upright and with no more support than a hand on Heidi's shoulder. Grandmamma looked on in amazement. They turned and walked towards her, and she saw their two rosy faces, aglow with happiness. Half laughing, almost crying, Grandmamma embraced first Clara, then Heidi, then Clara again, but could for the moment find no words to express her feelings. Then she noticed Uncle Alp, who had come out, and was watching with a pleased smile. She took Clara's arm in hers, and together they went to the old man. Mrs Sesemann was greatly moved at having her granddaughter walk beside her at last, and she grasped his hands, saying warmly:

'My dear Uncle, how can we ever thank you! It's your care, your nursing that has done this.'

'And God's good sun and His mountain air,' he added.

'And don't forget Daisy's lovely milk,' put in Clara. 'You ought to see what a lot of it I drink, Grandmamma! It's so good!'

'Your rosy cheeks tell me that,' answered her grandmother. 'I really should not have known you. You're quite plump, and I do believe you're taller! I can't take my eyes off you. It's a miracle. I must telegraph at once to your father in Paris and tell him to come immediately. I shan't tell him why. He'll have the happiest surprise of his life. Now how can I send off a telegram from here, Uncle? Have the men gone yet?'

'Yes, they have,' said Uncle Alp, 'but if you're in such a hurry, I can send Peter to take it.' And he went aside and whistled so piercingly through his fingers that the rocks above re-echoed with the sound. Almost at once Peter came running down, white as a sheet. He knew that whistle, and feared that the awful moment had arrived, and he was about to be arrested. When he found he was only to take a piece of paper, on which Mrs Sesemann had written a message, down to the post office at Dörfli, he was much relieved and set off immediately.

The little party then sat down to dinner in front of the hut and Grandmamma was told the whole story from the beginning. 'I can hardly believe it!' she kept saying. 'It's too good to be true' – which kept Clara and Heidi bubbling over with delight at the success of their great surprise.

As it happened, Mr Sesemann also had been planning a surprise. He finished his business in Paris earlier than he expected, and was so longing to see his daughter again that, without a word to anyone, he took train for Basle and went from there straight to Ragaz, arriving just after his mother had left. When he heard where she had gone, he hired a carriage, and drove on at once to Dörfli. From there he set out on foot, and hard going he found it, for he was not accustomed to such exercise. After a long climb, when he had not even come to the goatherd's hut – which he knew, from Clara's letters, lay midway between the village and Heidi's home – he began to think he must have taken the wrong path. He looked about anxiously for someone to ask, but there was not a soul in sight, nor a sound to be heard except the humming of insects and the occasional twittering of a bird.

Mr Sesemann grew very hot, and as he stopped to fan himself, Peter came running down the path with the telegram in his hand. Mr Sesemann beckoned to him as soon as he was near enough, but the boy seemed suddenly reluctant to approach him.

'Come along, lad,' cried the poor traveller impatiently. 'Can you tell me if this path leads to the hut where the old man lives with a child called Heidi, and where some people from Frankfurt are staying?'

'*The policeman!*' thought Peter, in such a panic of fright that he only uttered a little wail, and dashed off down the mountain, and in such a hurry that he tripped, and went head over heels, head over heels, just as the chair had done – but fortunately for him, he did not, like the chair, break into small pieces! But the piece of paper he had been holding, blew away and was lost.

'Dear me!' Mr Sesemann said to himself. 'How shy these mountain folk are!' for he thought that the mere sight of a stranger on his native mountain had sent the boy flying off like that. He stood watching Peter's wild descent for a moment or two, then went on his way; and Peter went bowling on, quite unable to stop and get to his feet again, until at last he fell into a bush and lay there, trying to get over his fright. Then –

'Hullo, here comes another one!' said a jeering voice near by, 'I wonder who'll be the next to get pushed over the top and come tumbling down like a sack of potatoes.'

It was the baker who spoke. He had come out for a breath of fresh air after work. His words made Peter jump up in fresh alarm. They sounded as though the baker knew what had really happened to the chair, and the miserable little goatherd went scrambling up the mountain again, as fast as his bruises and his guilty conscience would let him. He wished he could go home and hide under the bedclothes. That was the only place where he would have felt really safe, but the goats were still up on the pasture, and Uncle Alp had told him to hurry, so that the animals were not left alone too long. He did not dare disobey Uncle's orders.

Mr Sesemann trudged on, and soon after leaving Peter, he reached the goatherd's cottage and knew that he was on the right path. He went on from there with new heart, and it was not long before he saw the hut with the three fir trees a little way above him. The sight spurred him on, and he stepped out briskly, chuckling to himself at the surprise he hoped to give them up there. That was not to be, however, for he had already been observed, and the happy little party outside the hut were hastily improvising a welcome for him.

As he stepped thankfully on to the level ground on which the hut stood, he saw two people coming towards him, a tall fair girl, leaning slightly on a smaller dark one.

He stood still and stared, and suddenly his eyes filled with tears, for he was so strangely reminded of Clara's mother who had had just such fair hair and delicate pink

and white cheeks. He hardly knew whether he was awake
or dreaming.

'Don't you know me, Papa?' Clara cried. 'Am I so
changed?'

At that, he strode towards her and took her in his arms.
'Changed indeed!' he cried. 'Is it possible? Can I believe
my eyes?'

He stepped back a pace to look at her better, then drew
her close again. His mother joined them, anxious not to
miss a single breath of this great moment.

'Well, what do you think of that, my son?' she inquired,
and added, 'You thought to give us a surprise, a lovely

one, but as it turns out, it is nothing to the one we were preparing for you, is it now?' She kissed him affectionately as she spoke. 'Now come and make the acquaintance of our good Uncle Alp to whom we owe our great joy.'

'We do indeed,' he replied, beaming, 'and to our own little Heidi too. I'm glad to see you looking so well again, my dear, and so happy. Those must be Alpine roses in your cheeks.'

Heidi smiled up at him, immensely pleased that it should be here on the mountain that her good friend had found such happiness. Then Grandmamma took him over to Uncle Alp, and Mr Sesemann thanked him with all his heart for what he had done.

While the two men were talking, the old lady wandered away to the fir trees. There, in a little space between the lowest branches, she was enchanted to discover a clump of beautiful blue gentians, looking as fresh as if they were actually growing there.

'Oh how exquisite!' she cried. 'Heidi my dear, come over here. Did you do that to surprise me? It was a lovely thought.'

'No, I didn't,' Heidi replied, 'but I know who did.'

'They grow just like that up on the mountain,' Clara told her, 'lots and lots of them. Guess who gathered them for you this morning.'

She looked so happy that, for a moment, her grandmother wondered if she could possibly have done it herself.

They were interrupted at that moment by a little scuffling noise from behind the trees. It was Peter, who had seen the stranger outside the hut with Uncle Alp, and so was trying to creep by unnoticed. Mrs Sesemann caught sight of him, however, and the thought struck her that it might have been he who had brought the flowers, and that the slipping away was out of shyness.

'Come here,' she called, meaning to reward him in some way. 'Come along my boy. Don't be shy.'

Peter was too frightened to run away any more. 'It's all up with me now,' he thought, and he came slowly towards her with an agonized expression on his face.

'Be brave,' said Mrs Sesemann, trying to help him out. 'Just tell me plainly, was it you who did that?'

Peter did not look up, so he did not see what she was pointing at, but he felt Uncle's eyes upon him from the angle of the hut, and he muttered a shaky, 'Yes.'

'Well well,' she murmured, 'what is there to be afraid of in that?'

'It's ... because ... because ... it's all broken ... and can't be mended.' He brought the words out with great difficulty, and his knees were knocking together so that he could hardly stand.

After a thoughtful glance at him, Grandmamma went over to Uncle Alp, and asked quietly if the boy was half-witted.

'Oh no,' he assured her, 'not in the least. But he was

the "wind" that blew your granddaughter's chair away, and now he's expecting to be punished for it, as he richly deserves to.'

Mrs Sesemann found it hard to believe this of him. He did not look to her like a bad boy, and she could not think why anyone should have wanted to destroy such a necessary article as an invalid's chair.

Uncle Alp, however, had had his suspicions from the very beginning. He had not missed the scowls Peter had cast at Clara, nor his whole air of resentment of everything that had been happening on the mountain. Uncle had put two and two together, and had spoken with conviction when he accused Peter. He explained all this now to Mrs Sesemann, who said at once:

'Oh poor boy! He mustn't be punished any more. We must be kind, and try to see things from his angle. Think, here are we, complete strangers, keeping Heidi away from him for weeks on end – and of course he regarded her as very much his private property – and he has been left all alone to brood on it. Of course his feelings got the better of him and drove him to this foolish act of revenge. We are all foolish when we are angry.'

She turned and called Peter to her, as she sat down under the trees.

'Come, my boy,' she said in a friendly voice, 'stop trembling and listen to me. You sent Miss Clara's wheel-chair rolling down the mountainside so that it was smashed to bits, didn't you? And you knew all the time that it was wrong, and that you would deserve to be punished for it, but you've been trying to hide it, hoping that no one would find out. Isn't that it? I thought so. But you make a great mistake if you think you can do wrong and no one will know about it. God sees and hears everything, and when He notices someone trying to hide what they have done, He stirs up the little watchman we all have inside us – a little watchman who sleeps until we do something wrong. Then he wakes up, and he has a little goad to prick us with, and he does not give us a moment's peace after that, but goes on pricking us and telling us in a nagging little voice, "*Someone has found out. Now you'll get into trouble.*" Isn't that what has been happening to you lately?'

Much ashamed, Peter gave a little nod, for those had been exactly his feelings.

'And things haven't turned out as you expected, have they?' she went on. 'Instead of injuring her, you've actually done her good. Without her chair, Clara has had to make a special effort to walk, and you see she has succeeded. That's the way God brings good out of evil. You, who did wrong, were the one to suffer. Do you understand, Peter? Remember what I've been saying, and the next time you feel inclined to do something you know you shouldn't, think of that little watchman with his goad and his disagreeable voice inside you.'

'Yes, I will,' said Peter, very subdued but still anxious as to how the matter was going to end, for the 'policeman' was still standing beside Uncle Alp.

'Then we'll say no more about it,' Mrs Sesemann told him. 'And I should like you to have something as a pleasant reminder of the visitors from Frankfurt. Now tell me. What would you like most of all for a present?'

Peter raised his eyes at that, and stared at her in amazement. His head was in a whirl. He had been sure that something terrible would happen to him. Instead, he was to be given a present!

'Yes, I mean it,' she assured him. 'I want you to choose something really nice to remember us by, and to show you that we bear you no ill will. Do you understand?'

The truth slowly dawned on Peter. This kind lady was going to stand between him and the policeman. He had nothing more to fear. He felt as though a weight like one of the great mountains themselves had dropped off his shoulders. He began to see too that it might be better to own up at once when he had done any wrong, so he said quickly, 'I lost the paper too.'

This puzzled Mrs Sesemann for a moment, then she remembered the telegram.

'Ah, that's right,' she said kindly, 'you're a good boy to tell me. Always confess right away when you've done anything wrong, and it will save a lot of trouble. Now, what would you like for your present?'

Peter felt quite giddy at the thought that he could choose for himself anything in the whole world. He thought of the fair that came to Mayenfeld once a year, and of all the wonderful things he had seen on the stalls there, without a hope in the world of ever being able to buy any of them – nice red whistles, for instance. He could use one of them for calling the goats together. And those strong clasp-knives which made short work of cutting hazel twigs. He thought and thought – what should he choose? Then a grand idea came to him, and he spoke up clearly.

'A penny,' he said. Then he would have all the time between now and the next fair to decide what to buy with it.

Mrs Sesemann could not help laughing. 'What a modest request!' she cried, opening her purse and bringing out some coins. 'Come over here and we'll settle our account at once. Look, here are as many pennies as there are weeks in the year, and every Sunday you can take one of them to spend.'

Peter looked at her open-eyed. 'Every Sunday for ever?' he asked.

She laughed again, and the two men came over to hear what was going on.

'Yes, for ever,' she promised, 'I'll put it down in my will: *To Peter, the goatherd, a penny a week for life,*' and she turned to her son and added, 'Do you hear that? You must put it in your will too. A penny a week for Peter as long as he lives.'

Mr Sesemann agreed with a nod, and joined in the laughter.

Peter looked again and again at the coins in his hand, to be sure he was not dreaming. Then he thanked her and ran off up the mountain, in the highest spirits, leaping and jumping for joy. His troubles were over, and he was promised a penny a week for all the rest of his life!

Later, when they were all sitting outside the hut after a pleasant meal, Clara took her father's hand and said, 'Oh, Papa, if you only knew all that Uncle Alp has done for me! I shall never forget it. And I keep thinking, what could I ever do for him that would give him even half as much pleasure as he has given me?'

'I should like to know that too,' her father replied, turning to their host, who was engaged in lively conversation with Grandmamma. He put out his hand and grasped Uncle Alp's large rough one warmly. 'Dear friend,' he said, 'let us have a quiet word together. You will know what I mean when I say that for years I have never known real happiness. What were all my money and success worth, if they could not make my poor little daughter well? Now, with God's help, you have given us both something to live for. That can never be repaid, but tell me if there is any way in which I may show my gratitude. I will do anything that is in my power: only tell me what it shall be.'

Uncle Alp listened quietly, smiling at the happiness he saw in the other's face, then with simple dignity he replied, 'I have a share too in your joy at your daughter's recovery. In that lies my reward. Thank you all the same for what you have said, but I want nothing. So long as I live there will be enough for me and for Heidi. There is only one thing I wish for. If you could give me that, I should have no cares left.'

'Tell me then what that wish is,' said Mr Sesemann.

'I am old,' Uncle Alp began. 'I cannot expect to live much longer, and I shall have nothing to leave the child when I die. She has no one but me in the wide world except that one who has taken so little care of her. If you could promise me that Heidi need never have to go and earn her living among strangers – that would richly reward me for what I have been able to do for you and your daughter.'

'That is something you need not even ask,' Mr Sesemann returned quickly. 'Heidi is already like one of my family. Ask my mother, or Clara: they will bear me out in that. We shall never allow her to be left to strangers. I promise you that. Here's my hand on it. I will make provision for her during my life, and afterwards.

'While she was with us, we saw how hard it was for her to live away from her own home, though she made good friends among us, as you know, and one of them is winding up his affairs in Frankfurt at this very moment. I mean our dear Dr Classen, of course. He intends to retire very soon, and to settle somewhere near you. He was so happy with you and Heidi last year. So, you see, in future, with you and him, Heidi will have two good friends at hand, and I hope you will both live for many years yet.'

'Amen to that,' cried Mrs Sesemann, shaking Uncle Alp warmly by the hand. Then she put her arm round Heidi and kissed her. 'And now, my dear, what about you? Have you a wish to be granted?' she asked.

'Yes, I have,' Heidi replied readily, looking up into her face.

'I am glad. Tell me what it is.'

'The bed I had in Frankfurt, with its three pillows and the warm quilt – I should like to have it for Grannie, so that she won't have to lie with her head so low that she can hardly breathe, and she wouldn't have to wear her beautiful shawl in bed, either, to keep her from freezing.'

In her eagerness, Heidi hardly paused for breath.

'What a good child you are!' said Mrs Sesemann. 'It's easy, in our own happiness, to forget those who are not so well off. It shall be done. I will telegraph to Frankfurt at once and Rottenmeier shall pack up the bed and send it off. It ought to be here then in a day or two, and I hope Grannie will find it very comfortable.'

Heidi skipped with delight, and cried:

'I must just run down and tell her. I haven't seen her for so long, she'll be wondering what's happened to me.'

'Heidi,' said her grandfather, gently reproving, 'what are you thinking of? You can't run off like that while we have company.' But Mrs Sesemann stopped him.

'The child's right,' she said. 'Poor Grannie's been neglected lately because of us. Let us all go down together to see her. I can wait for my horse there, and I'll send off the telegram from Dörfli. What do you say, my son?'

Mr Sesemann had not yet had a chance to speak of his own plans, so he began now to explain them. He had thought of spending a little time in Switzerland with his mother, taking Clara with them for at least part of the time, if she was well enough. Now it looked as though he might have his daughter's company for the whole trip, and in that case, it would be the greatest pity to miss any of these last lovely days of summer. He thought therefore of spending the night in Dörfli, and fetching Clara next day. They would go then to Ragaz where they would meet Grandmamma, and from there start their little holiday. At first Clara was a little upset at the prospect of leaving the mountain so soon, but she had so much that was new to look forward to, that she could not feel unhappy for long.

Taking Heidi's hand, Mrs Sesemann was preparing to lead the way down to the goatherd's cottage, when a thought struck her, and she turned back. 'But how will Clara manage?' she asked. Uncle Alp smiled and picked the child up in his arms as he had so often done before, and like that they set off. On the way, Heidi told Mrs Sesemann a great deal about Grannie, how much she felt the cold in winter and that she had not always enough to eat, and Mrs Sesemann listened thoughtfully to all she had to say.

Bridget was hanging Peter's spare shirt out to dry as they approached the cottage, and when she saw them, she hurried indoors to tell her mother. 'They're all coming down the mountain,' she announced. 'Going home evidently, and Uncle Alp is carrying the invalid girl.'

'Oh dear,' sighed Grannie. 'Are they taking Heidi with them? I wish she'd come in, just for a moment. I'd like to hear her voice once more.' And then the door was flung open and Heidi bounced into the room and threw her arms round the old woman.

'Grannie, Grannie,' she cried, 'what do you think? My bed is coming from Frankfurt for you with three big pillows and a warm quilt! And Grandmamma says it will be here in a few days.' She expected to see Grannie's face light up at this news, but saw instead only a sad little smile.

'She's very kind. I ought to be glad you're going with her, but I think I shall die without you.'

'What's that I hear?' cried Mrs Sesemann, coming in and speaking in her usual kind tone. 'No, there's no question of that. Heidi's going to stay here with you. We know what a comfort she is to you. We shall want to see her too, of course, but we shall come to her. We shall come every year to the mountains to give thanks for our child's wonderful recovery.'

At that Grannie's face lit up, and she pressed Mrs Sesemann's hand, quite speechless with gratitude. Heidi hugged her again. 'Hasn't everything turned out finely?' she cried.

'Oh yes, child, I did not know there were such good people in the world. It renews my faith in God to have them bother about a poor old thing like me.'

'We are all poor in the sight of God,' Mrs Sesemann reminded her. 'We all need His care. And now we must say goodbye for the present but, as I say, we shall be back next year, and you may be sure we shan't forget to come and see you then.' She shook hands warmly, while Grannie thanked her again and again and called down blessings on her and her family.

The older Sesemanns then went on to Dörfli while Uncle took the girls back to the hut.

Clara could not help crying a little next morning when it came to leaving, but Heidi did her best to console her. 'Summer will soon come round again,' she told her, 'and you'll come back, and then you'll be walking right from the beginning. That will be much more fun, and we shall be able to go up to the pasture every day and see the flowers.'

Clara dried her eyes at that, and said 'Say goodbye to Peter and all the goats for me, especially Daisy. I wish I could give her a present in return for all her lovely milk.'

'Send her some salt then,' laughed Heidi. 'You know how she loves that.'

'I will. I'll send her a hundred pounds of salt to remember me by.'

Meanwhile Mr Sesemann had arrived, and had been talking to Uncle Alp, but now he said it was time to leave. Grandmamma's white horse was at the door to carry Clara down, and soon Heidi was left waving goodbye. She ran to the edge of the slope, and stood there watching till they were out of sight.

Only a few days after that, the bed arrived, and when it was put up, Grannie got into it with new pleasure and slept soundly all night. Grandmamma had noted all that Heidi had told her of winter's coldness in the mountains, too, and with the bed came a big bundle of warm clothes, as well, also from Mrs Sesemann.

Nor was that all, for soon afterwards Dr Classen came back and took up his old quarters at the inn at Dörfli. Then, on the advice of Uncle Alp, he bought the derelict old house there and had it rebuilt so that he could live in one half, and Uncle Alp and Heidi could use the other half during the winter. He had a new goat-stall built on at the back for Daisy and Dusky too.

The friendship which had begun between the two men the year before grew steadily so that they both looked forward to the day when the house would be ready for them. The doctor thought also, and with pleasure, of having Heidi near him.

One day as they were watching the men at work on the house, the doctor laid a hand on Uncle Alp's arm and said, 'I believe we think alike about that dear child, but I want to tell you all the same what she means to me. I have come to love her almost like my own child. I should like to be allowed to share with you in all that concerns her. It would warm my heart if I could know that she would be with me in my old age, as though she were indeed my daughter, and I shall leave everything I have to her at my death. So she'll be well provided for when we're no longer here.'

Uncle Alp said nothing, but he took the doctor's hand, and a look of deep understanding passed between them.

Just about the same time Heidi and Peter were sitting with Grannie, and Heidi was telling them all about what was going on, and recalled much that had happened during that hot, eventful summer. As the eager voice ran on, the three heads got closer together and so Bridget learned for the first time about Peter's weekly penny, and beamed all over her face.

At length Grannie asked Heidi for a hymn. She said,

'If I spend every moment, for the rest of my days, thanking God for all His goodness to us, that still would not be enough.'

PUFFIN
IN
BLOOM

HEIDI

With Puffin Classics, the adventure isn't
over when you reach the final page.
Want to discover more about your favorite
characters, their creators and their worlds?
Read on . . .

CONTENTS

Name: Johanna Louise Spyri
Born: 12 June 1827
Died: 7 July 1901
Nationality: Swiss (*Heidi* was originally written in German)
Lived: mainly in the city of Zurich, Switzerland
Married: to Johann Bernhard Spyri, in 1852
Children: one son, Bernhard Diethelm

What was she like?

Johanna is one of the most famous children's writers in the world but little is known of her life. Once, when she was asked to write her autobiography, she replied with the words: 'The external path of my life is very simple, and there is nothing special to be mentioned. My inner life was full of storms, but who can describe it?'

Where did she grow up?

Hirzel, a small village with beautiful views in the mountains of Switzerland. Johanna's parents were quite well-off, so she and her five brothers and sisters had comfortable lives. There were lots of books and music in their house, and friends and relatives often came to visit. Johanna didn't leave home properly until she got married when she was twenty-five, although she went away to school for a while when she was a teenager.

One thing Johanna didn't do when she was young was

write much, although she read a lot. Her first book wasn't published until she was over forty years old.

What did she do apart from writing books?
She gave a lot of her time and money to charities, and loved travelling, music and discussing books, art, music and politics with other people.

Johanna often struggled to be happy. Although she lived in Zurich for most of her adult life, like Heidi she sometimes found city life difficult. This is probably one of the 'storms' she spoke of, as was her experience of losing and then finding her faith again.

Where did she get the idea for Heidi?
Dörfli isn't based on Johanna's home village, but on a different part of Switzerland where she spent many family holidays. Mayenfeld, Ragaz, Prättigau and Domleschg are all real places. Heidi's homesickness in Frankfurt, however, is probably based on Johanna's own experiences of leaving her country home.

What did people think of Heidi when it was first published?
Heidi was first published in two parts, the first in 1880 and the second in 1881. Johanna was over fifty, and although her previous books (mainly for adults) had been quite successful, nothing had prepared her for people's reaction to *Heidi*. Within five years the book had been translated into English, and it soon became famous all over the world.

What other books did she write?
Johanna wrote over twenty-five books, but today only *Heidi* is well known. Two books she *didn't* write are the two sequels to *Heidi* – *Heidi Grows Up* and *Heidi's Children*. These were written by her original English translator, Charles Tritten.

Main Characters

Heidi (christened Adelheid) – at the beginning of the story, Heidi is about five years old, and by the end ten or eleven. Heidi is free-spirited, bright, brave and sympathizes with anyone suffering or in trouble.

Tobias and Adelheid – Heidi's dead parents.

Detie – Heidi's twenty-six-year-old aunt. When her parents died, Heidi was left in Detie and Detie's mother's care. Detie isn't bad, exactly, but she is selfish, careless of other people's feelings and ready to lie to get her own way.

Uncle Alp (Grandfather) – Heidi's gruff but, at heart, kindly grandfather. In his youth Uncle Alp gambled and drank away his fortune, and in later life when his son, Tobias, died, many local people claimed it was a punishment for the sins of Uncle Alp's youth. His anger at them is why, as the story starts, he lives alone on the mountain.

Peter – eleven-year-old local goatherd. Peter has a good heart, but he isn't very bright. He can be a little selfish, as well as jealous of Heidi's friendships with other people.

Bridget – Peter's mother.

Grannie – Peter's blind grandmother. Very religious, at the start of the book she is suffering so badly from cold, loneliness and fear that she is finding it hard to be sustained by her faith.

Clara Sesemann – wealthy twelve-year-old friend of Heidi's, who lives in Frankfurt. Detie virtually kidnaps Heidi to be the invalid Clara's companion – nevertheless, the two girls become firm friends.

Mr Sesemann – Clara's father, who loves Clara dearly but is often away on business.

Mrs Sesemann (Grandmamma) – a firm and kindly old lady, Mrs Sesemann is Mr Sesemann's mother and Clara's grandmother. Following Clara, Heidi calls her 'Grandmamma'.

Miss Rottenmeier – Mr Sesemann's housekeeper – a cold, silly and occasionally cruel woman. Heidi is often in trouble with Miss Rottenmeier due to her inexperience of the ways of a wealthy family in a big city.

Mr Usher – Clara's tutor.

Sebastian and John – manservants in the Sesemanns' house. Sebastian is an enemy of Miss Rottenmeier and an occasional accomplice of Heidi and Clara's.

Tinette – snooty maid in the Sesemanns' house, who looks down on Heidi as a country bumpkin.

Dr Classen – a friend of Mr Sesemann's and later of Heidi and her grandfather. The great grief in the doctor's life is the death of his daughter.

Barbie – a friend of Detie's.

Ursula – an old lady in Dörfli, who used to look after Heidi while Detie was working.

What do you think of the character of Heidi? What qualities does she have that make her such a powerful force for good in the novel – and is she too good to be true?

In *Heidi*, what are the positive and negative things about living in or near Dörfli, and living in Frankfurt? What does Heidi learn from her trip to Frankfurt?

What did you think of Heidi's grandfather at the start of *Heidi*? How and why does he change during the book?

Who do you think are the baddies? What makes you think these characters are bad?

Heidi is famous for Johanna Spyri's descriptions of the mountain landscape. Find a descriptive passage you like (for example, when Heidi goes out with Peter and the goats for the first time), and look at the words Johanna Spyri uses. What kinds of positive words does she use, and how? Are there any negative words, and if so, how do these affect the description?

There are many film and TV adaptations of *Heidi*. Watch one of them and compare it to the original book. Which do you prefer, and why?

Beat Johanna Spyri at her own game! Write a beautiful description of a natural place you've been to, a sunset, or a plant or animal you've seen.

Choose a scene from the novel and adapt it into a playscript – then act it out!

Heidi's visits and presents light up blind Grannie's life. Think of a grown-up (a parent, relative, friend or neighbour) you could surprise with a gift or do something nice for – and make it happen.

Imagine you are working on the soundtrack for a new film of *Heidi*. How would you want the music for the mountain scenes to be different to the scenes set in Frankfurt? Find some songs or instrumental music you think would work well on the soundtrack for each place.

Imagine that you and your family are moving house – to a hut like Uncle Alp's! You're going to live there for a year. There's clean water and plenty of wood, but no electricity, and the nearest shop (which only sells basic supplies) is two hours' walk away. Make a list of everything you'd need to take to keep you alive, comfortable and entertained – but remember, whatever you take you've got to carry it up the mountain with you, so pack light!

Lots of things in Switzerland are better now than they were in Johanna Spyri's day. People have better medical care, cleaner water and more effective sanitation. They're richer, and they live longer.

One thing, however, that *isn't* better is the mountain environment *Heidi* is set in. The fresh air in the mountains is less fresh today, and the vast expanses of grass, flowers, rocks and snow are less vast, less clean and less empty. And it's not just Switzerland (which actually looks after its mountains better than most countries). Mountain areas are in danger all over the world. Read on to find out what's threatening them – and what you can do to help.

THE THREATS

* **Air pollution** – our cars, factories and power stations release soot and poisonous gases into the atmosphere. Air pollution causes health problems, and because mountain valleys often trap pollution, people living there are particularly at risk.
* **Acid rain** – air pollution also causes acid rain. Gases such as sulphur dioxide combine with water in the clouds to make deadly acids, which may be carried hundreds of miles before falling in the mountains as acid rain and harming trees, plants and wildlife.

* **Litter** – people have always dropped litter, but today the problem is more serious. There are more of us polluting the world, and many modern materials (such as plastic bottles) don't decompose naturally.
* **Mining and quarrying** – many mining and quarrying companies who extract useful rocks and minerals from mountains are careful to protect the environment – unfortunately, some are not.
* **Tourism** – people visiting mountains provide local people with jobs and create reasons to protect natural areas. However, tourists can badly damage mountain environments unless they respect the places they visit, and unless good laws are in place to prevent unscrupulous people from building hotels, restaurants and car parks wherever they like.
* **Climate change** – the world is getting warmer. Temperatures rose on average by 0.6°C (1°F) between 1900 and 2000, and today most scientists agree this warming is due to the greenhouse effect. In the mountains, glaciers are melting, snow is falling less often and less heavily, and animals and plants adapted to cold mountain conditions are struggling to survive.

SIX THINGS YOU CAN DO

1. Save energy. Turn off anything (such as lights, TV or computer) if you're not actually using it.
2. Don't be lazy! If it's safe to do so, walk, cycle or take a

bus, rather than asking your parents to take you in the car.

3. If you visit a mountain area (or any natural place), stay on the path so you don't damage plants and erode the soil, and don't disturb or feed wild animals.

4. Don't drop litter – in a mountain area or anywhere else.

5. When you're shopping, use your own bag instead of a plastic one from the shop.

6. Companies care what people say about them. If you hear about a company damaging a mountain environment, write to its president and tell them what you think.

Where is Switzerland exactly?

Switzerland is a small country situated in the middle of Europe, with many mountains but no coastline. Switzerland has remained a mostly independent, neutral republic for hundreds of years.

Because French, German and Italian are all spoken in Switzerland, its official name is actually in Latin – *Confoederatio Helvetica* – to avoid offending anyone. That's why Swiss internet addresses end '.ch'.

What does it mean to be a 'neutral' country?

It means that Switzerland won't attack other countries, but also that it won't intervene to help another country or people, even if, for example, that country is a small, innocent one being attacked unfairly. Switzerland was neutral in the Second World War, and many people think it was wrong of Swiss banks to allow Nazis to open bank accounts and deposit millions of dollars – some of it stolen from Jewish Holocaust victims.

Is Switzerland as beautiful as it sounds in Heidi?

Yes! The Swiss Alps are famous all over the world (not least for their association with *Heidi*!). The Swiss people are very proud of their country, and look after it carefully – they have many laws designed to protect the environment.

Uncle Alp makes his own cheese from goats' milk. But how exactly does liquid milk become solid cheese? Here are the basics of the science of cheese:

* If you looked at fresh milk under a powerful microscope, you'd see large drops of fat and smaller pieces of protein, floating in a sea of sugary water.
* Although the protein pieces are naturally attracted to each other, a substance coating the outside of each piece prevents them from joining up. The secret of making cheese is to destroy this substance, allowing the pieces of protein to join up.
* Cheese-makers kick-start the necessary chemical reaction by adding an enzyme. Traditionally, this enzyme comes from a dried piece of calf's stomach (called rennet), which is added to the milk. Today, there's also vegetarian rennet.
* Cheese-makers also add a weak acid, usually produced by special bacteria added to the milk, as this helps the enzyme to work.
* It takes several hours for the proteins to join up and set the milk into a gel.
* This gel has lots of sugary water in it, but if the gel is squeezed, pressed or just allowed to drain, the water comes out, leaving a solid (the curds, containing most of the protein and fat), which looks a lot like cheese.

★ The type of cheese you get is determined by what happens next. There are many options, all producing different flavours and textures. Curds can be stretched, washed, heated, pressed and deliberately allowed to go mouldy. 'Fresh' cheeses (such as cottage cheese or mozzarella) are eaten soon after they're made, while 'aged' cheeses (such as brie, cheddar or Monterey Jack) have to mature for days, weeks or even years.

Collect the Puffin in Bloom classics!

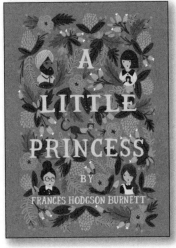

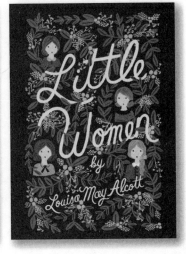

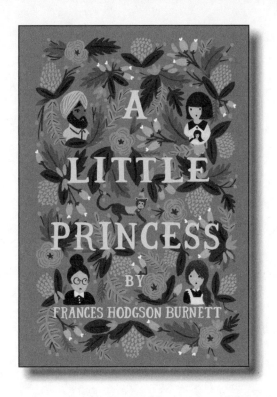

Alone in a new country, wealthy Sara Crewe tries to settle in
and make friends at boarding school. But when she learns
that she'll never see her beloved father again, her life is turned
upside down. Transformed from princess to pauper, she must
swap dancing lessons and luxury for hard work and a room
in the attic. Will she find that kindness and generosity are all
the riches she truly needs?

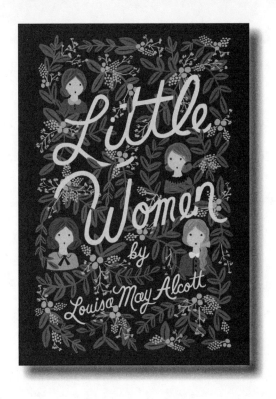

Grown-up Meg, tomboyish Jo, timid Beth, and precocious Amy. The four March sisters couldn't be more different. But with their father away at war and their mother working to support the family, they have to rely on one another. Whether they're putting on a play, forming a secret society, or celebrating Christmas, there's one thing they can't help wondering: will Father return home safely?

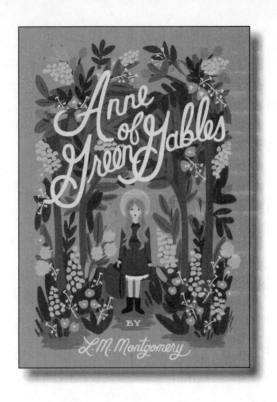

Marilla and Matthew Cuthbert are in for a big surprise. They're waiting for an orphan boy to help with the work at Green Gables—but a skinny, red-haired girl turns up instead. Feisty and full of spirit, Anne Shirley charms her way into the Cuthberts' affection with her vivid imagination and constant chatter. It's not long before Anne finds herself in trouble, but soon it's impossible to imagine life without her.